The Outer Rim

by

D L Bell

ISBN: 069291658X
ISBN-13: 978-0692916582

DEDICATION

For my beautiful eternal companion Eunice and our children, who never gave up on me.

CONTENTS

ACKNOWLEDGMENTS

Edited by
J W Troemner
jwtroemner.com/editing-services/

Cover art by
Jeffrey Ward
jsward0120.deviantart.com

Technical support by
Tim Bell
youtube.com/user/raekuul

"There go the ships: there is that leviathan, whom thou hast made to play therein."

Psalm 104 verse 26

INTRODUCTION

THE ALIEN RACES

Concerning the home star systems of the alien races in this book, I chose to use the names from the Human star charts to make it simpler to map locations and distances. For instance, the Alamani home world is located at Rigel. That of course is not what they would call their star, but it is much easier to tell the story in this manner.

Strovats
System: Unknown
Home world: Unknown
Affiliation: None
The Strovats are huge insectoids who live in hive societies ruled by a royal family headed by a grand queen. These insectoids move from planet to planet in search of food and water, and they will eat most anything organic. The Strovats prefer to subjugate worlds and then set them up as food farms, enslaving the inhabitants and then harvesting them, their livestock, and their crops over time. Their first line warships are spherical supercruisers, each of which has a diameter of approximately twenty miles. The Strovats are known to be able to endure massive battle losses and keep coming due to seemingly endless reserves. They attack in mass numbers, usually in phalanx formations, but their basic military unit is a hundred drones commanded by a lieutenant. While lieutenants and the other officers are capable of independent thought, the drones are completely dependent on their leaders for direction, and they

become confused and erratic without them. Thus, Strovat armies are much more susceptible to breakdown of command and control when their officer corps take high casualties. The standard Strovat drone appears as a huge ant-like creature, standing almost six feet tall on three spidery legs, with four arms and a big head that contains antennae, pincers, and bulbous eyes. They have finger-like claws for hands, and possess a nasty, long, tube tongue with which they can penetrate bodies and suck out the juices and internal organs of their victims. The drones are all white. The lieutenants are larger, averaging six and a half feet, much stronger, and they are all red in color. The dukes and other members of royalty are even larger and all black. There are no known accurate descriptions of Strovat queens, but one rumor states that they are giant, black, spidery creatures, each of which can lay millions of eggs.

Alamani
System: Rigel
Home world: Alaman
An ancient kingdom with warrior codes similar to chivalry, the Alamani are tall and lanky, averaging six and a half feet in height. Their bodies are humanoid and covered with either golden or brown hair, with the golden ones belonging to the ruling class. Their skin is the same color as their body hair, and they each possess a high forehead, a pug nose, and two round eyes. They wear long, braided beards, and they have canine teeth in the front of their mouths. The Alamani are very proud, having been around for nearly seven million years, and they believe themselves to be the chosen ruling race of the galaxy. For much of their existence they have been at war with their mortal enemies, the Burbesenys (whom they consider to be filthy, water-polluting fish), and the Amali (whom they refer to as "Grogs", meaning "toad people").

Heruli
System: L1 Puppis
Home world: Herul
Affiliation: Alamani
The Heruli are an ancient warrior culture governed by clans, with the most dominant clan ruling by sheer strength. They are large,

nitrogen-breathing reptilians that average between six and seven feet tall, and their thick, tough hide skin is either green or gray. Each Heruli possesses two powerful arms and legs on a thick, muscular body, and a short, tentacle-like tail which can be used to wield an additional weapon in close combat. They have big, crested heads with large, toothy mouths and three eyes; one in front and one on each side. The Heruli are the most feared race in the quadrant, and have a nasty reputation. Seemingly created for warfare, the Heruli love hand to hand combat, especially gladiator style, which is how most of their prisoners meet their fate. They are allies with Alaman, and run a small but very strong empire between Alamani and Tellopian space. Whenever the Alamani need work done which goes against their code of honor, they call upon the Heruli and their other allies, the Nephilim.

Tellopians
System: Pollux
Home world: Tellops
Affiliation: Tellopian League
The Tellopians are an old representative democracy run by elected consuls. They are short, averaging five feet in height, with yellow or brown skin. Each possesses a humanoid head with two eyes, but without a nose or any hair. They reside on an arid planet, and their bodies are round due to humps on their backs and sides for water storage. About the year 1200 AD, having grown weary of being used as pawns in the incessant warfare between the Alamani and the Burbesenys, they formed a military and trade alliance with four other worlds: Nerva, Gutay, Kirhar, and Zuz. Over the years many other independent worlds joined in this Tellopian League. The headquarters of the League is at Tellops, and the other members elect or appoint their own officials to represent their worlds in the High Council, which is the ruling body of the league. The High Council then elects its own Premier to act as the executive officer for a designated term, while a separate Security Council is appointed to handle the military. While most of the members of the League joined their space fleets with the Tellopians, they were not required to do so, and the strongest members maintain their own navies. Nevertheless, they are all required to give full support to League military operations. In 2099 the Tellopians came to

Earth and ended the apocalyptic wars which otherwise would have wiped out the Human race, and the Earth was brought in as the League's twentieth member.

Burbesenys
System: Deneb
Home world: Burbeseny
Affiliation: Tellopian League
The Burbesenys are hydrogen-breathing water dwellers. They are fishlike, with round, flat heads, large, toothy mouths, scaly skin, six-foot-long bodies, and four tentacles instead of arms and legs. Their ships are filled with water as opposed to gas, and while in a gas environment they must walk about in very large powered tank suits which either use four legs or tracks for mobility. This is an ancient military society, ruled by its admiralty, which is almost as old as the Alamani, who have been their enemies since ancient times. At one time the Burbesenys owned a vast empire which rivaled the Alamani in strength. About the year 2104, they first encountered the Strovats. In a long, grinding war, the Strovats slowly overcame them, and the Burbesenys were eventually reduced to becoming refugees like the Amali and the Antearians. Still possessing a formidable fleet, they joined the Tellopian League in 2134, and they were relocated to a terraformed world in the Errai system. Known for military prowess and pragmatism, the Burbesenys do not possess the same codes of honor as the Alamani. As far as they are concerned, the ends usually justify the means.

Nervii
System: Errai
Home world: Nerva
Affiliation: Tellopian League
The Nervii are short, stout reptilians distantly related to the Heruli. They stand upright, averaging five feet in height, with two short, strong legs and two powerful arms. Their heads are very similar to the Heruli, and they each possess three eyes in the same fashion. However, their necks are very short, and their mouths are larger and alligator-like. Their skin is grayish green or dark green, and thick and rubbery. The Nervii are a warrior race and they are ruled

by their military. Much like their larger cousins, they love a good fight. They are one of the charter members of the Tellopian League. It was the Nervii who first recognized the fighting quality of the Humans and their potential to strengthen the League, and it was they who lobbied for the Tellopian intervention. The Nervii have studied Human military tactics extensively, and incorporated them into their own. Their implementation of Human guerrilla warfare, heretofore unknown to the other races, has given the Strovats much trouble.

Sagobians
System: Epsilon Perseus
Home world: Marciana
Origin: Alaman.
Affiliation: Tellopian League
Originally members of the lowest caste of Alamani society, the Sagobians revolted circa 23,000 BC (see Appendix A). They were supported by the Burbesenys and the Amali, who later terraformed a new world for them at Epsilon Perseus when they were forced to leave Alaman. They thus became allies to the Burbesenys and the Amali, and bitter enemies to the Alamani and especially the Nephilim, as Epsilon Perseus had formerly belonged to them. The Sagobians are shorter and darker cousins to the Alamani. They possess many of the same features, except that their hair is either dark brown or black, and their legs are shorter and a bit bandy. They average five and a half feet in height. They reluctantly joined the Tellopian League in 2136, when the Strovat menace reached their borders.

Solarians
System: Nunki
Home world: Solari
Affiliation: Tellopian League
The Solarians are carbon-dioxide breathing Humanoids. They look like pudgy, blue-skinned Humans with no body hair, and they average five feet in height. The Solarians were an old, independent mercantile kingdom which had joined the Tellopian League in the year 2039. They were renowned as the best traders in the quadrant,

but they also possessed a strong space navy to protect their trade routes. However, in the year 2114 the kingdom was overthrown and replaced by an oligarchy. This group of powerful industrialists formed a parliament. This caused friction with the other members of the League, as this Solarian government proved to be more interested in profiteering than allied cooperation.

The other alien races are listed in Appendix B at the end of the book.

PROLOGUE

At the end of the 21st century the Earth descended into chaos. The world economic community collapsed in a horrible domino effect. Beginning in Europe, one country went under, then another, and then another. The few stable countries in that region desperately attempted to prop up the weaker ones, but instead were dragged down along with them like a single lifeguard trying to save a group of drowning men.

Finally, the United States economy tottered and crashed. The government simply ran out of money. Riots broke out across the nation all at once, as masses of people who were dependent on government assistance suddenly found themselves without food. The US military, whose personnel had already gone without pay for several months, was called in to impose martial law. What followed was a chilling repeat of what happened in St Petersburg, Russia in 1917. After brutally putting down riots in Los Angeles, the soldiers there had had enough of killing Americans and they mutinied. The soldiers called in to get them in line also mutinied, and within two weeks the revolt spread like an infection throughout the entire US military. A top-ranking general, fed up with poor executive leadership and a bickering Congress, moved his army on Washington and took out the President and most of his cabinet. The Vice President found troops loyal to him and set up base in California. Congress and the Supreme Court quickly became irrelevant, and from that point onward the country was divided.

Soon afterward the governors of several states asserted their independence and seized control of the military bases within their borders. New York City seceded from the state of New York. The Governor of Hawaii was overthrown and the people there set up an independent kingdom. After that, other cities and states formed their own militaries with their own dictators and generals. Each of these new kingdoms began to wage war with each other over the oil, coal, and food-producing regions; for food and energy had become the wealth of the world.

The economic crash rolled on through Asia, and soon virtually every nation on earth shared the same fate as the shattered United States. Canada and Russia fell apart, as did China and Iran, both of which lost several provinces to independence. France split in two, and both Germany and Italy reverted to what they had looked like in the 15th century.

Only a few nations remained intact; some through military strength and good generalship, while others through wily diplomacy. The kingdom of Medes, headquartered in Damascus and comprising of the former countries of Syria, Jordan, Iraq, and much of Saudi Arabia, used its massive energy reserves to bribe the other nations. The King of the Medes had two other aces up his sleeve: Mecca and Medina. No one dared risking a gigantic Islamic jihad and the total loss of Middle Eastern energy resources if either of these Muslim holy places were desecrated.

War raged across the planet as nations fought with each other over food and energy resources. The constant fighting destroyed ecosystems, polluted water supplies, and destroyed crops. Uncontrolled industrial pollution decimated the ozone layer, and this combined with thousands of battlefield fires to fill the atmosphere with smoke. As less sunlight reached the surface, the mean temperature of the earth dropped. The resulting harsh winters and acid rain from the pollution choked the crops that did manage to survive the ravages of war. Year after year, food production dwindled and starvation increased, with no prospect for improvement due to the lack of cooperation among the warring countries. The Human race sat on the brink of a self-inflicted mass extinction.

The Tellopian League, a trade alliance of several nearby worlds, had been carefully monitoring Earth for several hundred years. They debated whether they should intervene before the Humans destroyed themselves. The High Council at Tellops had hesitated, thinking that the Humans were not ready to handle their advanced technology. However, the Security Council, led by the Nervii and the Kirharans, argued that Earth had far too many resources and too much manpower to be allowed to go to waste. The Premier of the High Council, who was a Gutayid, objected because the Humans were too barbaric and warlike. The Security Council contended that this was exactly what they needed. The Humans were strong, adaptable, and more importantly, good fighters, and the Earth was one of the most populated planets in League territory. The Humans had the potential to create massive armies and build a large space fleet, both of which would be of good use to defend against Alamani, Heruli, or even Burbeseny aggression. Furthermore, the Nervii argued that they needed to act soon or they might lose the opportunity to gain a very valuable trading partner with the potential for a very strong military. This won over both the Solarians and the Zuzims, and the High Council vote was swayed. The Premier gave in, but only on the condition that the Tellopians, not the Nervii, would have the authority to set up and enforce a new political system on Earth. The last thing he wanted was another military dictatorship in the League, which would have given the Security Council additional power.

The Tellopians landed in force in London, Sydney, Moscow, and Damascus. Soldiers put down their weapons and vehicles ground to a halt. Indeed, everyone in the world stopped what they were doing to watch. The Tellopians communicated to the entire Earth via hijacking the communication satellites, and their technological superiority was clear from the start. Every person could hear what they said in his own language. The Tellopian Consul spoke to the people, explaining who he was, where he came from, and then he gave an overview of the League. The Earth had been selected to join the Tellopian League, but first it had to become a completely democratic society, the same as what existed on Tellops. The Tellopians were there to assist the people of the Earth in doing so, and to help rebuild their infrastructure.

Over the next few weeks, the aliens established bases and organized relief efforts. They retained control over the communication satellites, both to control the media and to continually educate the Humans, who had a lot of catching up to do pertaining to galactic history and politics.

Human nature being what it is, some people were all for this alien intervention, and some were not. In New York City, the people had a referendum on the subject; voting in favor of the alien assistance, but against joining their League. The envoy they sent to London was informed that the Earth was now already part of the League, that this decision had been made by the High Council at Tellops, and that the good people of New York would soon be democratically redistricted. After this they would be allowed to choose the leaders of their new district. Until then, all referendums would be ignored. It was at this moment the Humans realized that joining the League was not voluntary.

Even so, the Tellopians did not act as conquerors. They worked with the leaders of nations to put down riots, control crime, distribute food and medical care, and end the incessant warfare; the last of which proved to be the most difficult. While many of the world leaders had the good sense to cooperate, thus relieving their people of starvation and general misery, many others did not. Unfortunately, quite a few world leaders had no intention of giving up their little bailiwicks to any redistricting, much less elections, and they refused to disarm. A few dictators got the crazy idea that the aliens would choose the strongest to rule, and they responded by going on the offensive and attempting to grab as much power as they could.

This was the opposite of what the Tellopians had wanted, and exactly the sort of behavior that the Premier had feared from the Humans. The Tellopian response was swift and effective. Once their primitive nuclear weapon systems had been disarmed by the Tellopians from space, five of these aggressive dictators were then eradicated by the advanced alien military within a week. This took the starch out of the other stubborn ones, and they all negotiated reasonable abdication terms. The world finally had peace.

The Tellopians set up a government similar to their own, and the old national lines were mostly done away with. The Earth was divided into two hundred seventy-five districts of roughly equal population. The people in these districts each elected a representative to serve on the Earth Supreme Senate. This was to be the governing body of the planet, and it would choose an executive officer to act as the President of the Earth. This senate would also choose men and women to represent the Humans in the League councils at Tellops. Because most of the worlds in the quadrant were ruled by some form of royalty, anyone chosen to serve either on the High Council or the Security Council was required to be of noble blood. The other races simply would not accept the authority of anyone who was not. In the case of some, such as the Alamani, any ambassador sent to them who was not of noble blood would be ignored, and the act itself would be regarded as an insult.

The districts themselves could organize and elect their own governors and individual legislatures. The Tellopians, with their respect for nobility, allowed some districts to be ruled by their royal families. The leaders of these districts could set up police and para-military to keep order, but they were not allowed to raise their own armies. The military was controlled by the Earth Supreme Senate. This body oversaw creating and maintaining both the Earth Defense Force and a space fleet, which would be designed and built with the help of the Nervii. As with the other worlds, the Earth was required to send elements of its fleet and military to aid in League operations.

As soon as the situation on Earth stabilized, officials came in from all parts of the League to help set up the new government and repair the infrastructure. Many others arrived and began to tap the resources of the other planets in the system. Within a year, the Earth was on its feet and operating as the newest member of the League. Within two years, the Humans controlled all the mining operations in the Solar system. Within ten years, with the help of the Nervii, the Humans had already built several warships, and they were well on their way to creating a significant space fleet. By 2139, forty years after the Tellopian intervention, the Humans possessed the seventh strongest military in the League, and they had their own seat on the Security Council.

Many inhabitants of the Earth were drawn skyward by the Human pioneer spirit. Some became educated in high-tech industry and relocated to work for corporations on other worlds. Tellopian military veterans who served for twenty years earned pensions and free homes on terraformed worlds, so many more people joined the military or government agencies in search of adventure and the ensuing benefits. In addition, the League had many terraformed planets which needed skilled workers, professionals, and farmers to work the land. Thus quite a few Humans who were in search of a new beginning left the Earth and became homesteaders elsewhere.

One such terraformed world was Dragos, a planet about the

size of Mars in the Nihal system, two hundred ninety light years from Earth. Dragos was a world mainly for homesteaders, as it had been created specifically for agricultural production, and because it lay on the border of the Heruli Empire. Here land was free, if you worked it, and the cost of living was cheap. Despite the close presence of the fearsome Heruli, Humans flocked to this world and its population swelled to over twenty million.

In 2104, five years after the Earth joined the Tellopian League, the Strovats began their long war with the Burbesenys, the Amali, and the Antearians. Within ten more years, the Antearians had lost their home world and were in full retreat. A tide of refugees entered Tellopian space, and soon afterward the Antearians negotiated a treaty and joined the League. The League assisted the Antearians in evacuating their last inhabited planet before the Strovats could take it, and a new home world was terraformed for them at Pollux. Due to the advanced Tellopian technology, this process took less than two years.

In 2134, the League was overrun with Amali and Burbeseny refugees. Nervii intelligence reported that a major battle had been lost, and many of the refugees were from the Amali home world. Soon afterward the Zuzims were approached by ambassadors from both the Amali and the Burbesenys. It became clear that the proud and once mighty Burbeseny Empire was at its end. After a valiant struggle, they were finally succumbing to the endless Strovat flood. Both the Amali and the Burbesenys negotiated treaties and joined the Tellopian League. The Nervii and Zuzims terraformed worlds for them, and the League assisted them in their evacuations and lent them military support.

At this point, the Tellopians attempted to negotiate with the Strovats. They sent two embassies to the Strovat base at Graffias, the former home of the Antearians. The embassies were never heard from again. Burbeseny intelligence reported that the ambassadors had been eaten. Soon afterward, the Sagobians came under the Strovat assault, and they joined the League. The Tellopians geared up for full scale war.

In the year 2138 the Strovats attacked Cera, one of the home worlds of the League located in the Alrami system, close to the Solarians. Cera was a small mining planet and trade outpost, and the Cerans themselves were not relatively numerous; possessing a population of only about twenty-five million. The Tellopians had fortified this system with a hundred of their own heavy battle cruisers and another sixty destroyers, but even this proved to be inadequate. The Strovats brought one hundred of their light cruisers, and fifty of their twenty-mile-wide Bisa supercruisers. The Strovat light cruisers were bigger and more heavily armed than the Tellopian destroyers, and each Bisa could deliver a terrific pounding. These massive ships were almost impossible to destroy without a nuclear strike, and they each possessed so many defensive lasers that no missile could hit them from long range. To their horror, the Tellopians discovered that any attacking vessel would have to get in close to nuke one of these monsters, and most ships who attempted to do so were shot to pieces. After a terrific fight, the Tellopians were forced to retreat. They had lost forty of their destroyers and sixty of their heavy cruisers while taking out forty-seven Strovat light cruisers, but only destroying twelve of the heavy Bisas. The Strovats took possession of Cera, and they brought in giant transports full of troops to occupy the planet and enslave its inhabitants.

Worse yet, the Tellopians found themselves in no position to counterattack. The League's two strongest members, the Burbesenys and the Amali, were tied up fighting the Strovats in Sagobian territory. The Kirharans, Solarians, and Humans were backing them up, and also assisting in the Sagobian evacuations. The Zuzims and Antearians were protecting the Ceran flank at nearby Solari, but they were not strong enough to both protect the Solarian home world and counterattack Cera. The Nervii were behind Strovat lines attacking their supply points and performing rescue operations. The Gutayids were not warlike by nature, and they did not have a large military budget. They had few heavy warships, and most of these were obsolete. Their fleet was mainly used for escort operations and guarding against piracy.

As for the main Tellopian fleet, which consisted of their own navy plus the combined warships of the thirteen other less populated worlds in the League, it was not in good fighting condition. The many decades of peace which the League had enjoyed had resulted in cuts in military spending. Maintenance schedules had been lax, spare parts had not been stockpiled, and many ships had been mothballed. When the Strovat war suddenly came upon them, crews performed poorly and ships broke down. Most of the ships in the Tellopian main fleet were badly in need of an overhaul, and the loss of a hundred actual working warships at Cera did not improve the situation.

After the defeat at Cera, the Tellopians immediately reached out to the Alamani to try to form an alliance. However, the recent admission of the ancient Alamani enemies into the League resulted in a cold reception. Trade had already been suspended due to the presence of the Burbesenys, and Golar Hassiid, the king of Alaman, was not about to negotiate a military treaty with them. He did agree to reconsider reopening limited trade, but that was all. Burbeseny intelligence later reported that Golar Hassiid was secretly negotiating with the Strovats.

CHAPTER 1

Dragos: Nihal system
2139 AD

Beta Leporis, also known as Nihal, is a yellow giant star two hundred ninety light years away from Earth. Nihal sits in the far back corner of Tellopian League territory, five days' travel at faster-than-light speed from Tellops, and six from Earth. Nihal sits closer to the fearsome Heruli and Alamani warrior races than it does to League headquarters. Less than two days' travel away at FTL, a mere ninety light years, lies 32 Eridanus; part of the Heruli empire. One hundred seventy light years beyond Nihal lies Bellatrix; the farthest outpost of the Alamani Empire.

Even though Nihal is a giant star, the Tellopians examined it and determined that its core would be stable for another half billion years. Thus, there would be no harm in either mining or colonizing any of the four planets in that system. The first planet possessed too hostile of an environment to be able to do anything which would be cost effective. The third and fourth planets were outer gas giants which could be tapped for resources. Both also had several moons which could be mined or used as military or commercial bases.

The second planet in the Nihal system was deemed to be at the right position for colonization. It was terraformed for agriculture and mining operations, and was soon named Dragos by its first colonists, who were homesteaders from Earth. The days on Dragos were essentially as long as those on Earth, but the

Dragosian circular year and seasons were longer due to its larger orbit. Time being relative, and Humans being what they are, they stubbornly held on to their Earth reckoning of weeks and years, no matter how much the seasonal weather suggested otherwise.

Despite the close proximity of the Heruli and the Alamani, many Humans migrated here to start a new life. The West and the Zemmarich families had both come to Dragos in the year 2124. Hugo Zemmarich was a retired naval pilot whose military aviation heritage could be traced back to Manfred von Richthofen's Flying Circus. The father of the West family had started out as a consultant working with the military, and had ended up in Army Intelligence. Both men were granted free land outside of the municipality of Portsmouth, the second largest city on Dragos, as part of their military pensions. They had set up their farms about thirty miles out from the city limits, where they could find peace and quiet. Their houses were built only about a hundred feet apart, and they quickly became the best of friends.

The Zemmarichs' only child was Franz, who had grown up to join the flying corps just as his father had done. Franz had tested into the Nervii Special Forces two years before, and he was currently off on a mission. The Nervii found Humans to be both resilient and imaginative in warfare, and often employed them in their own military.

The oldest West child was Tonya, who was one year younger than Franz. Franz and Tonya had practically grown up together on Dragos. They had been sweethearts ever since they could remember, and in the coming spring their long-awaited wedding day would finally come to pass, if Franz survived that long.

Tonya grew up knowing the life of a military family. Since Franz also came from one, she had always known what to expect. She was proud that Franz would serve as his father had, and often bragged to her friends that she would be married to a pilot. However, for most of the time in which their fathers had been active they were at peace. When war actually came the year before, Tonya wished that Franz had become a store clerk.

During his deployments, Franz would be gone for months at a time. The onset of the Strovat War had made this all the worse, for while he was performing special operations she had little contact with him. Months could go by with only an occasional letter or video chip. This was very difficult for her, not only because of the worry that he might be killed or maimed, but also because there were worse outcomes regarding fighting the Strovats. She heard constant news stories and eyewitness accounts of Strovat captives being devoured like spider bait, or worse; being enslaved and exported to conquered worlds, never to be heard from again.

Tonya prayed twice a day, every day for Franz's safe return, and return he always did. Her parents were originally from Kentucky, and they brought their southern-style faith with them to Dragos. Her deeply religious upbringing was reflected in her own faith, which often befuddled Franz. His parents were from Germany, and their religious views were much more relaxed. Still, he always respected her beliefs and agreed that their children would be raised accordingly.

She worked in Portsmouth as a part-time dental hygienist, commuting back and forth from her parents' house in her old fashioned, four-wheeled car. This was a candy apple red, two-door four-seater with a convertible top and a standard operating computer. Streamlined and low profiled, it somewhat resembled a late 20th century sports car, except that it ran on alcohol. It was, in fact, a replica sports car which had been manufactured on Dragos. Despite advancements in technology, the old style wheeled cars were still very popular among young adults, mainly because they were inexpensive.

On this day, she brought with her a message cylinder and several items for Franz. After work, she drove to the post office at the spaceport. She parked her car and reviewed the items she would send to him. She packed a video chip, letters from their families, and an intimate letter that she had written into the cylinder. She removed a 3x3 digital picture frame from her purse and scanned through the photos she was sending him. She paused on a picture of the two of them at her senior prom sitting at a table and making funny faces. She gazed at his blue eyes and his light blonde hair, which had been much longer before his military days. Looking into her own blue eyes, she saw a happier time. Her straight, long blonde hair had been much shorter back then.

"Hard to believe that was just three years ago," she sighed. "Seems like forever."

She wiped away a tear before packing the picture frame into the cylinder and sealing it shut with a twist of the top. She put the cylinder on the passenger seat while she rummaged through her purse for one of Franz's identity chips. Without one of these, the postal computer would not know where to send his package.

"Oh, come on!" she griped. "I know I've got at least one in here. He sent me like forty of them. I swear, If I have to go all the way back home to get one, I'm gonna throw up!"

She dumped out her purse onto the passenger seat, and Franz's elusive identity chip finally appeared. She heaved a sigh of relief, and slid it into the small address port on the side of the cylinder. The port snapped shut and a green light appeared. Everything was a go.

A cold wind swirled her long, blonde hair about and made her shiver as she walked across the parking lot. She entered the lobby of the unmanned, automated post office and headed for the wall that contained several cylinder deposit machines, which resembled large ATMs. She slid her identity credit card into one and entered her PIN. The machine quickly confirmed her identity and opened a port for Franz's cylinder. She placed it inside, and the machine swallowed it. Once it had read his identity, and figured which outgoing ship the cylinder should go to, the machine deducted the proper amount of credits from her bank account and spat out a receipt for her.

Tonya put her hand upon the shut cylinder port and closed her eyes.

"Come back to me, my eternal love!" she whispered.

CHAPTER 2

Alaman: Rigel system
2140 AD

The Alamani royal city of Golar sat at the base of a beautiful blue mountain range in the middle of the northern temperate zone of Alaman. The city itself was laid out in rectangular sections, with blue steel skyscrapers, stone pyramids, and golden domed government buildings. The largest dome sat away from the main part of the city on the side of the nearest mountain. There, hewn into the living rock, rested the citadel of the king of Alaman. This place was a fortified complex, complete with its own air spaceport, heavy air defense lasers, and a base containing ten thousand elite Blue Armored Guards; the king's own personal army of crack Alamani soldiers who had been selected for their fanatical loyalty to the Golars.

The Golar Dynasty had ruled Alaman for twenty-five thousand years, assuming power directly following the Sagobian Rebellion. During their reign, Alaman had never been conquered and she had never been forced to pay tribute, beyond the occasional concessions during peace negotiations. Golar Hassiid himself was the embodiment of an Alamani king. He was tall, almost seven feet, with broad shoulders, young, handsome, and strong. He wore a royal blue tunic over a golden robe with long sleeves. His long golden hair was braided in the back, and his golden beard was braided in the front with crystal blue sapphires.

21

His golden domed palace lay in the center of his mountain citadel. Deep inside, the king of Alaman met with his Witan, or council of five elders. All other military leaders, spies, governors, government officials, and industrialists were under these five who reported to the king, who himself had absolute power. All possessed the golden hair of the ruling class, and all had braided hair and beards, though not with the royal sapphires.

Ator, the General-in-Chief of the Army, was young like the king, but a few inches shorter and more powerfully built. He wore a black tunic laden with diamond-studded insignia over a blue robe. Karg, the Chief Admiral of the Fleet, was likewise dressed, except he wore a green tunic. Karg stood six and a half feet tall, was rather fat, and most of his hair had turned white with old age.

Both Eblock, the Minister of Empire, and Pekota, the Minister of Industry, were ordinary looking, middle-aged Alamani nobles possessing a mixture of gold and white hair. Lastly, Nurgud, the Minister of Finance, was the shortest and the youngest of the group. He was a brilliant, young professional, the top of his class, with a genius for keeping everything running smoothly and under budget. All three of these ministers wore blue, toga-like robes with long, wide sleeves; the business suit of high class Alamani government.

The five elders of the Witan sat at a U-shaped table, with Golar Hassiid positioned in the center.

"My lord, we cannot do this thing!" Ator pounded the table with his hairy fist. "We cannot sign a non-aggression pact with the Strovats!"

"I must agree with Ator," Karg said. "These Strovats have no regard for life. They enslave weaker folk, and treat conquered sentients as livestock. They have no honor. I do not believe they will keep their word."

"It would be better for us to ally ourselves with the filthy water breathers than to make peace with these Strovat animals," Ator grumbled.

"My king, honor is one thing, but reality is another," Nurgud cautioned. "Since the Tellopians have allied themselves with the water breathers and the Grogs, we cannot justify any assistance to them with our people, our industrialists, or our banks. Any such help to them could result in war with the Strovats, and any war with the Strovats would be long and protracted, perhaps even devastating. It is in our best interest to stay out of this fight."

"Yes, as of yet we do not know the true Strovat strength," Eblock added. "They incurred tremendous losses in taking Burbeseny and Amal, yet they still have the power to attack the Tellopians. Our spies report that their supply centers are massive, asteroid-sized stations, and they have reported the presence of over a thousand of those Bisa supercruisers in this sector of the galaxy."

"My lord," Pekota said, "as strong as we are, we cannot compete with Strovat industrial might, especially since we do not know where their factories are. If a war started today, we could not strike at their industrial base, but they surely could get at ours."

"But, don't you see?" Ator implored. "The Strovats must think themselves stretched too thin. The dirty fish and the Grogs must have hurt them, or why else would they ask us for a truce? They do not wish to fight both us and the Tellopians. They have no intention of keeping any treaty with us. They are trying to separate us so that they can defeat Tellops now, and then attack us later. Can you all not see this?"

"Divide and conquer," Karg sighed.

"I am aware of this, General Ator," the king finally said. "However, I fear that the Tellopians are too weak. Our Heruli friends think as such. Baron Hareseth believes that Tellops will fall whether we help them or not. I wonder if by helping them that we perhaps may stretch ourselves too thin. It may be better for us to sit back and build our strength. For this reason, a non-aggression pact with the Strovats could also benefit us."

"My king your armies stand ready," Ator said. "Why sit back and wait for them to come to us? If war is inevitable, then let us begin it now."

"Have you seen my reports on Strovat industrial potential?" Pekota asked. "They are like the sands of the ocean. We may as well fight against our own sun."

"Better to die fighting the sun than make peace with sentient eaters!" Ator argued.

"My lord, our ancient enemies are no longer a threat to us," Karg pointed out. "However, the Strovats are a very real threat. After what they did to the inhabitants of Cera, it would be honorable to join the Tellopians in their fight."

"Why?" Eblock asked. "The Strovats have unseated our enemies for us. Why stop them? Why not allow the bugs to get rid of our enemies once and for all? I can tell you that neither the Heruli nor the Nephilim care to assist the water breathers."

"Neither do they care for the Strovats," Karg scoffed. "Do you not read your own reports? The Strovats have entered Marciana. As we speak, they are taking it from the Sagobians. You should not need me to remind you that that was once Nephilim territory, and King Zoar is in a rage over this. He is demanding that the Strovats hand it over to him, and he is ready to go to war if they do not."

"Let us join with the Tellopians, my lord," Ator entreated.

"They have allied themselves with our enemies," Nurgud said.

"Enough." The king calmly held up a hand. "War is easy for us to debate, but very difficult to implement, and much more difficult for our people to bear. I am afraid that Nurgud makes a valid point. To go to war to assist our ancient enemies would not be a popular move. Our soldiers may not be motivated to fight. We would be sending many young Alamani males to die, and for what purpose? How do we convince our people that we should risk their lives to defend the Tellopians? I have studied all your reports, and I cannot sanction war with the Strovats at this time. To join with a questionable ally and make war for honor's sake against a foe of yet unknown strength would be foolish."

"But, my lord, what if we were to have a deterrent?" Karg inquired. "A good deterrent can be more effective than ten victories, if used properly."

"You speak of the Nova Bomb." The king stroked his beard, and then he looked at his industrial minister. "Pekota, you have not reported on the progress of this weapon in some time."

"That is because there has been no progress in some time, my king." Pekota gave Nurgud a stare. "The financing for this project has been cut."

The king fixed his gaze onto his finance minister and said, "I do not remember authorizing any cuts in the Nova Bomb project."

"Er...no Sire, you did not." Nurgud shifted nervously in his seat. "However, that project is completely over budget, with few tangible results. The scientists involved are using theoretical physics, and frankly, they may be tampering with forces of nature that they cannot control. Also, they have yet to find an appropriate target in which to test their theoretical device."

"Maybe they are not looking in the right place," grumbled

Ator.

"I will decide that," the king said, "and I also will decide on the viability of this weapon. For now, the funding will resume and the research will continue."

Nurgud capitulated. "Yes, my lord."

"But I expect results," Golar Hassiid warned Pekota. "Tell your scientists that this is not a college experiment in which they may learn as they go. They do not have unlimited funds or unlimited time with which to work. They have one more month to produce a viable model for testing, else they can all go back to their classrooms."

"Yes, my king."

The king ended the meeting and then walked with his ministers and bodyguards to the grand hall of the palace. This was a spacious assembly room at the front of the building where embassies met, banquets were held, celebrations were had, and where the king sat in judgement on his golden throne. The room was shaped as a half sphere with a high ceiling. The lower parts of the walls were covered with paintings, tapestries, and murals; all of which depicted past rulers and victorious battles. Here and there were displayed sculptures and ancient weaponry. The highest portions of the walls were lined with stained glass, which provided wondrous beauty when the Alaman sun would shine through. The king's seat was placed in the corner of the far wall opposite the entrance. It rested at floor level behind a great table, at which his wives and any counselors who attended him would sit.

Few surprises awaited the king of Alaman in his great hall. Everyone who entered the citadel was thoroughly scanned, and then scanned again before being allowed through the front door of the palace. Once inside, they were greeted by Ator's finest Blue Guards, who lined the walls, the rafters above, and surrounded the king's table. Each Blue Guard wore shiny blue supersteel armor, a broadsword at his side, and wielded the deadly Alamani plasma rifle. This weapon shot superheated bolts of ionized gas that had the effect of either blowing holes through, catching afire, or melting its targets.

Once a week, Golar Hassiid did as his fathers had done; he sat in court of his people for an afternoon. This was not the time for industrialists or the nobility, but the time set aside for the king to meet specifically with the common folk of his realm. Any commoner could set an appointment and have an audience with the king to ask him to decide a civil or family matter, discuss a grievance, ask for clemency, or appeal a court decision. Sometimes the people, particularly the children, had questions they wished to ask their monarch. Several citizens who had appointments with the king this day had already been led inside and were seated in a waiting area near the front door.

The king entered the hall and sat at his great table. Seated to his right was his oldest and favorite wife, Radi. She was also very wise, and he valued her counsel as much as anyone else in the realm. To his left sat both Karg and Ator, but the other ministers left the king's presence to perform their duties.

Waiting for them was Urudo, Executive Secretary to the king. Urudo's sole job was to schedule appointments for the king, and he had been doing it for two generations. He was tall and hoary-headed, with a very long white beard. He waited for the king to be seated, and then he rose and began a very extensive oratory.

"All hail the great Golar Hassiid, ruler of all Alaman, chief sovereign of the sector, protector of the weak..." he announced.

He rambled on and on, spewing the speech which he himself had written. The king allowed this for but two minutes before signaling Urudo to get on with it.

"Thank you, Urudo." The king waved a hand. "Let us proceed."

"Windbag," Ator muttered under his breath.

Radi overheard him and covered her mouth to conceal her grin. Urudo, though annoyed, motioned for the captain of the guard to bring up the king's first appointment, who had white hair and was bent with age. He slowly walked with a cane, and a guard politely helped him as he moved along. After a short time, the old citizen finally reached the table opposite the king. He wore a clean orange jumpsuit, which was the ordinary uniform for the working class. He looked at the king with sharp blue eyes, and bore a worried expression. He bowed, with the help of the attending soldier.

"Welcome, citizen." The king smiled. "What is your name?"

"I am called Orizah, great one," the old citizen replied. "I am a laborer in your vineyards."

"And why have you come to see me?"

"To deliver a message, my king."

"A message?" The king sat back and raised his eyebrows. "From your fellow laborers?"

"No, Great One." The old gardener gave his king a steely stare. "I bring a message from the Lord God Alè."

Everyone stopped what they were doing to stare at the old citizen. Karg rested his chin on his arm and listened intently. The king, who had expected the old worker to present some sort of organized labor dispute, momentarily hesitated, but quickly regained his composure.

"Go on." He motioned with his hand. "Tell me this message."

"Thus saith Alè, Lord God of the universe," Orizah spoke with authority, "make no peace or alliances with the Strovats. Make no agreements and no promises. Do not trade or associate with them any longer, for by the word of Alè the Strovats are wicked, and they shall soon be swept from this quadrant!"

Ator's eyes grew wide, and then angry. He tried to order the guards to arrest Orizah, but Golar Hassiid held up a hand and stopped him.

"And what business is this of yours?" The king scowled. "What do you know of diplomacy, old one? Who has told you that we have any dealings with the Strovats? You are but a gardener."

"I am a spokesperson," Orizah stated. "I am Alè's servant. He reveals many things to me."

"So, you claim to be a prophet?" the king scoffed. "There has not been a prophet in Alaman for over two thousand years."

Golar Hassiid sat back and laughed. He looked around his table, but no one else was amused. Ator fumed, Urudo stood speechless, but both Radi and Karg had their eyes fixed on Orizah as if they were listening intently. This threw the king off his mark. He coughed and composed himself.

"I have been sent to warn you, great king," Orizah calmly but firmly continued. "You must not make peace with the Strovats."

"And what if I do?" the king growled.

"You must turn and fight them," Orizah warned, "or else Alaman will be destroyed!"

Radi gasped and covered her mouth.

"By whom?" Golar Hassiid smiled mockingly. "The Tellopians perhaps?"

27

"Nay, my lord," Orizah said. "There is something else coming. Something terrible, which none can withstand. The wrath of God is returning from the Outer Rim. It is the Leviathan!"

"What is that?" Golar Hassiid blinked and looked about him. "What is Leviathan?"

No one could give him an answer. Even Karg, himself a student of religion and history, shook his head as if he knew nothing.

"They are coming," Orizah continued unabated, "like a storm on the horizon!"

"Take him away." The king stood and pointed. "He is mad. Get him out of my sight!"

The guards roughly plucked Orizah from where he stood and dragged him off.

"They come for *you*, Golar Hassiid!" Orizah raved as he was taken away. *"Repent, or the Leviathan will destroy this city before your eyes! Repent!"*

Golar Hassiid sat down in a huff. Everyone in the great hall was silent, except for Orizah, who continued his rant until he was finally evicted from the palace. The king shifted nervously on his throne. After a minute or so, he finally looked up at Urudo.

"Well?" he demanded. "Proceed!"

"Yes, of course, my lord," Urudo quietly replied.

He called forth the next commoner, but Golar Hassiid paid little attention to what this farmer had to say. His mind was now elsewhere.

"He threatened me!" the king interrupted. "Did you hear that prophet? How dare he threaten me?"

"No, my king, he warned you," Radi replied. "There is a difference."

The poor farmer tried to continue, but Urudo stopped the proceedings. He apologized and then announced that all those who had appointments that day would be rescheduled. The remaining common folk were led out, and most of the guards dismissed. Urudo excused himself, and the king was left alone at his table with his wife and two counselors.

"My lord," Ator beckoned, "there must be a security leak if somehow this one knew of our impending deal with the insectoids. Perhaps we should detain this so-called 'prophet' for questioning."

"And what if he tells the truth?" Karg asked. "What if he is a prophet? What then?"

"My lord," Radi leaned and whispered into Golar Hassiid's ear, "if this one is mad, then leave him be. Nothing will come of this and he will be exposed. But if he is what he claims, you cannot fight against God. I think you should wait and be moderate. Imprisoning him before we know who he truly is can bring to pass no good."

"Yes, you are right." The king exhaled. "Ator, leave him alone. Find out information about him and keep an eye on him, but do nothing else. Perhaps we may find this security leak you speak of through him."

"Yes, my lord."

CHAPTER 3

The Battle of Algenib

Epsilon Perseus was the center of Sagobian civilization for twenty-five thousand years, until the Strovats appeared.

The Sagobians were at war with the Nephilim when the tide finally turned in the long Burbeseny-Strovat war. Both the Burbesenys and Amali were hard pressed, and they compelled the Sagobians to end their war with the Nephilim. On the other side, Golar Hassiid had been pressuring King Zoar of the Nephilim to also end that war, and not to be too greedy in the settlement. Thus, the Sagobians were able to bow out under somewhat agreeable terms.

Golar Hassiid's motive was not one of charity. Alarmed by the Strovat presence in the sector, he did not wish his ally to be drawn into a war with them, not even accidentally. He preferred his friend King Zoar to sit on the sidelines, assess Strovat strength, and watch their movements from a safe distance.

The Burbesenys and the Amali struggled valiantly against the overwhelming Strovat onslaught. In each battle, they inflicted tremendous losses on their foe, but the Strovats would always come back the next time with more of their giant Bisa supercruisers. Slowly the Burbesenys and Amali were pushed back, until finally their home worlds were threatened. At this desperate moment, the Burbesenys did the unthinkable: they made an alliance with the Tellopians. The Amali followed suit, but the Sagobians balked because the Tellopians were also seeking open trade with Alaman.

The irresistible tide of the Strovats eventually overran both the Amali and Burbeseny home worlds. The mighty Burbesenys had been reduced to refugee status, though they managed to keep the remainder of their military intact. Before open war broke out with the Strovats, the Tellopians sent embassies to the Alamani, inviting them to join their triple alliance in an effort to create a united front against the Strovats, but the Alamani reception was frosty. Golar Hassiid had already suspended trade with the Tellopians once they had allied themselves with his ancient enemies. As far as he was concerned, there would be no alliances between Alaman and the dirty fish people of Burbeseny.

Bite by bite, the Strovats made their way to Epsilon Perseus and the Sagobian home world of Marciana. The Sagobians beat back the first Strovat offensive against them, but they suffered heavy losses. Knowing that they could not withstand a second such Strovat strike, the Sagobians reluctantly joined the Tellopian League. The Tellopians assessed the situation, and immediately decided that it was untenable. They quickly came up with a plan to evacuate Marciana.

The Sagobians possessed another habitable planet in their territory at Algenib. This world, Algenib IV, had been altered to sustain life and colonized centuries before. It was teeming with cities, but still had vast tracts of open land. The Tellopian plan was to use this as a base. They would temporarily relocate the people of Marciana here, until a world further back from the Strovat front could be terraformed for them. A new world had already been selected for this process in the Pollux system.

However, despite recent events and the warnings from both the Amali and Burbesenys, the Sagobian leadership seemingly had no desire or plans to evacuate their beloved home world. When the first Tellopian transports arrived, they found, much to their dismay, that most of the Sagobians were not prepared to leave, despite intelligence reports that a new Strovat offensive was only weeks away.

The Tellopians were prepared, and they were able to safely move almost all of the Sagobians from Marciana to Algenib IV. Still, the reluctance of the Sagobians to evacuate took its toll. Their leaders had not set up adequate emergency services to cooperate with the Tellopians, and so the situation on Algenib IV quickly deteriorated into a confused and disorganized mess. Conditions in the camps were crowded and unsanitary. Food and water supplies ran short, garbage piled up, sewage disposal systems were overwhelmed, tempers ran short, and security was wholly inadequate. Sagobian officials were so busy trying to gain control of the situation that they completely failed to prepare for further evacuations, even though Algenib IV was only meant to be a temporary sanctuary. It was only a matter of time before the Strovats would be upon them again, and this time it looked like a disaster could not be avoided.

To make matters worse, several corrupt Solarian officials who had been sent to organize relief efforts decided to take advantage of the situation and engaged in profiteering. When Antigony, the king of the Sagobians, got word of this he arrested the Solarians and executed them. This caused consternation with the Tellopians, for this was done against League law, which required the use of proper channels and League courts in prosecuting League officials. The Solarians reacted by pulling all their support from the Sagobian sector. When the Strovats finally came, not a single Solarian warship or transport was at Algenib to aid in the evacuation.

The friction between King Antigony and the Tellopians did not improve the situation. Furthermore, because the Solarians had taken advantage of the desperate situation on Algenib IV to line their pockets, the Sagobian citizens now distrusted the Tellopians. When the first League transports arrived to remove the Sagobians, most of them refused to board, preferring instead their own ships or those of the Amali. Thus, the evacuation of Algenib IV progressed at a snail's pace.

Sadly, the Strovats would not adjust their timetable to accommodate this. Before they knew it, while over eight hundred million Sagobians were still on Algenib IV, the Strovats came upon them with a hundred of their giant Bisa supercruisers and two hundred of their light cruisers, more than even the Burbesenys had anticipated. Suddenly, the inhabitants of Algenib IV were not so picky about who was evacuating them. Every available vessel was sent to the planet surface, but all knew that it would not be enough. Panic set in, and ships on the ground were overwhelmed by mobs. Many Sagobians were gunned down by the crews of these ships in order to save their own lives. Many more Sagobians were killed by their own people in the violence to be first in line.

Worse yet, the Sagobian army seemed confused, and their help in controlling the mobs was sporadic. The home army commanders did not have any orders from their king as to what they should do. Indeed, King Antigony himself did not act like he even had a plan. When the massive Strovat fleet appeared at the edge of his system, Antigony retired to his palace, refusing all pleas to evacuate himself or the royal family.

In orbit above Algenib IV, among the swarm of League ships, sat Admiral Sir Nigel Clarke on the bridge of the Earth's flagship, the battleship *Ark Royal*. This wedge-shaped warship was four times as large as a 20th century supercarrier, and it represented the newest and best of the Earth's space fleet. It was fast and had excellent striking power, yet it was only a third the size of the conical Amali battle cruisers which accompanied them to assist in the evacuation.

Admiral Clarke was a tall English gentleman whose father had been Lord of the Admiralty, and whose ancestry in the Royal Navy could be traced back to Trafalgar. He and his Earth fleet had been ordered to the rear by Admiral Murko, the Burbeseny leader and overall commander of the League's fleet. The Humans and the Amali were to cover the evacuation and act as a rear guard.

Admiral Clarke had sent his liaison officer, Lieutenant Commander Dyson, and his personal shuttle to Antigony's palace with orders not to return without him and his royal family. However, thus far the Sagobian king had refused to meet with Dyson, or even to acknowledge his presence.

The rest of the League main battle fleet in the area consisted of fifty Burbeseny K class battleships, sixty Kirharan Landwaster battle cruisers, and one hundred thirty-four Sagobian battle cruisers and corsairs. The Sagobian battle cruisers were flattened spheres with fins and comparable in size to the *Ark Royal*, but their corsairs were only half that size. The Kirharan Landwasters were nearly the size of the Amali warships, and were shaped like fat eagles with short wings. The Burbeseny K battleships were massive cylindrical vessels that exceeded five times the size of the *Ark Royal*. However, even one of these monstrous vessels was less than a tenth the size of a Strovat Bisa supercruiser.

This portion of the fleet was heavily engaged with the Strovats three light hours away on the other side of the system. The good news was that even if the League forces did not prevail, it would still be almost two days before the Strovats would reach Algenib IV at sub-FTL speed. The bad news was that by the time Admiral Clarke would get word of the battle, the information would be three hours old. Because of the vast distances involved, all news in space was old news.

Admiral Clarke finally got the news, and it was bad. Despite inflicting significant damage on the enemy, they were still advancing toward Algenib IV. The League had lost several of its heaviest warships, the giant Burbeseny K class battleships. In addition, the Kirharans had also lost several ships of the line, and the remaining Sagobian fleet had done something completely irrational.

Admiral Murko had ordered the outer fleet to withdraw and reform in front of Algenib IV, where it could be reinforced by the inner fleet, which consisted of thirty-five Amali battle cruisers and twenty-five Human battleships. The idea was to make a stand and possibly stop the Strovats there. At the least they would be able to buy more time for the evacuation. This plan depended on the ability of Murko to disengage the Strovats while his outer fleet was still intact.

However, Lord Antedios, the commander of the Sagobian fleet, ignored Admiral Murko's order to withdraw and issued his own command, General Order Thirteen. All at once, the remainder of the Sagobian fleet did an about-face and headed straight for the massive Strovat cube-shaped formation.

Three hours later, Admiral Clarke and his bridge crew watched the live feed with the same dismay in which Murko had.

"What on earth are they doing?" the admiral wondered out loud.

It did not take long for him to realize what had happened three hours before.

"Good lord," he gasped, "it's a kamikaze attack!"

"Kamikaze, sir?" the helmsman turned and asked.

"A Japanese word meaning 'Divine Wind'. It was a type of desperate airborne attack from the Second World War, mid-20th century." The admiral stepped forward and pointed to the main screen. "General Order Thirteen is a suicide mission. Just watch. The Sagobians are going to try and ram them."

"They'll never make it." The helmsman shook his head.

They watched, frozen in anticipation, as the Sagobians charged at the wall of Strovat supercruisers in a wedge formation. Once their ships came within range of the Strovat long-range weaponry, they fell under a terrific bombardment. The enemy laid out a wall of nuclear blasts which fried nearly half of the incoming kamikazes. Once the Sagobians got in too close to safely use nuclear weapons against them, the Strovats hit them with a hailstorm of microwave laser fire which cut many of the attacking vessels to pieces.

"Utter madness!" Admiral Clarke shook his head. "To frontally assault a Strovat phalanx without supporting fire from the flanks is futile."

As the remaining Sagobian ships got close, the Strovats moved their remaining light cruisers, each of which a match for the heaviest Sagobian warship, in front to absorb the blow. This had the effect of neutralizing the Sagobian corsairs and forcing their battle cruisers to use most of their nukes just to punch a hole through the wall of these lighter enemy vessels. Thus, only a few of the kamikazes reached the Strovat Bisas. At the end, Lord Antedios' ship broke up under intense enemy fire just before it got to the enemy command supercruiser.

The enemy lost nearly a quarter of their light cruisers, but only five Bisas were destroyed in the assault, at a cost of all the remaining Sagobian ships. Between this and the earlier losses, the League fleet at Algenib was now at half strength, with seventy-five enemy supercruisers and eighty light cruisers still bearing down on them. Shortly after witnessing the wreck of the Sagobian armada, Admiral Clarke received new orders from his commanding officer.

"The situation here is no longer tenable," Murko slowly stated in his gravelly voice through his electronic translator. "You are to continue with the evacuation process until I arrive. When I reach you, the evacuation will immediately end, and we will withdraw the remainder of the fleet from Algenib."

The bridge of the *Ark Royal* remained silent for a few moments after Murko's message had ended. Each member of the crew knew that this would mean slavery and death for the eight hundred million Sagobians who were still trapped on the planet surface. Finally, Admiral Clarke sighed and contacted his liaison officer at the palace. Lieutenant Commander Dyson was to report back to the ship in forty hours, with or without the king of the

Sagobians. Clarke also notified all ships under his command of Admiral Murko's order to retreat as soon as he arrived at Algenib IV.

King Antigony was meeting with his counselors when news of the defeat came to him. He sent his advisors home to be with their families, with the promise that he would soon issue orders. He then retired to the inner court of the palace to be with his family, without giving Lieutenant Commander Dyson the time of day and without returning Admiral Clarke's personal calls. The king stayed in seclusion while his world crashed around him.

Admiral Clarke was shocked by Antigony's response, or lack thereof, to the impending doom of his people. The Strovats were coming, nothing could stop them, and the king of the Sagobians did not even so much as address his own people. Nor did he bother to order his own army to assist in the evacuation process.

"It's terrible down there, sir!" Clarke's communications officer, Commander Davies, lamented. "It's utter chaos. The Sagobians are mobbing our ships as soon as they land. They are killing each other trying to escape. We've lost three transports to rogue Sagobian military hijackers, and several others have been damaged or lost crewmen because of the mobs. Once the ships are full, the crews are having to fire on the people in order to take off, and then many Sagobians still hang on the outside of the vessels after takeoff and fall to their deaths! Where are the Sagobian security forces? What is their king doing?"

"It's sad." The admiral shook his head. "On the day when the Sagobians need a strong ruler, they have instead another Honorius."

"Honorius, sir?" Davies asked.

"A Roman emperor." Clarke sighed. "When the Goths sacked Rome, he was elsewhere tending his garden."

A day and a half passed, and still the situation on Algenib IV had not changed. Though hundreds of thousands of Sagobians had been evacuated, hundreds of millions remained trapped on the surface, and the window was closing. Soon the remainder of the League fleet would be forced to withdraw. The Strovats advanced like a tide, time was running out, and still the king of the Sagobians did nothing.

Finally, Admiral Murko got close enough so that he and Admiral Clarke could have a real conversation. Murko was utterly flabbergasted by the kamikaze tactics of the Sagobian fleet. He warned Clarke about what it could mean for the rest of the Sagobians.

"I do not like this," Murko complained in his gravelly voice. "Antedios disobeys my orders and destroys nearly half of our fleet in a suicide attack, and now the king of the Sagobians takes a vacation? This is insanity!"

"This is their last home world," Admiral Clarke calmly explained with his hands behind his back. "They know that we cannot get them out in time. I expect that King Antigony has decided to stay with his people and make a stand; to fight it out, sir."

"I do not think that you should expect anything at this point," Murko grumbled. "If I were you, I would get my people out of there."

A few hours later, the Sagobian Prime Minister entered the palace press room and issued a statement from the king. All foreign ships were to leave the planet at once. The evacuation was officially over. All Sagobian military personnel were ordered to return to their bases and prepare for planetary bombardment. The Sagobian people were told to return to their homes and await further instructions from the king, but few of them obeyed. Rioting and looting continued unabated in virtually all the major cities.

Admiral Clarke grudgingly recalled all the Earth vessels from the planet surface. Unfortunately, three of their transports had been rendered inoperable by the violence of the mobs, and their crews still needed to be rescued.

"We have known about this for hours!" Admiral Clarke barked. "Why hasn't Evac-Rescue got them out by now?"

"Evac-Rescue has been overwhelmed sir," Davies explained. "They're behind schedule on everything."

"Then get them on schedule!" Clarke ordered. "Rescuing our own personnel should have been top priority!"

Davies nodded. "Yes sir."

"Very sloppy!" Admiral Clarke complained. "This operation has been mucked up from the start!"

"Yes, sir."

Captain Fitzgerald, the man in charge of Evac-Rescue, was contacted and put on the big screen. He explained in his heavy Gaelic accent that two earlier attempts at rescuing the stranded crews had to be aborted due to ground fire, and that his people did not have clearance to return fire on the offending Sagobians. Admiral Clarke bristled over the fact that somehow this had not been reported to him, and then he gave Captain Fitzgerald his clearance.

"Do whatever you have to." Clarke frowned. "Interracial incidents no longer matter at this point, particularly if the Sagobian military is now part of the problem."

"Aye, sah!" Captain Fitzgerald saluted. "I will see to it myself."

An hour later, Captain Fitzgerald was on the surface performing the rescue operations, and Lieutenant Commander Dyson was back on the bridge of the *Ark Royal*. A transmission came in from the surface. King Antigony had emerged from his seclusion with his family and entered the palace press room. He finally addressed his people, but it was a short announcement.

"To all government and military officials," he said, as if he was swallowing a tough steak. "Initiate Program Thirteen. Those of you who have made preparations have one solong before these orders are carried out."

The king then kissed his wife, picked up their youngest child, and returned to the inner chambers of the palace. The transmission ended.

"How long is a solong?" Admiral Clarke asked Dyson.

"About fifteen minutes, sir," Dyson replied. "I think the question, sir, is what on earth Program Thirteen is?"

"Considering that General Order Thirteen was a kamikaze attack," Clarke said, shaking his head, "I don't think that Program Thirteen can be anything good. Commander Davies..."

"Yes, sir?"

"Send a message to Captain Fitzgerald. Tell him he's got fifteen minutes to get out of there."

Moments later Captain Fitzgerald's dirty, sweaty face appeared on the big screen.

"The situation down here is worse than before, Admiral," the captain reported. "We had to shoot our way in, and we shall have to shoot our way out. We have wounded that must be tended to before we can move out. We cannae do it in fifteen minutes, sah!"

"Move them anyway," Admiral Clarke ordered. "Good lord, man, get out of there!"

"I'll not leave me men behind, Admiral!" Fitzgerald barked back, and then he cut off the transmission.

"Pompous English arse!" he spat, and then he turned to his men and pointed. "Well, let's get a move on lads! There's more work to be done here."

"Get him back on!" Admiral Clarke demanded.

"He's not responding, sir." Davies sweated.

"This is insubordination, that's what it is!" Clarke griped indignantly. "I'll have his Irish hide before a tribunal for this!"

The tall Englishman took a deep breath and gathered himself.

"Never mind him," he said to Davies in a calm voice. "Call Antigony's people. Tell them we've still got men down there, and we need time to get them out."

For the next ten minutes, Davies tried in vain to contact Sagobian government officials. Then, suddenly, all communications and transmissions from the planet went dead, including those from the stranded transports and the government news station. A moment later, the Sagobian capital city disappeared under a huge fireball which could be seen from space. Similar fireballs consumed every other city on Algenib IV. Admiral Clarke, his crew, and the crews of every other ship in orbit watched in stunned horror as the world below them burst into flames. The view from space was that of hundreds of tiny red mushrooms popping up all over the surface of the planet below.

"Scorched earth." Admiral Clarke quietly gulped. "Program Thirteen is scorched earth. The Sagobians have decided to leave nothing behind for the Strovats to harvest, except for a radioactive wasteland."

He looked at Davies.

"Fitzgerald?" he asked.

"You won't need to worry about that tribunal, sir." Davies shook his head.

CHAPTER 4

"Good morning, Tonya," said the pleasant-sounding female voice which emanated from her computer mounted in the wall by her bed. "It is 9 AM, Saturday."

This was a terminal of Alice 1000, the household computer, which was a smaller, family version of a ship's computer. Alice controlled the temperature, humidity, and oxygen levels of the house, and she also ran everything from water filtration to waste disposal. In addition, she controlled all of the robots which performed most of the work on the farm. She kept track of maintenance schedules and potential hazards such as storms. She helped them control their food storage and inventory, manage their finances, and even handled their event calendar. In fact, computers did so much in Tonya's society that she feared people had become too dependent on them. She was afraid that one day her family would wake up and Alice would no longer work, and then they would discover that they had forgotten how to count.

Tonya stirred but did not arise, because she had been out with Franz the night before and did not get home until two in the morning. Regardless, she had set the alarm so she could spend as much time as possible with her fiancé. The computer repeated the greeting one minute later, only this time slightly louder. Tonya sat up and rubbed the sleep from her eyes.

"Good morning, Al." She yawned.

"Happy twenty-first birthday, Tonya," the computer stated. "Would you like to listen to music this morning?"

"Yeah," Tonya replied while stretching. "My program six."

"Tonya program six," Alice 1000 echoed. "20th century Earth classical rock."

The computer began by playing Pearl Jam. Tonya was suddenly reminded that she had left the volume turned up from the day before.

"Not so loud." She winced. "Level two is fine."

She got up and faced the full-length mirror on the opposite wall, standing five-feet-six inches tall. She lifted her pajama top, exposing her belly, and sighed.

"Four weeks until my wedding day and I'm gaining weight," she mumbled as she fingered her very expensive engagement ring.

"You weigh one hundred thirty-two pounds of Earth mass," the computer said, loud enough for the dead to hear. "You have gained one pound in the last six days due to water retention because..."

"I know why I'm retaining water!" Tonya snapped.

She stomped about her room, searching for clean clothing to wear. She removed a pair of black jeans from a basket and a nice purple top from her closet, and then she dressed for the day. She kissed her framed picture of Franz which she kept on her dresser, instructed Alice to shut off the music, and then stepped into the hallway which led to the front of the house. She was immediately greeted by her two-year-old little brother, Benjamin, who was still in his pajamas. He had dark hair and dark eyes, just like their father.

"Tonya!" he exclaimed while jumping up and down with his arms outreached.

"Hi, Benny." She smiled and picked him up.

She carried him past the other bedroom doors and out into the house library, where she found her father working at his computer desk. She walked up behind him.

"Hi, Dad." She leaned over and kissed him on the cheek.

Ben reached out to him. "Dada!"

Their father took the toddler and sat him in his lap.

"Hello, again, Benjamin." He smiled. "It's Tonya's birthday today. Can you say 'Happy birthday'?"

"Hap birthday." The little boy smiled.

"Thank you." Tonya kissed him, and then she looked at their father. "He looks just like you."

"That's a good thing." Her father nodded. "And you look like your mother did twenty-five years ago."

"You make it sound like I don't look so good now," her mother said from behind them.

Tonya's mother also had blond hair and blue eyes, but her hair was short. She put her arm around Tonya and kissed her while wishing her happy birthday. She then picked Ben out of her husband's lap so that he could continue working.

"You aren't hard to come home to," Tonya's father said, and then he resumed his typing.

"Go on in the kitchen." Her mother motioned with her head. "I fixed breakfast for you."

"Mom, you didn't have to do that."

"Consider it a birthday present, and enjoy it while it lasts. A month from now you won't be getting those from me anymore."

"Thanks." Tonya smiled.

She walked into the kitchen, sat down, and proceeded to stuff herself.

"My baby is grown up." Her mother sighed. "In a month she'll be gone."

"You make it sound like she's dying," her father stated while typing. "She's getting married and moving into Franz's apartment in Portsmouth."

"But Adam, it's so far away," she fretted.

"It's only thirty miles, Violet." He stopped working and looked at her over the top of his glasses.

"She'll be by herself when he's on duty."

"I'll buy her a German Shepherd if you like."

"You're taking this rather well, considering your only daughter is about to get married. Most men get a little crazy over that."

"Well, Franz is a good young man, and he's the son of our best friends. I can certainly think of far worse scenarios."

"So can I." She kissed him on the head. "Are you working on another report?"

He nodded.

"You're supposed to be retired."

"No one's retired during a war," he said.

"How's it going?"

"Don't ask."

Once Tonya finished eating, she grabbed her purse and walked downstairs to their garage under the house. Resting next to her father's blue hovercar was her old fashioned four-wheeled car. She climbed into it and activated the computer with a command. No one used keys or cards any more. Anyone who couldn't get a vehicle's computer to operate with his voice would have to walk. Tonya asked Alice 1000 to open the garage door, and she drove out of the subterranean carport and onto the main road to Portsmouth.

"Call Franz," she instructed as she drove.

A moment later, his smiling face appeared on the small screen at the top of the dashboard. Franz's blue eyes looked happy to see her.

"Hi Franz!" She beamed at him.

"Hi, Honey," he replied, pressing his face against his computer screen and looking very silly in the process. "I love you!"

"I love you, too," she giggled. "You're fogging up the screen."

"Sorry." He backed up and wiped his screen clean. "Are you in your car?"

"Yeah. I'll be there in about twenty minutes."

"You know," he said, wagging his finger, "you shouldn't drive and talk. It's a very bad habit."

"I know how to do more than one thing at a time." She smirked. "You always tell me how good a driver I..."

A collision warning signal popped up, and her car suddenly jerked to the right by itself to avoid an oncoming truck which was straddling the center line.

"WHOA!" she yelped, and then cursed at the truck driver as he flew by. The rush of wind pushed her further over, and she had to veer sharply to the left just to stay on the road.

"Tonya! Are you okay?" asked Franz.

"Yeah." She frowned. "I'm okay. I just passed a truck driver who got his license from the back of a cereal box."

"Maybe we should wait until you get here before we talk."

"Hey, that wasn't my fault. That guy was in the wrong lane!"

"I know he was," he admonished, "but you like to drive fast, and that doesn't mix well with talking. I prefer you to get here in one piece, so we can talk later. Bye."

"Bye." She exhaled and shut off the call.

A few minutes later, she entered the city limits and had to slow down considerably, for here there were speed limits. With a population of over half a million, Portsmouth was the second largest city on this mostly agrarian planet. To say that Dragos was sparsely populated would be an understatement. It was yet a new world, and possessed entire continents which were still uninhabited.

Portsmouth had been built using the standard Tellopian galactic city layout. The spaceport was in the center of town, with the local military base right next door. Surrounding this area were the business and industrial zones, intermingled with the low rent housing areas and several red light districts. Toward the outer edges of town lay the main residential areas and the shopping centers. Franz and his engineer (and commanding officer), Jim Washington, lived together in this section.

Off base housing was one benefit Franz received from being in the Nervii Special Forces. Another was that he would get extended leave. Sometimes he could be home for three or four months at a time. This particular furlough was for three months, and they had planned their wedding around it. They would spend the first month with their families and friends and then get married, because they knew that once they finally did so, no one else would see much of them. They planned to live in Franz's place, so the extra month also gave Jim time to relocate.

He had arrived on Tuesday night, and spent the next two days at his parents' house. On Friday she had to work all day, and he had moved back into his apartment in town.

She pulled her car onto the carport of Franz's place, which was a modest one-level rental house in a quiet neighborhood. He sat, waiting for her on his front doorstep wearing his green fatigues, with a .45 caliber handgun holstered on his black waist belt. When Tonya arrived, he stood, and she rushed to greet him. He was over six feet tall and weighed over two hundred pounds, with broad shoulders, fair skin, and a muscular v-shaped torso. She jumped into his arms and he twirled her around.

"I love you!" He smiled.

"I love you, too!" she replied, and then she kissed him very passionately.

He put her down and she put her hands on his waist and kissed him again. She moved her hands down further, encountered his gun, and then frowned slightly.

"I wish you didn't have to wear that all the time," she said.

"You know regulations," he said.

"I know," she said. "You're told to always be in a state of readiness, but it's stupid. We're in the back corner of the Tellopian basement, and everyone knows it. There's nothing here. The Strovats aren't going to jump over all those other crowded worlds to get to us."

"Well, the Heruli and the Alamani are just next door." He shrugged. "I need it anyway. We're planning to go target shooting at the base this morning."

"How romantic." She clasped her hands together and made a sarcastic happy face. "I'm sure you and Jim will have a lovely time."

Franz opened the front door and they both entered his apartment. It was a standard place with a large living room, a kitchen off to the left, and a hallway in the back which led straight to a bathroom. The two bedrooms were on either side of the bath. A very large, muscular African-American man sat on their living room couch. He wore fatigues, a baseball cap, and ate cold cereal while watching Saturday morning cartoons.

Tonya had known Jim Washington ever since Franz had been put under his command two years previously. He stood six-feet-five inches tall, with broad shoulders and a chiseled frame which only comes with years of serious strength training. He was the commander of their special unit, which was a two-man operation. Together, with the assistance of several robots, they flew a Nervii frigate. Most of their missions were behind the Strovat front, where they conducted organized raids and rescue operations. The two men were good friends, and Tonya always told Franz that it was a good thing that they got along so well. Being confined together for long periods of time in space always had the potential to drive men batty, and in extreme cases it could lead them to kill one another.

"You'd better be nice to Jim," she had teased Franz one day. "I'd be very upset if he squashed you like a grape."

"I can take care of myself," Franz had replied. "He may be bigger, but I could take him."

"Yeah, while he's asleep," Tonya had giggled. "But while he's awake you ought to be really nice to him."

Tonya walked over to Jim, leaned over and gave him a hug.

"Hey, Baby." He smiled. "You goin' with us to target practice?"

"Sure." She shrugged. "Can I use your .357 Magnum this time?"

"No, actually," Jim said, "I think your boyfriend has something for you."

"Really?" Her eyes lit up.

"Yes." Franz nodded. "I have your birthday present. Let me get it for you."

After Franz disappeared into his room, Tonya leaned over and whispered to Jim, "What is it?"

"It's a secret," he whispered back.

She playfully smacked him on the head and he laughed, as Franz emerged with a small jewelry box. He opened it, revealing a gold necklace with a diamond pendant in the shape of an angel. Tonya was breathless as he put it around her neck.

"Happy birthday, my love," he whispered into her ear.

"Thank you." She put her hands on his cheeks and kissed him.

Jim rolled his eyes as they continued to kiss. Eventually he emitted a not-so-polite cough, which had the desired effect.

"Now," he ordered, pointing toward the bedrooms, "why don't you go and get her the other present? The one we both bought for her."

Franz disappeared again into the back and emerged with what looked like a black shoebox.

"This one is more practical," he said as he handed it to her.

"This is too heavy to be shoes." She held it up and then saw the handle. "Is this a gun case? Did you two buy me a gun to protect myself with?"

"I knew she would figure it out," Franz said. "I told you. She's clairvoyant."

"More like a lucky guess this time," Jim replied. "Anyway, it's not just any gun. Open it up."

She did so and found a handgun inside, but not one of any fashion which she had before seen. It resembled Franz's .45, except that it was larger and looked to be of heavier design. The chamber was cylindrical and three inches in diameter. The barrel was cylindrical as well and only slightly less wide, and it was six inches long. The handgrip magazine was the same as Franz's gun, except it was slightly longer and bigger. Tonya saw that she would need to use both hands to fire this weapon. It had a trigger and safety button the same as other pistols, but there appeared to be no way to cock this weapon. Instead it had a power switch. Several bullets were in the lining of the case. Tonya gaped at them. They were the size of shotgun shells.

"Uh...thanks, guys," she managed to say. "Do you think it's big enough?"

Jim pointed. "Try it out."

"You're kidding, right?" She gave them a funny look.

"It's not as bad as it looks," Franz said. "Pick it up."

She did so, and despite its bulk it was remarkably light. She pressed the red power button and it hummed. The word 'EMPTY' appeared in green light on the top of the chamber.

"Whoa, this is cool." She looked it over. "I mean...I kinda expected you guys to get me a gun at some point, but...wow."

"You were expecting a gun?" Franz asked.

"Well...yeah, at some point," she replied. "You're military guys and I'm an army brat, and we go target shooting enough, so I figured you'd get tired of me using your guns all the time. But....because I'm a little person I thought ya'll would buy me a small gun, like a .32 or something, and here you go and get me a bazooka. Silly me."

"As you know, Strovats have very hard exoskeletons and they attack in bunches," Franz said. "I've seen nine millimeter guns fail to stop them, so a pea-shooter like a .32 would be useless against Strovats, or Heruli for that matter."

"You know, it's funny." Jim smirked. "With all the technology they have, those bugs can't stand up to our old fashioned guns. We can mow them down with automatic rifles, machine guns, and even shotguns if we use the heavy shot."

"And best of all, our old-style weapons are cheap," Franz added. "You can take off a Strovat's head with a cheap, high caliber pistol just as well as with an expensive laser, and our old fashioned grenades kill them just as well as the plasma ones do. Even the sound of our guns firing messes them up."

"Yeah, that makes sense." Tonya nodded. "My dad says they communicate through their antennae. The gunfire noise could certainly vibrate those things and stun them."

"But you gotta use either high-caliber or high-velocity guns to stop them," Jim said as he held up his .50 caliber semi-automatic pistol. "This baby here can take a Strovat's head right off, or shatter his thorax with one shot. I can stop eight of them with one clip. With a nine millimeter, I might have to fire three or four times just to stop one, and like he said, they attack in bunches."

"Yes, the higher calibers are better," Franz said. "We have two Tommy guns on the ship."

"Tommy guns?" Tonya gaped. "You mean the old Al Capone machine guns?"

"Yes, but they're better, modern versions of the Thompson," Franz replied. "They have fifty-round magazines just the same. The smaller caliber submachineguns aren't as effective, but the Thompson can cut a bunch of Strovats to pieces. It really tears them apart at medium or short range."

"So, wouldn't I do better with a regular gun? This one looks like it'll knock me down every time I fire it."

"No, that's just it." Franz smiled. "Let me show you."

He stretched out his big hand, and she handed it to him.

"The only problem with our old guns is they won't fire in a vacuum," Franz explained. "But this gun can fire in zero atmosphere, because it's not gas operated, it's magnetic. There's no explosion, so there's virtually no kick. When you pull the trigger, a magnetic field moves rapidly up and down the barrel and spins the bullet out like a rifle shot. The round comes out at over a thousand feet per second, which is comparable to my .45. When you turn it on, the gun will automatically cock itself. If it's empty you will see the green light here. To reload, you simply press the trigger while it's empty, like this."

He pulled the trigger and the top of the chamber opened up. He showed her how to load the gun by inserting six of the large rounds into the chamber, and then closing the chamber by pushing the safety button. The number six appeared in red where the word 'EMPTY' had been.

"Wow, this is really cool," she said while looking it over. "I've heard about guns like these, but never seen one before. My dad said the Heruli use magnetic guns."

"Yes, that's true," Franz said. "The Heruli use nasty, high-powered, magnetic auto-rifles that fire supersteel needles at high velocity. Those things can make Swiss cheese out of almost anything."

"Gosh, what size are these rounds?" she asked. "They're huge."

"Eighteen millimeter," Jim replied. "About .70 caliber."

She whistled and said, "this looks really expensive, guys.

Thanks."

"Oh, it is." Jim nodded. "These guns are good but very expensive. That's why we use the old guns. We've got a couple of bulky rifle versions of that on our ship, but we almost never fight in zero atmosphere, so they just sit in a locker. Our ship's got a .70 cal magnet machine gun mounted on it which can fire in either atmosphere or space, but we only use that when we're attacked by Strovats on the ground during rescue operations."

"So," Tonya asked with a smile, "when do I get to try this out?"

"Thought you'd never ask." Jim grinned.

They locked up the apartment and exited through the back door. They climbed into Jim's wheeled car, which was a replica of a Cadillac. Franz and Tonya snuggled together in the back seat as Jim drove them to the military base.

"Hmmpf!" he complained. "I feel like a damn chauffeur. I really need to get a girlfriend."

The base in town was surrounded by a reinforced concrete wall. However, the main entrance was not closed off by a gate of any kind. From a distance, it appeared that nothing existed at the front door to prevent intrusion. As they drew closer, the air in front of the entrance shimmered slightly. Tonya knew what it was, for she had been through that gate thousands of times. Her parents came here every week to shop for groceries at the commissary.

All entrances to the base were protected by an energy force field. This field also extended over the top of the concrete wall. Anyone who attempted unauthorized entry, whether through a gateway or over the wall, would end up looking like a burnt French fry. When Tonya was in middle school, a group of radicals had tried to force their way through a gateway in a stolen armored car. Their improvised tank got stuck in the force field and melted.

Jim stopped his car in front of the entrance. He got out and walked over to what appeared to be a black brick in the concrete wall. He removed an ID card from his wallet and held it close to the black box.

"Lieutenant Commander James L Washington," he announced.

"Lieutenant Commander James Lionel Washington," replied a pleasant female voice.

A thin red beam quickly scanned his face.

"Retina scan positive," the female voice stated. "Hair DNA confirmed. Identification confirmed. Security level one. Access approved to all sectors."

They entered the base and he parked his car next to a large building that was not far from the front gate. This was the practice facility, and it was full of indoor firing ranges and other training areas. Tonya had been to this place several times. Her father had first brought her here when she was ten years old to teach her how to shoot.

They went to the supply center to purchase ammunition. Tonya bought a box of a hundred shells for her gun, and Franz purchased a waist belt and holster for her. He put the belt on her and slid her gun into the holster which extended down her thigh.

"It's a little bulky," she said while examining herself. "Does it look okay?"

"You look very sexy." Franz smiled. "Now I want to buy you a tight leather outfit to go with it."

"For our wedding night, by the sound of it." She smirked and put her arms around him. "Trust me, I've got something else to wear that you'll like a lot more."

"Get a room." Jim rolled his eyes.

The practice facility was built like a single-level mall. They walked through a long concourse that had training rooms on either side. Some rooms contained battle simulation, some contained tanks for Zero-G training, and there were quite a few shooting ranges. Tonya had tried the battle simulation on a beginner's level and found it to be quite scary enough. She decided against going up any levels on that. The other chamber she did not like was the G-Force simulation, which she compared to like being in the spin cycle of a washing machine. She had tried that once before and was sick for the rest of that day. However, she liked the zero-gravity chambers, which simulated the weightlessness of space. She thought that was fun, and teased Franz that after they were married they should find a hotel that had Zero-G rooms.

Along with Humans, many different races from throughout the League were also there. Tonya saw several short, yellow, hairless, humanoid Tellopians, as well as a few tall, Viking-like Kirharans. She also noticed a few of the short, green, alligator-like Nervii, and quite a lot of the strange three-legged reptilian Gutayids. She had seen these races many times before, but she was surprised by the next one she saw.

"Wow, Burbesenys," she said. "Don't see them much way out here."

"They're starting to show up all over," Franz said. "They're now the right arm of the fleet. When they came into the League they brought with them over a thousand ships of the line, half of which were K class battleships, and all of which were bigger and better than ours."

"I've seen diagrams of Burbeseny battleships," Tonya said. "They're huge. My dad says they're like five times bigger than our biggest warships."

"And yet they're small compared to the Strovat Bisas." Franz exhaled. "And we don't know how many Bisas are out there."

The trio got out of the way and watched the two Burbesenys go by them. They wore rectangular, armored tank suits which were filled with water. Each of these was six feet tall, five feet long, and trundled along on bulldozer tracks. Burbeseny tank suits had four tentacles and a clear front, through which the creatures could see out, and through which they could be seen. Their heads were large and fish-like, with wide, toothy mouths. They communicated to each other by an unknown form of aquatic radio technology. Indeed, of all the races in the quadrant, it was the Burbesenys whose culture and technology was truly alien.

The three friends picked one of the less crowded firing ranges, one which had lifelike targets made from ballistic material. These were very realistic statues, which could be made to stand still, retreat, move back and forth, or even advance upon you as you fired. One could choose to fire at simulated animals, or those of virtually any race in the quadrant, including Strovats, Alamani, and Heruli. These targets took damage in a very realistic fashion, including emitting fluids. Thankfully, Tonya thought, they did not emit any odors.

As they entered the range, they placed small plugs in their ears and donned eye protection glasses. They walked past a group of Nervii who were trying out Thompson submachineguns on fake Strovats. Just as Franz had stated earlier, these old-style Human weapons made mincemeat out of their targets. One of the Nervii gave Tonya a toothy grin and held up his submachinegun, signifying that he liked it. She waved politely at him, and the Nervii soldier returned to demolishing simulated Strovats with absolute glee.

Tonya noticed a Tellopian firing a pistol like hers. He set the target to charge him, and made ready as a simulated Strovat rose out of the floor. As it rapidly approached, he held the trigger down, emptying his magazine. He blew off two of its arms, but failed to score a kill shot. It stopped ten feet from him and a red light flashed, signifying that the target had killed him. His friends responded with scornful laughter.

They each chose a station and selected their language and targets via touch screens. Both Franz and Jim started shooting with their usual competitive fervor, but Tonya took her time on stationary targets so that she could get used to her weapon. It was lightweight, but bulky, and she found that she needed both hands to fire effectively, even with virtually no recoil. Upon firing, she heard no loud, explosive noise, but instead her weapon emitted a strange sort of humming sound as it discharged. It devastated her chosen targets, which consisted of a couple of giant spiders and a few Strovats. She thought her gun was every bit as deadly as Jim's .50 caliber, if not more so.

After a few more tries she became comfortable enough to attempt the charge setting. She punched up a Strovat on her screen and ordered it to come right at her. Franz noticed that she had increased her target difficulty, and he motioned for Jim to stop and watch.

A Strovat rose from the floor and charged her. As it rapidly approached, she widened her stance and steadied her weapon. When it came within fifteen feet, she squeezed off a shot. The round struck the Strovat at the top of the thorax and completely removed its head. The target stopped moving and a green light flashed, signifying a kill, and "Good job!" appeared on her station console. Both Franz and Jim came over and gave her high fives.

"This thing is great." She smiled. "Thanks, guys!"

Just then Tonya noticed a yellow light flashing on her station's computer console. She looked around, and the same thing was occurring at the other stations.

"Something's up," she said as she shut off her gun and holstered it. "That's the news signal."

As Franz typed on his console, Tonya looked about and discovered that all the others in the shooting gallery had also stopped what they were doing. Many headed toward the exits.

"It says there's news about the war." Franz shook his head. "But it won't tell me anything else."

"They're probably not connected to anything outside of this room," Jim said. "We need to go to an outside source to see what's going on."

They did not bother to try their phones, because the buildings on the base had been built to withstand a nuclear blast. They packed up their stuff and headed for the parking lot.

"We may as well get something to eat," Jim said. "You know, whatever it is, it's at least a week old. We're five days away from Tellops. The Heruli could come here and own this system for a week before anyone in the central government could find out about it."

"That's why land is so cheap here," Franz remarked as they walked out into the concourse.

"But it's crazy," Tonya complained. "We have all this technology, but if I try to send any message to another star system it's like I'm suddenly back in the 18th century. I either have to send it by courier, or a drone, or go there myself. I can call the other side of the planet, but not Earth? You'd think that if we can travel faster than light that we could also call faster, but noooooooooo! We still have the same phone technology we had a hundred and fifty years ago."

"We can cure radiation disease with a pill, but we still get the flu," Jim said with a shrug. "The more things change, the more they stay the same. The news stations are all close to the star docks, because the only way they get any outside info is from ships coming into port. Even the military has to use drones to communicate between star systems, Babe. We have to go station to station like everyone else, because normal transmissions are useless across deep space. That's just the way things are."

"Yeah, but it's so stupid!" she fussed. "You guys could lose an entire fleet, and a major world could get taken by the enemy and no one, including those bozos at Central Command, would even know about it. I mean, how can they even confirm information that might be a week old when they get it? Oh, and we can forget about any advance warning if for some reason the Strovats want to come here."

"Preachin' to the choir, Babe," Jim said. "Trust me, it's just as frustrating to us when we have to communicate long-distance to our commanders. It's one reason why we get so much leeway to make our own decisions. It drives our commanding officers nuts, too."

"You'd think it would be a top priority for them to fix that during a war," she murmured.

On their way out, they stopped at the food court and picked up lunch. They walked outside, and since the weather was clear, they found a table. Jim tuned his phone in to the local English news station and caught the reporters in mid-discussion.

"There is no word on exactly how many refugees were able to get out before the battle took place," a female newscaster reported. "But we fear that most of them could not possibly have escaped. Two weeks ago, we reported that that area was flooded with millions of refugees from their home world. It was a complete mess there, and the government had little control over the situation."

"Yes, that's true," the anchorman added. "At Algenib, there were reportedly over eight hundred million of their citizens, half of which were refugees. The Sagobian government had been decimated during the loss of their home world in the Epsilon Perseus system, and here it seems they were simply overwhelmed. They were seemingly powerless to stop this tragedy, even though they knew it was coming. The central government sent literally an army of personnel and a good portion of the fleet to assist the Sagobians, but now it appears that help may have been too late."

"Once again," the anchorman said, turning to face the audience, "there has been a huge battle in the Algenib system, in which lies the last home world of the Sagobians..."

"This is bad." Jim shook his head.

"How far is Algenib from here?" Tonya asked.

"It's on the other side of the Nephilim kingdom," Franz replied. "At least ten days away."

"More than that," Jim said. "I'd say this battle happened at least two weeks ago."

"...This was a major offensive on the part of the Strovats," the anchorman continued. "Unconfirmed reports indicate that there may have been as many as one hundred of their Bisa supercruisers which took part in this battle..."

"One hundred Bisas?" Franz gasped.

"We lost, didn't we?" Tonya asked.

"I'd say so," Jim said. "I've seen one of those Bisas take out five Tellopian cruisers at once. They were as big as our battleships, only slower, and that Bisa just pulverized them like they were nothing."

"Bisas can both dish out and take a mountain of punishment," Franz said. "Our frigate is longer than a football field, and it would be like a gnat to one of those monsters."

"...The Sagobians were desperately fighting to save their people," the anchorman persisted. "Most of the remaining Sagobian fleet is reported to have been destroyed in the battle. Though inflicting heavy casualties on the enemy, the League fleet was forced to withdraw. The Algenib system is now in Strovat hands. What will become of the millions of Sagobians on Algenib IV is now unknown..."

"No, it's not," Tonya sighed. "We all know what'll happen to them."

"Maybe," Jim said. "Both Algenib and Epsilon Perseus are still claimed by the Nephilim. I doubt if they're just going to sit back and let the Strovats take it. I'll bet the Nephilim are looking for any excuse to fight the Strovats right now."

"Yes, but they're also probably not upset that the Strovats are killing their old enemies, either," Franz pointed out.

"Neither are the Alamani," Tonya added. "Since the Strovats have spent the better part of the last thirty years getting rid of Alamani enemies, they might more likely join up with those bugs than fight them."

"You know there are rumors that the Alamani are talking to the Strovats," Franz said.

"Great." Tonya frowned.

They did not touch their food as they listened to the reports trickle in.

CHAPTER 5

Thunder awakened the king of Alaman. He sat up in his vast, circular bed and listened in the darkness. He thought to himself that it must be a great storm outside for him to feel it, for his bed chamber was buried deep inside his mighty fortress, and very few sounds could filter through from outside. He gazed for a moment at Radi, who slept peacefully next to him.

However, he could sense that something was not right. He tried to ignore his intuition and laid back down. A second noise came through, one which was much louder and shook the very foundation of the citadel.

"That is no storm!" he said, leaping from his bed.

Another shudder came and nearly knocked him off his feet. He threw on a robe and dashed through the entrance to his bedroom and out into the corridor. The guards were not there, and the post up the corridor was abandoned.

"*Lieutenant!*" the king bellowed.

There was no response.

"Balzi will pay for this," he growled.

Another shock wave hit. Parts of the ceiling came loose, and dust fell. Golar Hassiid braced himself against a wall and bated his breath. He scooted along the wall and slowly approached the guard post at the end of the hallway.

When he arrived there, he found that all the guards' equipment had been destroyed. The computer, the holographic displays, everything had been smashed. Incredibly, the large support beam in the center of the area was cracked down the middle, with a strange, alien weapon protruding from it. The king stepped toward it and stumbled over Lieutenant Balzi, or rather what was left of him. He had been split in two, and he lay in a pool of his own ooze. His supersteel armor had been sliced through as if it was paper.

"What manner of weapon has done this?" the king gasped.

He stepped over to the broken beam to examine the weapon, which had the look of a huge tomahawk, with a three-foot-long haft that was curved near the top and shimmered like some form of hardened crystal. The bladed head was made of some unknown black alloy, and it was embedded deep inside the beam.

The king could not believe his eyes, for both the support beam and Balzi's armor were made from Alamani supersteel; an atomically bonded alloy considered to be the hardest metal in that quadrant of the galaxy. Alamani swords were feared, for they could penetrate titanium with ease, and their armor could withstand most any slugs. Even lasers took time to cut through supersteel, but this alien weapon had sliced it like paper. The angle at which it protruded suggested that it had been thrown, and the trajectory passed over the dead body of Balzi, as if it had cut him in two and split the beam with one blow.

The tall, strong king of Alaman wrenched the weapon from the support beam, and found it to be very heavy. Golar Hassiid thought it must be made from extremely dense materials, and whoever could have thrown it must have been of great strength. What was more incredible was the fact that its blade had not at all been nicked. He dropped the malicious alien device. It clanged and took a chunk out of the stone floor.

Suddenly a flash of light appeared, followed by a clap of thunder which shook the walls. Now the storm seemed inside the citadel. This was not at all correct, so the king thought to himself. He ran down the hallway, past two more destroyed guard stations, and headed for the ramp which led upward to his great domed hall. When he approached the final corner, he was nearly trampled by a group of emergency medical personnel who brought past him a score of mangled soldiers.

They hardly noticed the king as they pushed by him, carrying the wounded on pneumo-stretchers - self-supporting cots that could be guided with a single hand. These Alamani soldiers, from the finest of Golar Hassiid's legions, were badly mauled. Some were missing limbs, and others had gaping holes torn through their armor, as if they had been struck by cannon shot. The look in their eyes reflected inconceivable terror.

Once they had passed, Golar Hassiid was free to round the final corner and move up the ramp to his great hall. However, this brave king who had personally led troops in battle as a prince now hesitated. What came over him was a strange, instinctive fear which he had never before felt. For the next few moments, as more thuds shook his citadel, he fought a desperate inner battle to keep himself from bounding back to his bedroom and hiding under the covers.

At last he composed himself and proceeded up the long ramp. He entered the great hall, and what he encountered stunned him with utter horror. The giant dome had been blown off, and the front wall was reduced to rubble. The king could see his Blue Guards crouched among the ruins, as if they were bracing for an assault. Looking up he could not see any stars, for the sky was filled with smoke. Looking down he saw the most terrible sight of all. His great capital city, engulfed in flames!

He stumbled forward, but someone grabbed his arm and pulled him behind a large slab of fallen stone. It was Ator, and his face was lit with primal fear.

"My king, you must go from this place!" the general exclaimed. "It is not safe here! They are coming!"

"Who?" Golar Hassiid grabbed Ator by the top of his breastplate. *"In the name of Alè, what is going on?"*

"It is the Leviathan!" Ator huffed and pointed toward the ramp. "My lord, you must go!"

"What happened to our security alert systems?" the king demanded. "Why have we been taken by surprise? Where is Karg? *Where is my fleet?"*

"They are gone." Ator looked down, crestfallen. "The fleet is destroyed."

"No!" Golar Hassiid shook his head. "This cannot be!"

"They came upon us out of nowhere." Ator clenched his fist in frustration. "Our warning systems did not see them, and our ground defenses could not lock onto their ships! It is all gone...*everything is gone!"*

The brave king of Alaman tried to respond, but he was speechless. He looked down at his once great city and watched it burn.

"Here they come!" yelled the sergeant at the front of the citadel.

A small, blue, grenade-like object arced over the sergeant's position. With a crack of thunder, it exploded into a ball of light. A small, concentrated electrical storm erupted to form a spherical, hellish oven of interconnected lightning which lasted for several seconds and cooked every member of that platoon. It finally dissipated, leaving only charred bodies behind the rubble of the front wall.

Suddenly giants, terrible to behold, charged over the lip of the remains of the front wall. It was only then that Golar Hassiid remembered Orizah's warning. They were massive grayish-green reptilians, each one of which was nearly eight feet tall and four feet wide, with legs like tree trunks and long, powerful arms with huge hands. Their bright red eyes were like tree fruit, and their huge, gaping mouths were filled with crystalline, slavering fangs. One of the monsters looked directly at Golar Hassiid, opened his mouth wide enough to bite someone's head off, and emitted a terrifying roar that froze the king's blue blood.

The Leviathans blasted elite Alamani troops into oblivion with huge, double-barreled machine guns that fired bullets the size of small cannon shot. These high-velocity projectiles punched through supersteel armor, pulverized stone, and tore bodies to pieces. They mowed the king's soldiers down, no matter what cover they sought. The ones who hid behind stone and steel rubble may as well have crouched behind cardboard.

Two of the monsters fired wicked looking rifles with three-pronged barrels that shot lightning bolts. These static guns reached over and around cover and electrocuted multiple targets, and anyone wearing, using, or even next to anything conductible was vulnerable. The static from these weapons killed many more by detonating the defenders' grenades, and causing one unfortunate guard's plasma rifle to explode.

All of the aliens carried the dreadful throwing axe which Golar Hassiid had already encountered. Some used them hand to hand, and others threw them at their targets. Either way, the results were the same. These axes sliced through supersteel like soft butter.

The giant invaders rolled over the rubble like an irresistible gray-green tide. Nothing could stop these behemoths. Supersteel swords broke over their crested heads. Lasers did not cut them.

Armor piercing grenades did not phase them. Even the dreaded plasma rifles were useless against these monsters, as their superheated bolts simply bounced off. Golar Hassiid's men put up a withering fire, yet not a single monster alien went down. The king of Alaman watched in frozen terror as his elite Blue Guards, thought to be the best troops in the galaxy, got slaughtered like sheep before him.

The monarch turned to look at his golden throne, which had been mangled by the double-barreled machine gun fire. Hanging above it was the Sword of the Fathers. This ancient weapon of generations past gleamed at him with its supersteel haft and black blade wrought from meteorite metal. Golar Hassiid rushed to it and plucked it from the wall, just as Ator and the last of his men threw themselves in front of the advancing monsters. The king turned to attack the enemy, but was stopped in his tracks by Ator's head rolling into his feet. He looked up to see Karg's head bounce off his chest. The mighty king of Alaman reeled as the monsters mocked him, while battering him with the heads of his other ministers. Their cold, hideous alien laughter froze his spine.

Only the sight of Radi's head awakened him from his trance. Golar Hassiid flew into a rage, spun about and chopped at the closest alien's trunk-like neck. The Sword of the Fathers broke apart at the haft, stunning the king and forcing him to stumble backward. The behemoths ceased their laughter and raised their awful axes. They uttered horrible roars, and then charged the king.

King Golar Hassiid awakened on the floor beside his bed, screaming in terror. Radi rushed over to him and put her arms around his shoulders. He clutched her as if he was hanging off the edge of a cliff. The royal guards burst into the room, led by Lieutenant Balzi.

"It is all right," Radi said. "He was having another nightmare."

Balzi bowed, and then he and his men returned to their post, closing the door behind them on the way out.

"A...another n-nightmare?" Golar Hassiid shivered.

"Yes, my lord." Radi kissed his cheek. "It was only a dream."

Golar Hassiid closed his eyes, took a deep breath, and composed himself. A moment later, he opened his eyes and looked at her.

"No." He shook his head. "This has gone on for five nights. This is more than a dream. I must do something, or we will all be destroyed."

He stood and she retrieved a robe for him. He wrapped himself in it, and she gave him a worried look.

"What I do now, I do for you." He smiled at her.

He looked over at the console on the wall, and ordered his computer to contact Admiral Karg. It came to life, and moments later the bleary-eyed old admiral appeared on the screen.

"Good morning, my king." Karg smiled as one of his servants handed him a hot drink.

"Admiral," the king calmly ordered, "I want you to summon an emergency session of the Witan."

"For the morning at first light?" Karg asked.

"No, this night," Golar Hassiid instructed. "Assemble the elders as soon as possible."

"Yes, my lord." Karg nodded. "Is there anything else?"

The king stroked his beard and thought for a moment.

"Yes, two things," he replied. "Summon Talg the Lore Master, and have Ator detain that prophet."

CHAPTER 6

Later that morning, before their sun rose over the horizon, the Witan assembled in the palace council chamber. The king ordered the palace servants to prepare both food and drinks. Each minister was provided with bread and hot, clear fruit drinks which were called Koolas. As they awaited their king, the five ministers refreshed themselves and gathered their thoughts. They quietly discussed the nature of this meeting among themselves.

"But, if there truly is no military emergency, as General Ator has reported, then why call for an emergency meeting in the middle of the night?" a weary-eyed Nurgud argued.

"I do not know," Ator grumbled, "but whatever it may be, I am glad of it. I cannot sleep any more this night, nor do I wish to."

"Nor do I," Pekota agreed, with a sullen look. "Ever since that prophet showed himself, I cannot sleep without terrible dreams. I think I must be going mad."

"I as well." Eblock put a hand over his face. "For five nights now I have dreamed of horrible monsters from the Outer Rim, just as that gardener said. Last evening, I rolled out of my bed. Kala, my second wife, told me that I was screaming."

"And what were your dreams about?" asked Karg, who propped up his chin and raised his eyebrows.

"My dreams are all the same, as if every night I am caught in a horrid time loop," Eblock murmured. "I am with Baron Hareseth and his Stosstrupen, the Heruli's very best soldiers. They are under attack by monstrous aliens which we have never before encountered. The Heruli can neither track nor lock their weapons on the alien warships. No weapon we possess can stop them, and they have terrible weaponry. Every night it is the same outcome. We are all slaughtered."

"It is the same in my dreams, every night," Karg stated. "An alien armada appears out of nowhere, attacking us from the direction of the Outer Rim of the galaxy. Their ships have incredible power readings, and our own weapon systems cannot lock onto them. They annihilate our grand fleet before my eyes. They board my flagship and storm the bridge, and then I awaken. I learned years ago how to control my dreams through psionics, but I cannot stop these nightmares."

"Each night I and my best soldiers are cut down in the great hall defending the king." Ator clenched a fist. "Swords, grenades, lasers, even our plasma rifles are all useless against these Leviathans!"

At that moment, the double security doors opened. The ministers stood as Urudo entered the room and then took one step to the left.

"All hail King Golar Hassiid, emperor of Alaman," he announced.

The king entered and with one voice everyone in the room said, "Alè tu Alaman," which is to say, "Lord of the Lord's people." Golar Hassiid motioned with one hand for everyone to sit, as Alamani custom dictated that the most important person in the room should be seated last. Urudo left the room, closing the doors behind him, and then the king sat at the center of the U-shaped table.

"Six days ago, we had a rather unusual visitor in the great hall," the king began. "As many of you know, since that time I have experienced...dreams, which are very disturbing to me. They are all the same, and they fulfill what that prophet foretold. I see the end of Alaman."

For a few moments, which seemed like hours, no one said anything. The king stared at the table as his ministers looked at each other.

"I have called this meeting to try and get to the bottom of this," Golar Hassiid finally proceeded. "We must find out about this Leviathan which Orizah spoke of. I realize that some of you may fear that I may be mad. I have questioned this myself."

"Nay, my lord." Karg shook his head. "If you are mad, then so are we, for we have all shared similar nightmares since that prophet spoke his warning."

"Truly?" the king asked. "Please, tell me of your dreams."

One by one the king's ministers related their versions of the same nightmare. The king was astonished at how their dreams interconnected, especially Ator's description of dying in front of him, just as his own dream had revealed.

"The Heruli are worthy warriors," Eblock finished. "I have never seen them back down from a fight. Yet they flee like frightened children before these monsters, whatever they are."

"Whatever they are, the Strovats would fare no better against them," Ator said. "Their vast numbers would mean nothing. These giants would exterminate them like cockroaches. My lord, if that prophet is correct, if we are to choose between the Strovats and these Leviathans, then let us fight the bugs."

"But what if this is some sort of trick?" Pekota asked. "What if that prophet has put some sort of spell or curse upon us? Maybe this is some sort of ruse to trick us into following him."

"You forget, my friend, that we were not all in the room with the king when this gardener made his prediction," Nurgud pointed out. "How could he curse you, myself, and Eblock if we were not present?"

"Also, he did not bid us to follow him," Ator said. "He did not ask for money or favors. He only gave the warning. There was no motivation other than to obey God, or so he said."

"Perhaps..." Karg thought out loud, "perhaps there is truth in this. Our dreams all coincide. This cannot be mere coincidence, can it? Could it be that this gardener told us the truth? Maybe these dreams we are having are some sort of premonition of future events."

"Maybe." The king nodded. "Or perhaps it is a warning from God. Either way, we will hear more from that gardener this night, for he shall come and explain himself. I also have summoned Talg, the Lore Master. Perhaps he may shed some light on these Leviathans, whether they be real or not."

"They seem real enough," Ator said.

The king tapped his wrist communicator and said, "Balzi, bring them in."

Talg the Lore Master was led in. He was a venerable Alamani

64

with hoary hair, but still in good health for his age. Talg had been the guest of the king many times, and oft times acted as a historical consultant for the Witan. He carried with him a very large and very old book. He smiled and bowed low before being led to his seat at one end of the table.

Orizah was then brought in, blindfolded and bound. He was old, bent and haggard. The guards led him to the opposite end of the table. They seated him and removed his bonds and his blindfold. Orizah's eyes beheld a sight not normally seen by ordinary Alamani who usually lived to see another day; the king and his Witan in their council chamber. The old gardener tried to appear calm, but he silently gulped.

"Orizah," the king addressed him, "do you know where you are?"

"Yes, my king." The old gardener looked around. "Unless, of course, I am dreaming."

"You are not," Golar Hassiid stated. "Do you know why I have brought you here?"

"I presume that it is because of what I said to you six days ago, my king," Orizah replied.

"That is correct." The king gave him a stern look. "Your life now depends on how you answer my next question. Orizah, if I agree to reward you and your followers, will you recant your statement about the destruction of Alaman?"

"No, my king." Orizah looked him in the eye. "What I said to you was from Alè. I cannot recant the words of God, even if my life depends on it."

"Well said." The king sat back and exhaled. "That was the correct answer. Now I know that you have not done this for personal gain."

Orizah heaved a sigh of relief and bowed his head, silently thanking his God.

"I did not bring you here to pass judgement," the king continued. "You are here to clarify what you said to me in the hall of my ancestors. What is this Leviathan you speak of?"

"I do not know." Orizah shook his head and closed his eyes. "But for the past month they have haunted me in my dreams. I see them destroy our fleet, lay waste to our cities, and slay you, great king, in your own hall. When I inquired of the Lord, He revealed unto me that these are the Leviathans of old. That long ago they came from the Outer Rim to destroy the kingdoms that were once here, and that they will soon return."

Orizah went on to describe the exact same giant, seemingly indestructible beasts which both the king and his counselors had seen in their dreams. When he was finished all in the room were astounded, including Talg.

"Orizah," the king asked, "would it surprise you if I said that for the past five nights I also have had this dream, and so have all of the members of my Witan?"

"Truly, my lord?" Orizah raised his thick eyebrow. "I swear that I did not know anyone else has had these dreams!"

"They seem to be infectious." Golar Hassiid stroked his braided beard. "Talg, have you had these same nightmares?"

"No, my lord, nor has anyone else that I know," Talg replied.

"Orizah, can you tell me anything else about these rather...remarkable aliens?" the king inquired.

"Only that they are coming here, and that they have some ancient enmity with the Strovats, great one." Orizah gestured with his hands. "Therefore, we cannot ally ourselves with the insectoids. I can tell you nothing else which you have not already seen for yourself."

"Very well," the king sighed and looked at Talg. "This is why I also summoned you, Lore Master, in case Orizah could not or would not answer my questions. Tell me, in all of our histories, is there anything resembling the monsters which we have seen in our dreams?"

"If I hear you correctly, my lord, there is," Talg replied, wide-eyed.

Talg opened the old book which he had brought with him, and carefully thumbed through the pages.

"When I received the call, I felt impressed to bring this book," he explained as he searched. "I have recently been studying some of our most ancient records, and this particular book contains the oldest of the old. Some of these accounts are from the very beginnings of the Alamani, almost seven million years ago. A few days ago, while reading this book, I came across an account of the very aliens which you have just described, though I thought they were only an ancient legend."

"At least it is good to know that we are not all mad," Karg replied, looking around the room. "Talg, as you know I have studied our history extensively, including our ancient history. I do not recall reading about anything like what I have seen in my dreams, particularly considering the advanced nature of these creatures' technology. They make our best weapon systems seem like obsolete toys."

"Yes, that sounds like what I read." Talg nodded. "I am not surprised that you have not heard of these things, Karg. I myself discovered them only recently, and this book is one of the few sources in which I have seen them. The Leviathan exists only in an archaic legend; an ancient fairy tale if you will. We have no actual records of them. Our earliest writers speak of them existing in the past tense, before the beginnings of our culture. The legend states that our own civilization rose from the ashes of another, one which was destroyed by the Leviathan.

"Unfortunately, these records are written in Chiasmic Verse, a form of ancient poetry. They can be a bit difficult to sift through, which is why most students of history such as yourself, Admiral, do not bother to look through them, for they appear as archaic stanzas. You have to know how to read them."

"My king, if I may," Orizah broke in.

Golar Hassiid nodded.

"I do not believe that all of this together is coincidence," Orizah said. "My dreams, your dreams, this book which Lore Master Talg just happened to be reading at this exact time? This is all the work of Alè."

"As insane as this sounds, I think I agree," Karg added.

The king looked at his other ministers, and not one of them objected. Ator gave him a nod, while Nurgud, ordinarily the brash young professional, simply stared down at the table.

"Ah, here it is." Talg tapped a page in his book. "In one stanza, they are called the Leviathan, and in another they are referred to as Mentotians. They came from a place called Kolor that is located somewhere on the Outer Rim of the galaxy. They were huge in stature, larger than any other sentient race. Their technology was unknown, and their ships were invisible. It also says here that none could stand against them in close combat, for their very skin was tougher than stone."

The king looked at his ministers. All of them were speechless.

"According to this," Talg continued, "Alè called them forth to punish the wicked kingdoms. They swept forth as a mighty flood and destroyed the great kingdom that was here before us, and its allies."

The king looked at Orizah and asked, "and you say that these Mentotians are returning?"

"That is the word of Alè, my lord." Orizah nodded.

"May He help us!" Pekota gulped.

"What can we do?" Eblock fretted. "A war with the Strovats will devastate us, but surely we cannot stand against this. We are caught between a hammer and an anvil!"

"The first thing we must do is to decide if our dreams are in fact a warning of a real future, or not," the king calmly said. "If we agree on this, then we may pursue a course of action. Karg, you are the oldest and wisest of my counselors, so I put the question to you. Do I trust this prophet?"

"Just one more question," Karg asked. "Talg, have you ever seen Orizah before this day in your library?"

"I have never met Orizah before now," Talg responded. "Nor have I ever seen him in the archives. As you know, he could not possibly have had access to our ancient records without my consent."

"My king, I am now convinced of the truth of Orizah's words," Karg stated.

Golar Hassiid looked at Ator, who was crestfallen. All of his youthful haughtiness was gone.

"Let us make war with the Strovats, my lord," he said humbly. "Let me and my soldiers die fighting something that we have a chance to defeat. Though I am ashamed to admit it, we cannot stand against these Leviathans. They are monsters."

"Do not be ashamed, my friend," the king said. "I appreciate your honesty. I prefer my counselors to counsel me, not simply tell me what I wish to hear."

He looked at his other ministers, all of whom nodded in agreement.

"No agreement with the Strovats will save us from the beasts in my dreams, my lord," Pekota admitted. "Let us do as this prophet says."

"There it is." Golar Hassiid sat back and huffed. "I also am convinced by what Talg has said. I now believe these dreams to be the workings of Alè. My father taught me that even a king must answer for his actions. Who am I to go against the word of God?"

"You are wise, great one." Orizah smiled. "Alè has made you king now to save this people from destruction."

"That may be, but I am still faced with an evil choice," Golar Hassiid explained. "A war with the Strovats will be long and hard. Our females and children will suffer, as well as my own children. If these Leviathans do not come to our aid in a timely fashion, then we could lose everything. We could be overrun, and become as refugees like the Burbesenys. Orizah, can you tell us exactly when these Leviathans will return?"

"No, my king," the old prophet said. "The time has not been revealed, only the command to wage war against the Strovats without delay. I think Alè tests our faith in this matter, but I do not believe that He will allow the Strovats to overrun us before the Leviathan returns."

"Very well." Golar Hassiid exhaled. "The Witan and I must now decide on a course of action. Orizah, Talg, you are both dismissed. However, you are under oath not to reveal what was discussed in this meeting, under penalty of death. Do you understand?"

"Yes, my king," they both replied.

As the guards escorted them out, Orizah turned and thanked the king.

"No, it is you whom I should thank," Golar Hassiid said. "I wonder how many princes and captains of industry have the courage of my gardener."

Once Urudo had led them out and closed the doors behind him, the king and his counselors discussed their options. They immediately agreed that the non-aggression pact with the Strovats was no longer on the table.

"Shall we open full trade with the Tellopians?" Pekota asked. "After all, they will shortly be our allies."

"That is a bit presumptuous, I think," Eblock scoffed. "We may fight the same enemy, but that does not make us friends. As for our true allies, King Zoar will not easily give up his piracy network in their territory, and Baron Hareseth would just as well shoot Tellopians as he would Strovats."

"Yes, the Heruli are not prejudiced," the king replied with a smirk. "They despise everyone equally and fairly. I think, Pekota, that open trade with the Tellopians would benefit us. However, I do not want you to approach them until after we are at war with the Strovats. We will be able to negotiate better trade terms with them once we are fighting on the same side. I also do not wish to give the Strovats any clues as to what we are planning. If we suddenly become friendly toward the Tellopian-Burbeseny Alliance after nearly signing a treaty with the Strovats, then I fear that we will be seen as double-dealing, and both sides will be suspicious. I prefer our offensive against the bugs to be a surprise."

"My lord, I fear that this will not be so easy to accomplish," Nurgud explained. "As I have stated before, a war with the Strovats will be a hard sell to the people, much less to the financiers and the industrialists. We have no good reason to attack them, and many feel that it is a war which we may not win. A long, drawn out war without the support of the people could destabilize our government."

"My lord, another problem is logistics," Karg added. "We are not poised to strike them at this moment. It may take some time for us to mobilize and prepare an army and a fleet together for an offensive against the Strovats. If we are to wage war expeditiously, as Orizah warns, then perhaps we should look to our allies. If hostilities were to occur between the Strovats and our allies, then this could solve both problems at once. Now, if I may point out, as we discussed before, King Zoar of the Nephilim is not happy about the Strovat presence next to him."

"Yes, I have heard from him." Golar Hassiid nodded. "He wishes to meet with me next week and discuss this. The question is, Eblock, are the Nephilim actually willing to fight the Strovats over this matter?"

"Absolutely, my lord." Eblock smiled. "Zoar is utterly livid at the Strovats, and he has a legitimate grievance. When those overgrown bugs first offered to us this non-aggression treaty, they guaranteed that they would respect our territorial claims and those of our allies. Since that time, they have occupied three Sagobian systems, all of which were former Nephilim territories stolen from them by the Burbesenys. As you know, the Nephilim have never relinquished their claims on these three star systems, even though they have not owned them for several millennia. So, technically, the Strovats are already in violation of this treaty which they have offered to us. I can tell you that King Zoar and his generals are ready to fight over it. He has already called up his reserves, and he is currently gearing his industrial base for war. This is why he wants to meet with you, my lord."

"This does sound promising." The king stroked his mustache. "Technically, they have already provoked one of our allies."

"Why not send the Strovats an ultimatum?" Ator asked. "They must give those systems to the Nephilim, or else."

"And what if they do?" Pekota asked. "They may be so eager to keep the peace with us at this time that they may just give those systems away. What then?"

"Forgive me, my lord," Nurgud interrupted, "but I fear this technicality is a little thin by itself. To win over the people, the industrialists, and the financiers we would need more than a claim from one of our allies which no one's grandfather is old enough to remember."

"Yes, I agree." Karg grinned wickedly. "We need a little more."

"Do you have an idea?" The king raised his bushy eyebrows.

"The Strovats have a reputation for committing atrocities," Karg proposed. "What would happen if they did so against one of our allies?"

"Yes, yes, that may be it." The king snapped his long fingers. "If there was an incident between the Nephilim and the Strovats, then we would be bound by honor to assist them. We could obtain the public support we need, in view of atrocities committed against our friends."

"But, my king," Eblock politely coughed, "my intelligence shows no Strovat activity near King Zoar's borders. In fact, they seem to be going out of their way to avoid even accidental contact."

"I think that those reports may not be altogether accurate," Karg said. "You need to look at them again."

"What do you mean?" Eblock asked. "My intelligence is completely reliable..."

"He means change those reports, you fool," Ator derided. "Make it look like those bugs are harassing Nephilim border areas. Then we can have our incident."

"Others have seen those reports," Eblock responded with a scowl. "We cannot simply change them, simpleton."

"But I think this is a good idea," Golar Hassiid calmly stated. "Eblock it is not necessary for you to change anything. What we need is a new intelligence report for that sector. One that is a bit more...imaginative. Then, this new report will conveniently be leaked to the press. We will also be sure to release plenty of information regarding Strovat atrocities committed against the Tellopians at Cera. This should cause quite a stir. In the meantime, we will meet with the Nephilim and set up our incident."

"That is brilliant, my lord!" Pekota clenched a fist. "As the Strovats do not bother with public relations, they will have no effective means of denying our reports. So long as we control the media, no one will know the difference. We shall have all of the public support that we need."

"And this will also give us more time to mobilize our forces," Karg agreed.

"While we are mobilizing, we should also meet with the Heruli," Ator added. "We should plan for a combined offensive into the old Sagobian sector, and be ready to hit them hard immediately after we declare war. Let us knock those overgrown cockroaches off balance before they have time to react."

"Yes, very good." The king nodded. "Eblock, you will call the Nephilim Viscount and the Heruli Margrave that are stationed here in the city as ambassadors. I want messages sent to both Baron Hareseth and King Zoar, asking them for a summit as soon as possible. We have a lot of planning to do."

"Yes, my lord." Eblock smirked. "I think you will find that both of our allies are itching for a fight with the Strovats."

For the rest of that day the Witan met with the king and forged the Alamani plans. The next day, without announcement or fanfare, Karg and Ator called up their reserves. Eblock prepared new intelligence reports, Nurgud began to adjust the government budget, and Pekota quietly started accumulating energy and armament reserves. Within a week, Golar Hassiid held a secret war council with the rulers of the Heruli and the Nephilim.

CHAPTER 7

Tellopian Central Security Headquarters
Tellops: Pollux system

Curtis Baxter arrived early for his meeting in the Security Council chamber. He was a tall, fair-skinned English country gentleman with light hair and blue eyes. Though in his mid-fifties, he was in excellent shape and appeared to be younger. He wore a dark suit and carried a hand computer, and, as usual, he was the first one to arrive. He strode over to the huge, round, black electronic table in the center of the spacious room, which lay deep underground beneath the central government complex.

He plopped into one of the plush purple chairs and propped up his chin with one hand while the other tapped the table. For the next few minutes he sat alone in that room and brooded over how he had gotten stuck in this position. He was only thirty-six light years from Earth, or about a day's travel. However, as far as he was concerned, he may as well have been a thousand light years away on an Alamani moon mining colony. His heart rested with his family's estate in East Yorkshire, where he had a wonderful, stately mansion that he could not enjoy.

He sat at the hub of the League's central government operations; an important man in a place where many politicians dreamed to be. Yet, ironically, he had been sent to this place by his political enemies on Earth. This was not a promotion, but was simply a means to get rid of him. He had been exiled.

His family had survived the financial chaos of the previous century by investing in the armaments industry. His father had been in the House of Lords, and after the Tellopian reorganization he had become one of the leading members of the North England District Government. Naturally, Curtis had followed in his father's footsteps, but he had much higher political aspirations. Curtis Baxter sought after and attained the seat of the North England District Representative on the Earth Supreme Senate, the ruling body of all the Earth.

Unfortunately, his quest for government office became an obsession for power. This took a major toll on his family, for he would be gone for weeks and even months at a time. The extended time away from his family, and with female associates, resulted in more than one extra-marital affair.

During his last campaign to retain his seat in the Supreme Senate, his opponent found and exposed the details of his latest adultery to the media. Baxter won his re-election bid, but his marriage was over. The divorce was ugly, expensive, and public. His wife got half of everything, including half of his manor house. This had been in his family for generations, and he had no intention of losing it. In the end, he had to borrow money in order to pay his ex-wife off for her half of his family manor.

Two years later, he had recovered enough financially to finally pursue his ultimate dream: to become the Chairman of the Supreme Senate, and President of the Earth. However, this was not a publicly elected position. The chairman was selected by the members of the Supreme Senate, not the people, but one still had to campaign to gain the office. This turned out to be a very expensive undertaking for Baxter, as it required traveling across the globe to many representatives' districts in order to win their votes. Curtis Baxter's own appetite for luxury only added to the cost. In addition, his opponents used his scandalous divorce against him, and his ex-wife was all too glad to assist them. In the end, he could not overcome the bad press, and he ran out of money.

To make matters worse, his failed presidency bid had siphoned off so many of his resources that he was extremely hampered the following year in his own district election. The result was that he lost his seat in the Supreme Senate as well. For the first time in his privileged life, Curtis Baxter found himself unemployed and out of money. He was at the mercy of his political rivals, who still considered him to be dangerous.

Baxter's competitors offered him a job as an adjutant to the Earth's representative on the Tellopian High Council. While the salary of this new post was not what he was used to, it had its perks. Tellopian law stipulated that the Earth's government must sustain the assets and properties of anyone serving in the League government. If Baxter accepted the position, at least his 'friends' back on Earth would have to make his mortgage and tax payments for him while he was gone.

Baxter's enemies wanted him out of their hair, and what better place to send him than to a low-profile job on another planet? This, of course, was an insult to offer a gofer job to a member of the landed gentry, and a former candidate to the Earth's Presidency. However, Baxter had little choice but to accept or face financial ruin, and his enemies on Earth knew it. After nearly choking to death while swallowing his immense pride, Baxter took the job and moved to Tellops.

He was humiliated, broke, and as far as he was concerned he had been abandoned by his family and friends. He was also now forced to live a not-so-lavish lifestyle. This did not last long, for he was accustomed to luxury and he intended to have it one way or the other. He began to live on his family's reputation, and any credit which he could squeeze out of it. Thus, over the next few years he accumulated quite a lot of debt.

Embittered, he no longer cared for his world, or for that of anyone else. He became a true capitalist, and if the price was right he would sell his oldest and best friend to a Heruli gladiator school, though he would prefer to sell them his ex-wife. Thus, he would not have second thoughts about selling government or even military secrets to the highest bidder. The problem was not in finding a buyer, for spies and their contacts were seemingly everywhere on Tellops, like flies swarming about a bloated elephant carcass. The problem was in getting very juicy information for which they would pay a lot of money. Baxter had access to a few government matters, and he was able to make some money in satisfying the flies, but not enough for his expensive tastes. What he needed was a really big score, but ever since the Burbesenys had joined the League, security had been as tight as a hermetically sealed coffin.

Then came a stroke of fantastic luck. Prince Hussein Bin Ali, the Earth's representative on the Security Council, was killed when his space liner crashed while on a visit to his cousin on Dragos. This left a vacuum on the Security Council, for the Humans were highly regarded in military matters, and the Tellopians sought an immediate replacement. The only Human on Tellops who had the necessary qualifications for this assignment was Curtis Baxter. He was of noble blood, and due to his family business, he had much expertise in both armaments and logistics.

As far as the Tellopians were concerned, they had found the man for the job. They appointed Baxter to the Security Council before notifying the leaders of the Earth, much to their annoyance. As far as Curtis Baxter was concerned, this was his ticket to fortune and glory. He did not sell out right away, however, but decided to bide his time and wait for the right opportunity.

He quietly cackled, but then quickly composed himself as other members of the council arrived. General Blaaga of the Nervii, and Karnow, the Tellopian who was the head of the council, both entered and took their usual places. They each activated their hand computers and got to work. Baxter rather liked the warlike Nervii, even if they looked like miniature Heruli. It was they who assisted the Humans the most, and they who adapted Human guerrilla tactics to interplanetary warfare. As for the Tellopians, he did not care for them one way or the other. As far as he was concerned, the little yellow people were a means to an end. Once they were no longer useful, he would discard them like an old suit.

Karnow was preoccupied with whatever he was doing, but Blaaga donned his wireless headset translator and addressed Baxter. Once Curtis Baxter had put on his own headset, he could hear everything Blaaga said to him in perfect English, and vise-versa. However, one of the things that annoyed Baxter was that their chips were not universally compatible. He had complained for years that these headsets were bloody useless in speaking with virtually any race outside the League, and that the Tellopians really needed to come up with something better. Communicating with outside races still had to be done the old fashioned way, either through a linguist or by typing on a computer. Baxter had argued that this was not always convenient, particularly if you were dealing with trigger-happy groups like the Heruli.

"No, General, we did not lose any front-line Earth warships at Algenib," Baxter replied to Blaaga. "Our forces oversaw the evacuation, and Admiral Murko ordered a full withdrawal once the King of the Sagobians blew himself up. Our fleet did not come in contact with the enemy. We did, however, lose five transports and a frigate to the Sagobian rioters."

The automatic doors at the end of the room opened, and the Burbeseny Admiral Murko trundled into the room inside his tracked water tank suit. He rolled up next to Blaaga, bumping an unnecessary chair out of the way, and exchanged pleasantries with him. Baxter always felt that Burbesenys were a bit creepy. They appeared to him as huge, intelligent piranhas, and their presence always made him nervous. Murko especially did so, for he was always in a bad mood. On this day, after a defeat, he seemed particularly morose.

Next came Xanthar, an Amali duke, and Rashaa, a Zuzim prince. Both were methane breathers from swamp worlds. They each had strapped to their shoulder belts a small device which provided their bodies with the methane gas that they needed. The Amali were a warlike lot, and Baxter thought they reminded him of exceptionally large toads. He did not mind them so much, for they were at least sociable. However, he loathed the Zuzims, whom he considered to be snide and pretentious. He thought Rashaa, in particular, to be an extremely arrogant little creature from the Black Lagoon.

Alatheus, a Kirharan general, followed. The Kirharans were the most humanoid of all the other races. Alatheus himself reminded Baxter of portraits of ancient Vikings, except that he had white hair, pink eyes, and wore a suit-like black tunic. He could picture in his mind Alatheus standing next to Ivarr the Boneless as he sacked York in the year 866. He looked at the tall alien general and wondered if he had any relatives back on Kirhara named Harald Bluetooth, Olaf Tryggvasson, or Swain Forkbeard.

The last two to enter were Juman, a Tellopian military consultant, and Crown Prince Mocor of the Antearians. Mocor was also quite humanoid, appearing as a much smaller, less hairy version of Alatheus. Like Rashaa, he also had an air of superiority about him. In fact, Baxter had never met an Antearian whom he liked. He considered them all to be condescending albino pygmies.

Once everyone was in their places, Karnow officially opened

the meeting. He went over the itinerary before turning the meeting over to Alatheus to report on the defeat at Algenib. Alatheus activated the large electronic table in front of them, and a three-dimensional display of the Algenib system appeared above it. Every vessel which took part in the evacuation and the battle was represented in this holograph. The areas around Algenib IV and the battle with the Strovats were enlarged, and the planet looked as if it was surrounded by a swarm of bees.

On the other side of the system, the Strovat cube-shaped phalanx was fronted by a fleet of ships in a crescent formation. The nearby gas giant, Algenib VII, was the most outer planet in the system. The area around this planet had been mined heavily with drone satellites which were programmed to nuke any incoming vessels who did not have a proper access code.

The Strovats had encountered these minefields before, and they dealt with it in their usual manner by simply bludgeoning their way through it. They first sent in a group of captured ships and light cruisers to decelerate around Algenib VII. These ships were used as fodder to literally clear out the close mines, and then punch a hole through the minefield while the rest of the Strovat fleet arrived and formed its phalanx. Once they had done this, with the loss of twenty light cruisers, the rest of the fleet came through without any further losses.

At this point Murko interrupted, objecting to the use of this type of minefield, which in his opinion did more harm than good. He argued that due to the lag time in interstellar communications, and the fact that the drones themselves often malfunctioned, these minefields had the habit of destroying as many friendly ships as they did enemy ones. Commercial vessels coming in from far away as well as ships of refugees escaping the Strovats that did not have the needed deactivation codes would be blown up, and if the time came that Algenib could be retaken, then this minefield would have to be removed anyway.

"The best tactic," he stated while pointing a tentacle at Algenib VII, "would have been to position our ships here, close to the planet. In this manner, we could have hit and destroyed many of the enemy ships as they came in, before they could organize and form their phalanx."

"Yes, Admiral," Alatheus argued by pointing to Algenib VI, which was positioned on the adjoining quarter of the system, "but if we did as you say and the Strovats came in here, then they would have been in between us and Algenib IV. We did not have enough strength to divide our forces and guard both planets, so the best solution was to position your fleet halfway between the fourth and seventh planets. This way we also would not exhaust our fuel reserves trying to maintain two fleets at two different points on the outer edge of that system."

"We did not have enough strength because of the minefields!" Murko complained. "As you can plainly see, it did not prevent the enemy from forming his phalanx. He simply organized behind the minefield as a few expendable vessels punched through it. All the Sagobian minefield accomplished was to help the enemy organize himself while we watched."

"Why did you not simply go through the minefield and attack the Strovats as you suggested?" asked Juman. "After all, you had the access codes."

"Mine drones are unpredictable even with access codes," Murko grumbled. "It takes a year to replace just one of my battleships. I absolutely refuse to risk losing any of them trying to ford through a field of drones that may not recognize friend from foe."

"Even if we had attempted to do so, we could only have sent through two ships at a time, allowing the enemy to simply pick us off," Xanthar added.

"It was moot anyway," Murko carped. "By positioning ourselves in-between everything, we were too far away from Algenib VII to prevent the Strovats from organizing their phalanx. The fact remains that if the Sagobians had not foolishly mined the sixth and seventh planets, we might have had a chance to disrupt the enemy offensive. If you remember, I accurately predicted that the Strovats would use Algenib VII to enter the system. In my opinion, we could have averted this defeat by putting most of our fleet right at their point of entry, but of course the minefield prevented that."

"Thankfully the Sagobians didn't mine any other planets," Xanthar murmured. "Or else we might not have gotten out of there at all."

"And what if the enemy came in through Algenib VI?" asked Juman.

"Admiral Murko and I have been fighting these bugs for a

long time," Xanthar replied. "If the Strovats are anything, they are predictable. We knew they would use Algenib VII to decelerate their fleet because of where it is currently positioned in its orbit. It is the closest planet in that system to the Strovat front."

Baxter sat back and tried not to smile as they argued, but it was difficult. He thought it was hilarious that, although they were supposed to be the heads of the council, Juman and Karnow were continually interrupted by Murko and Xanthar at these meetings. Ever since the Amali duke and the Burbeseny admiral had joined, they had been in a power struggle with the Tellopians for control of the Security Council. The Tellopian leaders were often forced to acquiesce to the will of Murko and Xanthar, who represented the two strongest military powers in the League and who always agreed with each other. The only chance Juman and Karnow had to get anything done their way was to have most of the others agree with them. This was especially true of Alatheus and Blaaga, who represented the next two strongest military contingents and whom everyone respected. Whichever side won over Alatheus and Blaaga always won the day.

Eventually Alatheus interrupted the debate with a polite cough, and then motioned toward his paused holograph.

"My apologies, General," Murko said. "I merely wanted on the record that we should not use these minefields in the future. Please continue with your report."

Alatheus restarted the holograph and the battle resumed before their eyes. The Kirharan Landwasters at each end of their crescent formation moved in to attack the sides of the Strovat phalanx, and then quickly withdrew. This tactic was used to draw as many Bisas away from the group as possible and then pick them off one by one with concentrated fire. In this manner, they were able to destroy twelve of the enemy supercruisers, but with the loss of twenty-four Landwasters.

However, the main part of the phalanx continued to advance on the Tellopian center, and here is where the heaviest fighting ensued. The giant Burbeseny K battleships held their ground and slugged it out with the Bisas, while the Sagobians took on the flotilla of Strovat light cruisers. After destroying eight Bisas at a cost of fifteen of his K class battleships, Murko ordered his fleet to break off and move to the rear and reform. It was at this point that the Sagobian admiral broke ranks and charged his fleet headlong into the Strovat wall.

"As you will see, this proved to be our undoing." Alatheus exhaled. "The Sagobians represented almost half of our strength at Algenib. Here they will charge into the teeth of the Strovat defenses and be cut to pieces by the concentrated enemy fire."

After watching Antedios' ship get destroyed, General Blaaga could no longer remain silent.

"That was mere suicide, nothing more!" He pounded the table. "Ramming tactics against a wall of supercruisers? Why would they do such a foolish maneuver?"

"Such tactics are not unheard of." Curtis Baxter folded his hands on the table in front of him. "Certain cultures on Earth have regarded suicide attacks such as this as an honorable way to die. The old Japanese banzai and kamikaze attacks, for example, were meant to do as much damage on the enemy as possible. If done successfully, they can inflict both severe physical and moral damage on an enemy."

"I have studied some of your Earth history," Blaaga responded. "I know of these kamikaze tactics. They were done out of desperation, and while they did inflict damage, they did not decide the outcome of that war. The only thing the Japanese accomplished in the end was to further decimate their own population and waste valuable fuel reserves. This proved to be both fruitless and ruinous, for it was the fear of more suicide attacks which led to the American decision to finally use nuclear weapons on the Japanese populace."

"Ruinous is exactly what it was in this instance," Alatheus continued. "Up to that point, even with our losses, we had inflicted enough damage on the enemy that we still had a reasonable chance to make a stand, once we had retreated to Algenib IV and united with the Amali and the Earth fleets. However, Lord Antedios' rash decision decided the battle, and the fate of the Sagobians on the planet surface. Ninety-nine ships of the line were gone in one stroke. At that point we were well below half strength, even including the Amali and the Humans, and we faced a superior enemy fleet. Any further action would have put us at a severe disadvantage in firepower. We could not afford to waste any more ships in a battle which we had no hope of winning. We had no choice but to withdraw at that point, in order to live to fight another day."

At this point, Duke Xanthar enlarged the area around Algenib IV to where it was the only image that they beheld. He then began his part of the report.

"My friends," he began with a sad countenance, "the evacuation of Algenib IV was a complete disaster. I will not reiterate the problems we experienced which hampered our efforts leading up to the battle, for we all know of them. Once the Strovat invasion began, what little control we had on the planet surface was lost. The king issued no orders, and the Sagobian military did nothing to aid us. The result was that our ships were mobbed with panicked citizens. In the chaos, our combined fleets lost a total of twelve transports, two frigates, and hundreds of personnel on the ground. In the three-day period from the moment the enemy came into the system to the minute when we had to withdraw, we managed to evacuate only eight hundred seventy-six thousand. The total number of Sagobians evacuated since the process began more than two months ago is less than twenty million, or about two point five percent of the population. We left behind approximately eight hundred million Sagobians to the Strovats."

Xanthar paused for a moment and sighed. He gazed down to compose himself, and then raised his head and resumed.

"We did not anticipate King Antigony's actions on the final day," he said. "He was my friend, and he did not inform me of any such plans. I do not understand why he would do such a terrible thing. He destroyed his own people."

"I believe the tactic is called 'scorched earth'," Blaaga said. "In Human terms, it is better to destroy your own land than to let your enemy have it."

"Yes," Baxter stated, "but the idea of scorched earth is to deprive your enemy of the ability to supply himself on your resources, not necessarily to kill your own people in the process. Although, often that is the final outcome due to starvation."

"Perhaps the thinking was not only to make their planet undesirable, but also to deprive the Strovats of eight hundred million slaves," Murko said. "In any event, that is what has been accomplished. Even if we somehow can retake Algenib, the fourth planet may have to be terraformed again to be of any use. King Antigony was also my friend, and I mourn his loss."

Amazing, Baxter thought to himself, *that overgrown piranha had a friend.*

"We do not know exactly how many Sagobians survived the holocaust that Antigony initiated, but we do know there are survivors," Xanthar continued. "Our recon drones have reported heavy fighting on the planet surface between Sagobian and enemy units, mostly in the rural regions, the forests, and the mountainous areas. Reckoning the number of citizens and army units who did not inhabit the cities that were destroyed, we estimate that there may still exist between thirty to fifty million Sagobians on Algenib IV. Even if they all possess anti-radiation medication, which is doubtful, the planet's ecosystems are destroyed. Once the food on hand runs out, they will not be able to grow more. I can only implore this council to find a way to organize a counterattack, so that we can relieve what is left of them before they all succumb to starvation, or are horribly devoured by our common enemy."

"Thank you, Alatheus," Karnow said with a sullen expression.

The Kirharan general sat down and Juman stood.

"There is also a military reason to counterattack," Juman stated. "If the Strovats are allowed to build their usual supply bases at Algenib, then they can use that system to strike at any one of many populated worlds in the League."

He changed the holograph to a sector view, and pointed out several different star systems which were within striking distance of Algenib.

"As you can see, losing this system has opened up the front," he explained. "They can hit us anywhere, anytime, in any one of these areas. We are already spread out too thinly. We cannot possibly defend all of the exposed systems effectively, nor can we retake Algenib with what little we have available. We simply do not have enough warships."

"The simple truth is that a large portion of our fleet is still being refitted in the Nihal system," Juman said as he looked directly at Baxter. "Over two thousand warships are there. Half of this constitutes the bulk of the Gutayid and Tellopian fleets, with the remainder being ships from twelve other smaller worlds who belong to the League. Nearly a third of our navy is just sitting and doing nothing! When can we expect to have these ships, Mister Baxter? Can you at least replace the ones which we have recently lost?"

"A third of the fleet is not simply sitting and doing nothing," Baxter calmly retorted, "and you all know fully well why they are there. The Tellopian League had too many decades of peace, and most of the members became complacent and neglected their space fleets. Most of the vessels at Nihal III were barely space worthy, much less battle worthy, when they arrived there. Also, we did not have enough spare parts for the newer ships, and virtually none for the older ones. I assure you that Marshal Coriantumr, who is in charge of the base and is himself a Tellopian, is doing everything he can with what he has to work with. We cannot cure a hundred years of neglect overnight. Over the next few months we have several ships which will be made ready, but it will take at least six months or more to get you the replacements that you want. You are simply losing them faster than I can fix them."

"Can you at least give us a few heavy ships?" Juman practically begged. "Your latest report stated that a portion of the Gutayid fleet is operational, along with twenty-two Tellopian battle cruisers. Nihal is far behind the front. There is no need for any operational warships to remain there."

"The Gutayid ships which are ready are lighter class vessels, such as corsairs and frigates," Baxter replied. "As for the Tellopian battle cruisers, we are using them and the Gutayids to reinforce the twenty battleships and thirty destroyers from the Earth fleet which are stationed in that system. Combined they are a considerable force, and we cannot afford to leave Nihal unguarded, even though it's far behind the Strovat front. Personally, I did not choose to put all these ships in one place, and if I did I would not have chosen Nihal. May I remind you all that it is right next door to the Heruli? They could easily strike that base before we could react from here."

"I must agree," Blaaga added. "That base on Nihal III is like a ripe fruit just waiting to be picked. We must keep a strong defense force there. In my opinion, we should put more ships there, rather than send them out. If the Alamani become belligerent, we would have another disaster on our hands, one that would be twenty times worse than losing the Sagobian fleet."

"I assure you that we looked at all of our options before deciding to use Nihal," Rashaa said in his usual, condescending tone. "It is too far behind the front for Strovat probes to find it, and it is also out of the way of the mainstream media. Nihal III is far enough away from Dragos to hide the base. We were constructing a large mining hub there, and so we had previously put that world under classified restriction. The public already could not go there, or use the planet to enter or exit the system. We secretly converted the hub to a repair center and brought in the ships in small groups. The media and residents on Dragos are used to military presence due to the proximity of the Heruli, so a few extra warships and personnel going in and out was not noticeable."

"As for the concentration in one place, that was my decision," Karnow admitted. "I preferred to manage one large operation, rather than ten or twenty medium-sized ones scattered all over the League. Logistically, it is simply easier for us to ship massive amounts of supplies to one location. It is also much easier to keep one secret than twenty."

"Secret?" Murko laughed, making a deep, gurgling sound that sent chills up Baxter's spine. "The only secret at Nihal III is why the Heruli have not yet blown it up! Do not think for a moment that they cannot see the massive power readings emanating from that supposedly uninhabited planet. I agree with General Blaaga. You had better pray that the Alamani and Heruli do not decide to become hostile."

"As to that, this day we have acquired very good news," Karnow said with a smile. "Prince Mocor, would you please enlighten us with your latest intelligence report?"

"Fellow Leaguers." Mocor stood. "My intelligence from early this morning shows that the Alamani will soon be at war with the Strovats."

This news rushed though the room like a wave, with reactions ranging from jubilation to caution. Karnow held up a gloved hand to silence everyone, and motioned for Mocor to continue.

"As you know, we had previous intelligence which led us to believe that the Strovats and Alamani were negotiating some sort of agreement," Mocor explained. "However, recently the relations between the two parties has become strained, due to continued Strovat presence in Sagobian territory which has long been claimed by the Nephilim. We learned only last week of a reversal in Golar Hassiid's attitude toward the Strovats when he did not open trade with them as we had expected. He also formally requested them to hand over Epsilon Perseus to King Zoar of Nephil, a rather silly demand, considering it is no secret that system is now being used as a key jumping off point for future operations into Tellopian space. Since that time, an incident has occurred between the Strovats and the Nephilim."

"Can this be?" Rashaa leaned forward and asked. "Are our fortunes finally reversed?"

"If Nephilim have been killed by Strovats, the Alamani would be bound by their honor to support them," Alatheus said as his eyes darted back and forth. "This may be a fantastic stroke of luck!"

"That is indeed what has happened." Mocor grinned. "It seems that the Nephilim had recently placed a science colony along with a mining expedition in the Atik system. This system is a disputed area formerly held by the Sagobians. However, the Nephilim still claim it, and they apparently moved in when the Sagobians were forced to pull out to defend Algenib. The Strovats also moved in, encountered the Nephilim there, and they did what Strovats do."

"A Nephilim science colony?" Baxter asked doubtfully. "At Atik? There are no planets in that star system."

"No, but large asteroids do exist there," Juman pointed out.

"This is an obvious fabrication," Murko scoffed. "The Nephilim had no such colony there, or my intelligence drones would have detected it. We cannot trust that report."

"That is King Zoar's story and he is sticking to it," Mocor replied. "The truth of it does not matter. What matters to us are this morning's reports, which I am sure Murko's drones will also report later today. King Zoar has fully mobilized his entire military, including his reserves, and two of his elite Argolath Guard corps have disappeared from view. What's more, Baron Hareseth is also on the move. He has reportedly arrived at the Nephilim capital in Zeta Taurus with over a hundred Heruli battle cruisers and five legions of his Stosstrupen Strikers. In addition, all the major clan lords of the Heruli are raising their levies and gearing up for full scale war. There is a massive concentration of warships gathering at the Heruli home world at L1 Puppis, greater...far greater than we have ever seen before."

"All of the Heruli clans at once?" Xanthar asked, leaning forward. "Are you certain?"

"Yes." Mocor gave him a nod. "The drone recorded the clan symbol on each warship it counted. All of the known clans, plus four which we had never before seen, have ships at L1 Puppis."

"Exactly how big of a concentration is this?" Rashaa asked apprehensively.

"The probe which reported in this morning showed over a thousand battle cruisers of varying types, plus over two thousand smaller design warships," Mocor replied. "Some appear to be of older design, but they are all definitely Heruli. What's more, we do not believe that their mustering is yet complete."

"Thousands of Heruli warships?" Rashaa choked. "That is not possible!"

"Yes, it is." Xanthar cleared his throat. "The truth is that we have never been able to make an accurate assessment of Heruli strength. Even when we were at war with them decades ago, we did not encounter all of their clans. We have always assumed that they would never truly unite because of their dynastic rivalries, but if this report is true, then Baron Hareseth appears to have finally done it."

"If they are going to fight the Strovats, then the more of them there are, the better for us," Alatheus commented.

"Not necessarily," Murko grumbled.

"What about the Alamani?" Blaaga asked, gritting his teeth. "What word is there from Rigel?"

"There is no official word as of yet," Mocor answered. "However, our drones have picked up major activity inside the Alamani frontier. It seems that sometime after he sent his demands to the Strovats, Golar Hassiid called up his reserves. Somehow, we missed this before, but now it is definitely evident. Several army units have been moved out from their fortresses, and these fortresses have been garrisoned by the reserves. A huge Alamani fleet is assembling at Meissa, and another large fleet is gathering at Betelgeuse."

"We feel it is significant that two Nephilim Argolath Guard corps have disappeared," Karnow finished. "It is also significant that five Heruli Stosstrupen corps have appeared at the Nephilim capital. We do not believe that so many elite striker units moving about that close to the Strovats is a mere maneuver. Combine these with the Alamani fleets at Betelgeuse and Meissa and it can only mean one thing: this must be a buildup for an offensive into former Sagobian space."

"We will see," Murko stated. "But I would caution all of you that we do not know for sure what they are doing. I will check my intelligence reports today before I decide for myself what is going on. My question is, are they also assembling forces near our borders? Are there any Alamani fleets at Bellatrix, or any Heruli fleets at 32 Eridanus?"

"Nothing out of the ordinary," Mocor responded. "Except that the Alamani have moved their army units out of the Bellatrix system and replaced them with reserves."

"They are not positioning themselves to attack us at all," Karnow said. "I know you do not trust the Alamani, and for good reason. However, this time they are clearly pointing their weapons at the Strovats. Your own intelligence reports will tell you the same story. I predict that within the next two days or so we will hear their official war declarations."

"As I said, we will see," Murko murmured.

Karnow turned the meeting over to General Blaaga, who discussed several Nervii special operations behind the Strovat front. Most of these were rescue and evacuations of citizens and personnel from areas already overrun by the Strovats. However, there was one battle to report. Blaaga clicked on the holograph to display the action.

"As we previously discovered, the Strovats have a weakness, which is their own arrogance," Blaaga explained. "While they garrison their systems along the front with significant forces, the areas to the rear are virtually unguarded. They have been so successful for so long that they do not cover their supply lines. They simply do not expect us to attack them behind the front lines, and they have little or no conception of commerce raiding. Just over a month ago, we received intelligence that the Strovats were building a great supply station at Rho Ophiuchus, a small star cluster formerly in the Antearian kingdom, and behind the front."

Blaaga paused to give a nod of respect to Prince Mocor, with his hand raised palm upward. Mocor responded in like fashion, and then Blaaga continued.

"We acted immediately. Three weeks ago, we struck with a fleet of fifteen cruisers, twenty destroyers, and twenty frigates. Just as our drone had reported, we encountered no Bisas there. It seems that they had pulled them all out of the rear areas to attack Algenib. The only warships we found were two obsolete heavy cruisers, which were only about the size of Landwasters. These are dangerous but slow, and the Strovats only use them to guard the rear areas from pirates. We easily dispatched them, along with a convoy of thirty transports which they were escorting. We did not lose a single vessel, although two of our cruisers sustained heavy damage. We then moved on to our primary target."

"What we found was astonishing." Blaaga clicked the holograph to reveal a large floating rectangular object which made their ships look like flies. "This was the actual Strovat supply base. As you can see, it is utterly massive. We estimated that it was over one hundred miles across, and forty miles deep."

"But, how can that be?" Karnow gasped. "How could they transport such a monstrous space station to Rho Ophiuchus?"

"In much the same way that we assemble large mining centers on planetary moons," Blaaga replied. "Due to the lack of protection, we were able to take many images of the station before we destroyed it. Upon analyzing them, we have deduced that it was of modular design. It was manufactured in sections elsewhere, and the pieces were trucked into this system for easy and rather quick assembly. The good news is that it was unarmored and had no heavy defenses. It was made for a single purpose, to supply a large fleet of Bisas.

"Despite its huge size, it was not difficult to destroy, once we found its weakness. We tried hitting it with nuclear warheads, but that only damaged the outer hull areas. Then we nuked one of the fueling ports, and this caused a catastrophic chain reaction within the ship. We continued to nuke fueling ports around the hull."

The image of the ship bubbled with nuclear blasts, shuddered, and then blew apart in chunks. The surviving chunks were then mopped up with more nukes. Blaaga clicked off the holograph.

"The bad news is also the modular design," he stated. "We already knew they could do mass production on a gargantuan scale, but the fact that they can manufacture massive sections, transport them, and assemble them into a hundred-mile-wide space station in a relatively short period of time shows that the Strovats possess an industrial base that is much greater than even the Burbesenys had reported. Their capacity and potential for war production may be exponentially greater that of our own."

The sobering report tempered the news of Blaaga's victory, and took the air out of the elation over the Alamani mobilization. After a few moments of uncomfortable silence, Karnow moved to adjourn the meeting but was stopped by Admiral Murko, who said that he wished to discuss dealing with the Solarians.

"This is ridiculous," Juman protested. "The Solarians have

been staunch members of the Tellopian League for a hundred years."

"They were staunch members before the Hermenigild Royal Family was deposed," Xanthar complained. "But this government is more interested in profit margins than aiding any one of us. Their treacherous business with the Sagobians proves my words."

"Their flimsy excuse for pulling all Solarian support from the evacuation was that it was done in protest to their officials being executed by King Antigony," Murko spat. "Never mind that those 'officials' were nothing more than thieves profiteering from the misery of refugees. However, the Solarians offer no explanation for recalling their entire fleet from throughout the League. This has left two populated systems close to the front virtually unprotected, as their respective fleets are being re-fitted at Nihal III. Because of this, we will be forced to spread our forces out even more thinly to cover these two exposed systems. Any counterattack toward Algenib is out of the question, unless Mister Baxter can magically repair hundreds of ships overnight, a feat which he has admitted cannot be accomplished for several months."

"Both sides over-reacted to a few corrupt Solarian officials and their fate," Karnow said. "I hardly think the Solarians hurt the Sagobians any more than Antigony did, nor could they have made much of a difference in that disaster. As for the other matter, it is no wonder that the Solarians wish to have their fleet protect their home system, since the Strovat front also runs very close to them, especially after what happened to the Cerans."

"If the Strovats were actually threatening Nunki, then I would agree with you," Murko scoffed. "But for some strange reason, the Strovats halted their offensive in that sector, and then threw everything they had at the Sagobians. Couple that with the fact that the Solarians suddenly refused to assist the Sagobians in any way, and I'd say it looks more like an agreement than a coincidence."

"That is absurd!" Karnow objected.

"To boycott the Sagobians was one thing, but to completely withdraw military support from the League is another matter entirely," Xanthar complained. "The Solarians have no good reason to do this. There are no major Strovat fleets on the Solarian side of the front. Else how could Blaaga have won such an easy victory in that sector?"

"General Blaaga attacked behind the front, where we have

already established the Strovats are weak," Curtis Baxter argued. "The Solarians are right on the front. They have reported that there is still a significant Strovat presence at Cera. They also say there are as many as seventy-five Bisas in the Alrami system, which is practically next door to them. They have also reported a group of fifteen Bisas that they found prowling around the edge of their home system of Nunki. If this is true, then they may be the next Strovat target."

"If that is true, then why did we not discuss the defense of Nunki in the opening of this meeting?" Murko fussed. "I will tell you why. The Solarian reports are pure fantasy, and everyone here knows it. Last week they reported fifty Bisas at Alrami. This week they say it's seventy-five. As Blaaga has reported, the Strovats pulled all available forces to attack Algenib. Alrami has no more Bisas there than any other Strovat garrisoned system at the front; between thirty and forty. As for those fifteen Bisas patrolling outside of the Nunki system, this is pure paranoia. A group of first class warships such as Bisas would not be wasted on either reconnaissance or patrols. Like us, the Strovats mostly use drones for reconnaissance, and they use their light cruisers for patrols. Bisas are simply too expensive to maintain for such operations. The Strovats cannot ignore logistics any more than we can. Nunki is in no imminent danger."

"Murko is correct," Xanthar pointed out. "We have been fighting the Strovats longer than any of you have, and I can tell you that they do not behave in the manner which the Solarians are claiming. Look at our own drone reports for that sector from just this morning. The Solarian intelligence is contradicting everything our probes are seeing in that sector. It is simply not true."

"Maybe we need to probe the Solarian government," Murko said with a hint of malice.

"There is no need for that," Baxter dismissed. "Perhaps they are being a little...hyper vigilant. So what? In light of Strovat atrocities, can we blame them? Let's look at it this way, we now have a strong naval presence on our left flank. This is not a bad thing."

"It is if the Solarians have switched sides!" Murko smacked the table with a tentacle. "Even if this is merely hyper vigilance, as you say, it only benefits the Solarians. It does not help us to have them shore up the left when our right flank is collapsing!"

"We cannot ignore this any longer," Xanthar demanded. "We must find out what is going on at Solari. If indeed they have struck a deal with the Strovats, then our left flank is now wide open. We will have to deal with them."

"Do you mean to attack the Solarians?" Juman asked, clearly shocked.

"If they are traitors, yes!" Xanthar exclaimed. "We must stop them now, or they will be our undoing!"

"Enough!" Karnow intervened. "I will not have us fighting among ourselves. This is exactly what the enemy would want. If we fall into warring among ourselves, then the League is finished. We need to be united, especially in light of the Alamani joining the fight. If we fall apart now, there would be no alliance with Alaman. They could simply take over and have hegemony over the entire quadrant."

"Karnow is correct," Juman said. "If we even so much as begin spying on one another, then we will appear weak and the Alamani and Heruli will likely carve us up. We cannot allow this to happen. We must be patient."

"Still, the situation is what it is," Blaaga calmly reminded. "We cannot ignore the Solarian situation and hope that it will get better. I motion that we send drones to spy on them."

This took both Juman and Karnow by surprise. Before they knew it, the rest of the council agreed to vote on the matter. Juman, Karnow, and Baxter objected to the measure, but Murko, Xanthar, Alatheus, Blaaga, Mocor, and even Rashaa voted in favor of it.

"We must do something," Rashaa admitted. "They now control half of our left flank."

"It is the lesser of two evils," Mocor said. "Whether we appear weak to the Alamani or not, it would be far worse for us if the Solarians are indeed traitors and we ignore them."

"Very well," Karnow said in a defeated tone. "Admiral Murko, you may send your spy drones to Nunki. I am certain that if there is a problem, you will find it."

"I will holograph every inch of Nunki," Murko growled.

Karnow adjourned the meeting. Both he and Juman left the room without saying a word. Baxter watched Murko, Blaaga, and Xanthar discuss among themselves how to deal with the Solarians.

The League is finished, he thought to himself and smiled.

CHAPTER 8

Dragos possessed no moons. Therefore, even in the cities, on a clear night one had a clear view of the stars. In the countryside, where Franz and Tonya's families resided, the view was spectacular. One of the couple's favorite things to do on a clear night was to sit under the stars and talk. Franz and Tonya had been doing this together since they were children, and on this night the sky was lit with a panorama of millions of tiny, beautiful pinpricks of light.

After being on active duty for six straight months Franz would be off for the next three, according to the rotation for General Blaaga's corps. Franz had already been home for two weeks, and their wedding was but another two weeks away. Once he went back on duty, Tonya might not see him again for another six months.

They sat together in the grass on the side of the hill which their parents' houses rested. They had just enjoyed a fine meal, and had come outside to enjoy the stars an hour after sunset. Inside Tonya's house, Jim sat with her father watching a local sports channel. Tonya laid on her back and rested her head on Franz's lap as he ran his fingers through her long, golden hair.

"Do you remember Earth?" she asked.

"Is that a trick question?" he replied.

"What do you mean?"

"Well, I was just there about three weeks ago. We had to stop and refuel there on our way back here."

"You..." She gave him a look as if he had just said exactly the wrong thing. "...were just on Earth three weeks ago?"

"Yes, it's still quite polluted, particularly the east coast of North America and Central Europe," he replied. "Old Poland is very nasty. The air there is awful."

"I meant when we were little kids," she murmured. "Never mind. I never get to see our home planet, and I barely remember what it was like. But you go there so often you take it for granted."

"We can go to Earth if you like sometime, but you know how it will be." He shrugged. "It takes six days to get there, and six days to get back. Let's see, on a two-week vacation that's twelve days' travel time to spend two days on Earth."

"I can see it now." She rolled her eyes. "This is going to be the same as my mom and dad. You'll get to see the entire galaxy. Meanwhile I'm stuck waiting for you here on Planet Podunk."

"Planet Podunk is safe." Franz put his finger on her nose. "Here you're as far away from the Strovat front as you could be, and I prefer it that way. Yes, I'm seeing the galaxy. I'm seeing it get destroyed by the enemy. The Strovats either kill or enslave everyone they come across."

"Oh yeah? I'm safe here, huh?" she laughed, sat up, and pointed to a bright blue star. "What's that?"

"Rigel," Franz replied.

"Alaman," she reminded him, and then pointed to another, brighter blue star. "And what about that one?"

"Bellatrix," he admitted.

"An Alamani settlement with a big military fortress, so my dad tells us." She poked him. "It's actually closer to me than I am to the Tellopians, isn't it?"

"Yes."

"And what about that one?"

"32 Eridanus," he sighed. "But, Tonya..."

"The Heruli," she complained. "Not even two days away from here. They're close enough to spit on us. They can probably hear us talking right now."

"Yes, my love, but we aren't at war with them."

"No, but we shouldn't just trust them, either. If the Heruli attack while you're away, I'll end up in a gladiator arena before you ever find out."

"Not at all." He smirked. "They wouldn't waste such a fine

Human woman on gladiator games. They'd use you for breeding instead."

"Oh, that makes me feel better!" she laughed. "So, basically you're saying that I'm better off here with a bunch of hostile lizard men on one side, and the Planet of the Apes on the other?"

"Yes, that about sums it up. Even the Strovats don't want to come here."

"I don't blame them," she sighed, and then looked him in the eyes. "Franz, my dad says that the government is really downplaying the defeat at Algenib. He says it's a lot worse than what we're being told by the media. Do we really have a chance to win this war?"

"I don't know." He exhaled. "I suppose it all depends on what the Alamani decide to do. The Strovats are trying to avoid war with them, which means at least they don't believe themselves to be invincible. But I can tell you that what your father says is true. The central government is suppressing the news, because they don't want to cause a panic."

He looked back toward their two houses, which sat relatively close together.

"The news makes a big deal out of how many Strovats we killed at Algenib," he lowered his voice. "The truth is they can replace their losses, while we can't. They say that the Strovats will think twice about attacking one of our strongholds again. The only thing the Strovats will think about is sending more of their Bisas at us the next time. I've seen their industrial potential, Tonya. Their supply stations are as big as asteroids. The news won't report that, but it's true."

"No, I guess not, but at least the Strovats are slow. It takes them a lot of time to build up for an offensive. If we can use our hit and run tactics to knock out all of their supply stations, then we could stop them in their tracks. All those Bisas can't get to us if those bugs don't have any food or fuel."

"If General Blaaga could hear you, he'd put you on his general staff. Yes, an army runs on logistics, and that's where the enemy is vulnerable. Blaaga has studied our history, and he knows how effective the German U-boats were against Allied shipping in two world wars. We're hitting the Strovat supply lines, and we're giving them a lot more trouble than they expected."

"Still, I wonder." She looked down. "The other day I saw an

invoice on my dad's desk. Our parents have gone in together and bought an old mining scout ship. That's not a good sign."

"They're just being prepared." He put his arm around her. "Hope for the best, but prepare for the worst, my father always says."

"My dad doesn't like to talk about it." A tear streamed down her cheek. "It's like he's lost all hope. What if he's right, Franz? What if there's no hope for us?"

"Honey, there's always hope, as long as we're together," he answered as he wiped away her tears. "We've always had each other. We played together as children, and you were my sweetheart in school."

"And you were mine." She clasped his hand tightly. "Always!"

"Nothing has ever come between us, and nothing ever will."

"But...the war. What if I lose you?"

"Hey, give me some credit. I'm a pretty good pilot, you know."

"Yeah, I know." She exhaled in frustration. "To think, with your exam scores you could be in the Corps of Engineers, or a staff officer tucked away in some safe underground bunker in Tellops. But, noooooooo, you had to join the Special Forces."

"The Corps of Engineers supports the Navy and Marines," he explained. "They're in the thick of the fighting. The Marines get killed first, and then the engineers die second. As for the staff officer bit, too boring for my taste. Flying is in my blood. What would the Red Baron think of me if I became a staff officer?"

"Oh, don't give me that!" She put her hand on her hip. "The Red Baron doesn't care. He's dead. When are you Germans going to figure that out?"

"In my family? Never!" he laughed. "Look, I have one of the best Tellopian commanders there is. Blaaga isn't bloody, like the Burbesenys or the Kirharans. He's not interested in taking on the Strovats directly. He wants to give damage, not take it. The Nervii units have had the fewest casualties than any other in the League. I'm no dummy. I didn't join the military to get killed."

"That is so noble of you." This made her smile. "You better not get yourself killed. I don't know what I'd do without you."

"I promise I'll always come back to you." He stroked her hair. "If you are forced to leave I will find you. This is a big galaxy. The

Strovats can't possibly take all of it. We'll find somewhere safe to live. Somewhere in this galaxy there must be a race that can stand up to those bugs and beat them. If they exist, we'll find them. As long as we stay together there's always hope."

"I pray for you every day," she said, stroking his hair. "I know you don't believe in God, but I still do."

"Good. Someone has to."

"I love you!"

"And I love you!" He kissed her.

They lay in the grass and kissed passionately, again and again. He began to kiss her neck, but was interrupted by the sound of Jim shouting from inside her parents' house. He hooted as if he had just won the Solarian lottery, and then stuck his head out a window and grinned like a madman.

"Hey, you two!" he yelled.

"What?" came Franz's annoyed response.

"Get in here!" Jim ordered. "You gotta see this!"

"We're busy!" Franz yelled back, which made Tonya giggle.

"Get off your butts and come watch the news!" Jim exclaimed. "The Nephilim have attacked the Strovats!"

The young lovers looked at each other with wide eyes. Franz leaped to his feet and pulled Tonya to hers, and they ran, hand in hand, into the house. In the living room her father had enlarged the computer projection television to where it engulfed an entire section of the wall. He and her mother cuddled on the couch, while little Benjamin sat on the floor and played with his toys, oblivious to what was going on around him. Jim plopped into a chair and pointed at the TV projection. An excited news commentator sat at a studio news desk and rambled as different images appeared behind him. Franz and Tonya stood together for a moment and watched like a pair of deer staring at approaching headlights, before sitting together on the floor.

"Reports are still coming in." The newsman read his teleprompter. "Again, the central government has confirmed that a state of war now exists between the Strovats and the Kingdom of Nephil. The Nephilim have attacked the Strovats in the Epsilon Perseus system, which was the former home to the Sagobian kingdom..."

"That's behind the Algenib line," Tonya's father noted. "The enemy was probably using it as a supply base."

While the anchorman continued to speak, the broadcast switched to a variety of screen shots of Nephilim soldiers and warships. Tonya had seen images of Nephilim before, but now the pictures of these large, warlike reptilian centaurs mesmerized her.

"I'm glad those things are attacking the Strovats instead of us," she said.

"I'm glad the local news actually got it first this time," Tonya's mother commented.

"We never get fresh news here, Violet," Jim said to her. "This must have happened over a week ago."

"I didn't say it was fresh." Violet smirked. "I'm saying we've usually already heard it before they report it. Usually these guys are just confirming rumors that are already a day or two old."

"I think they do their best, Mom," Tonya responded. "I mean, these reporters all have to hang out at the spaceports. If they don't get any info drones from outside the system, then they have to try to interview people coming in to find out what's going on. The trouble is that the people coming in have already posted stuff on the net before they even get to the docks."

"Even if those reporters get the news as it comes in, they can't always tell us right away," Tonya's father said.

"What do you mean, Adam?" Jim asked him.

"Because any international news has to be verified by the government," Adam replied, "and the government suppresses anything that they think might cause problems. Do you remember what happened last year after our defeat at Cera?"

"They weren't here, Dad," Tonya pointed out. "They didn't get back on leave until three months after Cera."

"Well, we first heard about Cera from a group of refugees that got here about two weeks after it had happened," Adam explained. "They came straight from that place, and were posting stuff about the defeat all over the internet before they even landed. There were eyewitness accounts, pictures, and even home movies that showed what went on. All the news could do was to report what everyone had already seen as unconfirmed, because the government refused to comment. After about a week of the media looking silly, they finally were given a toned-down version of the events at Cera, and they were bullied into feeding it to us by the central government. Algenib was different in that no Sagobian refugees came here, and the news was able to just go with the government reports, which were skewed."

"Today's much different though," Violet added. "These guys look like they're having the time of their lives. I'd say they're getting the exclusive straight from the government, with no restrictions this time."

"That's because for once the news is good," Tonya said.

The news broadcast switched to a female reporter who was standing outside of the main government administration building in the capital city of Dragos. At this point, Adam adjusted the screen into four sections with his remote. Each reporter had a section, while images of Baron Hareseth and King Zoar showed on the other sections. This was something he did quite a lot, especially during sports broadcasts. It annoyed Tonya, who thought it was hard to watch TV that way.

"Yes, Tom." The female reporter gleefully read a piece of paper. "I've just been handed a dispatch from the governor's office. It states that the Nephilim, supported by elements of the Heruli Hareseth clan, have attacked the Strovats in force at Epsilon Perseus."

"Isn't the Hareseth clan the ruling party of the Heruli?" Tom the anchorman asked to make conversation.

"Yes, indeed they are." The female reporter played along. "And it's by far the most powerful. The fact that Baron Hareseth has sent his own house troops to support the Nephilim is very significant. It means that the Alamani are very likely behind this, though our government has yet to confirm it..."

"Well, duh." Tonya rolled her eyes. "Those guys don't go to the bathroom without the Alamani being involved."

"The official dispatch..." the female reporter continued, "...states that this attack was in retaliation for an earlier Strovat attack on a Nephilim colony in the Atik system. The Nephilim had recently claimed Atik during the collapse of the Sagobian kingdom, and apparently they had set up a research and mining colony there. The Strovats, thinking Atik was theirs, moved in and slaughtered the entire group of Nephilim miners and scientists..."

"The Nephilim have scientists?" Jim joked.

"Not anymore," Franz chuckled.

"We now have with us our resident political analyst, Doctor Yazell, who joins us from his home in Portsmouth," the anchorman stated.

A finely dressed Tellopian appeared at the top corner section of the screen. He explained how tensions had grown between the Strovats and the Nephilim in the last year because of the Strovat occupation of Sagobian territory, and the plundering of valuable planets upon which the Nephilim had ancient claims.

"But, Doctor, what about the rumors that the Strovats were negotiating some sort of agreement with the Alamani?" the anchorman asked.

"By all accounts, the rumors were true," Yazell said. "However, the Nephilim situation is precisely what would disrupt any Strovat-Alamani negotiations. This appears to be exactly what has happened, and frankly, this is exactly what our own government was hoping would happen."

"Doctor, is there any chance that this was an independent attack upon the Strovats by Alaman's allies, or are the Alamani involved?" the anchorman persisted.

Doctor Yazell laughed in a way which Tonya thought was very professional.

"Of course, the Alamani are involved." He smiled. "This is all being orchestrated by them. The Nephilim certainly would not take on the Strovats by themselves, and the Heruli have no good reason to join in, unless Alaman also intends to declare war. As was reported a few days ago, Golar Hassiid had recently requested that the Strovats give the former Sagobian systems to the Nephilim. Now it seems that it was not a request at all, but an ultimatum."

"So, Doctor," the lady reporter asked, "you admit that a month ago it seemed like the Alamani and Strovats were negotiating at least some sort of agreement. Why the sudden turnaround?"

"They were negotiating, but we do not know exactly what they were talking about," Yazell pointed out. "For all we know, Golar Hassiid was merely trying to keep the peace between the Strovats and his own allies. Meanwhile, both parties simultaneously moved in to claim Atik, and it all blew up. Whatever happened before Atik does not matter now.

"There are other forces at work inside Alaman as well. For one, since the fall of Burbeseny we know that many Alamani military leaders now see the Strovats as the biggest threat to their power in the sector. Also, it is well known that many prominent Alamani absolutely abhor the Strovats, particularly in the military.

The Strovats' long record of atrocities goes against their codes of honor. It is very likely that Golar Hassiid was feeling pressure from the military to take action while he still had potential allies to work with, meaning us."

"But Doctor," the anchorman pressed, "isn't it strange to think that Alaman would seek an alliance with us, since we are also allied with their ancient enemies, the Burbesenys, the Sagobians, and the Amali?"

"Strange, but not unheard of," the doctor replied. "It happened in your own Earth's history. During your Second World War the Americans and British allied themselves with the Soviet Union against a common foe, the Germans..."

At this point, everyone in the room gave Franz a teasing look, and Tonya poked him with her elbow. Franz rolled his eyes and cursed in German.

"Above everything else, Golar Hassiid is a realist," Doctor Yazell continued. "He realizes that his old enemies are no longer a major threat, but the Strovats certainly are. He could not sit back and let them become the dominant force in the sector. In my opinion, all he has been waiting for is a legitimate excuse to attack the Strovats. Now, he has one."

Adam turned the sound on the TV down.

"How convenient," he said. "Golar Hassiid feigns peace with the Strovats, and then sits back and lets them destroy his ancient enemies. Once the Burbesenys are no longer a threat, then he finds a way to start a war with the Strovats."

"Why die fighting your enemy when someone else will do it for you?" Franz asked.

"Exactly." Jim shrugged. "Let the Strovats do your dirty work, and then once you no longer need them, get rid of them. Not a bad strategy."

"Totally evil, but smart." Tonya raised her eyebrows. "Those Alamani are good politicians."

"It's more than just that." Adam shook his head. "Golar Hassiid is no dummy. If I can see that the Strovats are a far bigger threat than the Burbesenys, then he could see it, too, and so could his military. He had to know that war with the Strovats was inevitable. You either submit to them and be their slaves, or die. There is no alternative. Eventually he would have had to fight on our side, no matter how much they hate the Burbesenys."

"And now that's what they're doing, Dad." Tonya pointed to the TV. "So, what's the big deal?"

"The question is, why now?" Adam replied. "If you want to use the World War Two alliances as a comparison, then any alliance with Alaman should have happened twenty-five years ago, when the Burbesenys and Amali were still at full strength. Together we all would have had a much better chance to beat the Strovats then, rather than now."

"So they don't like each other. Who cares?" Tonya shrugged. "That doesn't matter anymore. We've just picked up three major allies. This is great!"

"Yes, the more the better for us." Franz smirked.

"You're missing my point." Adam wagged a finger. "I can only think of one good reason why Golar Hassiid waited this long to decide which side he's on. Hegemony."

"Say what?" asked Jim.

"Think about this for a minute," Adam said. "The Burbesenys have been weakened to the point that they may not even be as strong as the Heruli are right now. By waiting until now to declare war on the Strovats, the Alamani are in a much stronger position. I think that the moment they declare war on the Strovats, the Tellopian League is done."

"I don't follow you," Franz said. "How can all of this do anything but strengthen the League?"

"Because if they're stronger than us, they don't have to be our friends," Adam pointed out. "The moment they declare war on the Strovats they will become the strongest on our side, and it's not like they're going to join the League."

"But, why not?" Tonya wobbled her head. "We have the same enemy."

"Because we need them and they know it," Violet replied. "I see what you're getting at, Honey. The Alamani don't have to come to us, like the Burbesenys did. We'll have to go to them, and they're not going to play by our rules."

"Like it or not, our fortunes in this war now depend on Golar Hassiid," Adam continued. "He now controls the fate of this quadrant. Even if we win, it will be because of the Alamani and the Heruli. Do you think for one minute that they will let things stay the way they've been?"

Tonya quietly realized. "Oh."

Jim tried to respond, but no words came out of his mouth.

"They would have the advantage over us." Franz lost his grin.

"Not advantage, hegemony," Adam explained. "Golar Hassiid can literally send his top general to Tellops and dictate terms. What are we going to do, tell him no? What the news isn't reporting is that the League is one more major defeat from falling apart. Two of its members have been wiped out already. The Solarians have pulled their forces out of the front lines, and the Amali and Burbesenys are ready to take them out, just to keep everyone else in line. The government won't let the news report this because they don't want to create a panic, but it's true. You guys know this."

"Yeah, so we've heard," Jim admitted. "The Alamani timing is perfect. You're right. They've got us right where they want us, without having to fire a shot."

"They'll carve us up like a wedding cake," Tonya sighed and rested her chin on her arm.

"We're still better off." Franz gently stroked her back. "I've seen firsthand what the Strovats do to their prisoners. I'd much rather take my chances with the Alamani than end up in a Strovat meat locker."

"So would I," Jim agreed. "I doubt if they'll cut us up, Tonya. We'd be more useful to them as a satellite, like the Nephilim. They'll likely let us keep our military and govern ourselves, but they'll call the shots."

"More likely they'll let us fall apart," Adam warned. "One by one the members of the Tellopian League will have to choose either to submit to the Strovats, or become tributary allies to the Alamani. The only thing certain is that things will never be the same. But, I do agree that we'll fare better with the Alamani than the Strovats."

"Amen to that," Tonya quietly said.

CHAPTER 9

"It is now official. The Alamani have declared war on the Strovats..."

Curtis Baxter glanced up from his computer for a moment to frown at the television on the wall. He sipped the mug of very expensive lager which his personal assistant had recently left on his desk, and then resumed what he was doing. He sat in the study of his very expensive yacht, which was currently in orbit around Pollux VII, a very scenic gas giant on the edge of the Tellopian home system.

A face appeared in the bottom left corner of the TV screen. It belonged to Jack Nero, Baxter's chauffeur and personal bodyguard. Nero was a very large, Caucasian man from New York. He was a bruiser, albeit a sharply dressed one, who stood six-foot-five, was bald with a square head, a thick neck, and built like a gorilla. Baxter found him to be quite useful in a number of ways.

"Yes, Mister Nero?" Baxter addressed him.

"Mister Senzi has arrived, sir," Nero reported in his heavy Bronx accent. "Shall I bring her around to dock with his ship?"

"Yes, Jack." Baxter nodded. "Go ahead."

Nero's face disappeared and Baxter resumed what he was doing. Meanwhile the TV news continued as background noise.

"We now switch live to the Alamani Consulate Center at the capital, where we will hear a statement from Ambassador Ghali."

The screen switched to a tall, hoary-headed Alamani who sat in a throne-like chair and began to read from his hand computer. He started with the general greeting to all members of the Tellopian League, except this time, for the first time ever, he mentioned the Amali and the Burbesenys. He denounced the Strovats, calling them a wicked race who enslave and kill the innocent, waste conquered worlds, and who practice cannibalism. Ambassador Ghali then insulted everyone's intelligence by denying that the Alamani had ever tried to negotiate with them. He went on to elaborate about the incident which had occurred in the Atik system, which had led to war between the Strovats and the Nephilim.

"What happened at Atik was no misunderstanding," he explained. "The Nephilim were attacked. They successfully thwarted the first assault, and then tried to contact the Strovats. They were ignored and attacked again. There were no survivors. The following day a supply ship found the remains of the dead that were left behind and their colony's computer records. Among the dead and missing were several females and young.

"The Strovats possess no regard for sentient life. They show no remorse for anything that they do. There is no end to their wickedness. It is time for all races in the quadrant to unite against them. King Golar Hassiid has declared a holy war against the Strovats, and he invites all the other races to join in this venture. There will be no concessions or negotiations with the Strovats. They are to be given no quarter. They must leave this sector or die. We will fight them until either they are gone, or the last Alamani is dead. From this point onward, any negotiations with the Strovats will be considered treachery.

"This means that all races currently at war with our sworn enemy are now our allies," Ambassador Ghali stated. "Therefore, I have been empowered by his eminence, King Golar Hassiid, to sign non-aggression treaties with the members of the Tellopian League, the Amali and Antearian Kingdoms, and the Burbeseny Empire. King Zoar of the Nephilim and Baron Hareseth of the Heruli will also sign and honor these agreements. I am not here to ask for concessions or dictate terms. We simply wish for mutual trust and cooperation, so that we can effectively combine forces in this holy war against the Strovats..."

"Blah, blah, blah," Curtis Baxter sneered and shut off the TV. "Make all the alliances you want, Golar Hassiid. It will avail you nothing. You will be devoured. Meanwhile, I will be a thousand light years away setting up my new administration."

He removed a quarter-sized disk from his computer and then

shut it down. He held the small disk in his hand for a moment and smiled. Then he put it in a plastic sleeve and slid it into his suit pocket.

He left his study and entered the main corridor, where he bumped into his personal assistant, Debbie Parker. She was a pretty, young African-American woman with short hair and a slender body. Baxter had originally hired her for her looks, but then found her to be both intelligent and capable. In a short time, she had worked her way up his staff to become his personal assistant, and she had also worked her way down to his bedroom.

"Oh, hello, my dear." He smiled. "I'm afraid I've left a bit of a mess in there. Could you take care of it for me, please?"

"Yes, Mister Baxter," she reciprocated.

"And Debbie," he said as she walked past him, "when you're finished you may take the rest of the afternoon off. I'm going to be in a meeting, and I don't know how long it will take."

"Thank you, sir." She glanced over her shoulder and gave him a wry smile. "See you tonight."

Baxter raised an eyebrow and nodded with a lustful grin. He paused to watch her walk away, and then hurried off to his meeting.

Debbie entered the study and quietly cleaned up the small mess which her employer left behind. Once she had finished she did not leave, but instead crept over to the door and quietly closed it. She slinked over to his desk and clicked on his computer, then inserted a disk of her own and got to work.

"Come on, baby," she encouraged it. "Just get me in, and I'll be on my way to an early retirement."

Her heart raced with excitement as her disk did its thing. She thought about how close she was to accomplishing a goal that she had set in high school, and how she got to this point. In college she had majored in office management, and minored in computer science. The one skill landed her a job in a government office, and the other had helped her create this disk.

Her disk was a code cracker, a special and very illegal device created by hackers for breaking through computer firewalls and deciphering passwords. These disks allowed one to hack into a computer system and download files without leaving behind a log or any other kind of trace, and they were not the sort of thing one picked up at the local electronics store. Code crackers were usually homemade devices that were moved on the black market. While most major bank computers would eat such disks for lunch, they were highly effective for breaking into personal computers.

She wasn't too ambitious. She wasn't going to try knock off a bank, and embezzlers always seemed to be caught. Her plan for early retirement involved plain, old fashioned extortion.

Public officials were easy targets for such a plan, having to maintain some sort of cleanliness or risk having public opinion turn against them. A politician who lost his public either had to retire in disgrace, find another career, move two sectors away to start over, or jump off a building. However most important people preferred to remain important, so they usually would do anything to keep their reputations clean, including paying lots of money. She figured that even if she got caught, she could at least take a few important people down with her.

The sex came with the territory, and it helped her get into Baxter's inner circle. Besides, as Humans were concerned, they were out in the middle of nowhere, and she needed it like anyone else. At least, she had thought to herself, Baxter wasn't a fat, alcoholic pig.

She already knew that she couldn't use their relationship against him. He was divorced and had a reputation for being a ladies' man. However, he was also one of those guys who had moved two sectors away, and he did spend quite a lot of money. In fact, it was his taste for luxury which piqued her interest. His salary definitely could not cover his expenses. If he was loaded, then why was he way out here instead of playing golf at St Andrews? If he was borrowing the money, was he spending it all and not paying anyone back? No one could live like this for very long on credit. Therefore, she figured he must be on the take.

"Bingo." She snapped her fingers. "I'm inside your mind, Curtis Baxter. Now, let's check your personal files and see what you don't want anyone to know."

She scrolled down and found what she was looking for.

"Okay, here we go," she mumbled. "Show me your checkbook...Whoa!"

What she found was much, much bigger than she had expected. This was enough money to pay off a medium-sized country's national debt. She dropped her hands to her sides and gaped at all of the zeros.

"Jeez! Should I blackmail him, or marry him?" she gasped. "Who in the galaxy would pay this much to a burned-out, middle management politician in the central government?"

It took her but a few seconds to find the answer.

"State Bank of Solari?" she whispered to herself. "The Solarians? Why would they have anything to do with this guy? What could he possibly have that they would want?"

Then she found the file that Baxter had just copied to the quarter-sized disk. For a moment she sat, frozen in total shock and horror.

"I don't believe this!" she quietly exclaimed, shaking her head in denial. "No! This isn't real. This is a nightmare! He's...he's sold us out!"

"Yeah, it looks that way, don't it?" came a raspy voice from behind her.

Debbie nearly jumped out of her skin. She turned around to see Jack Nero standing in the doorway.

"Jack!" she stammered, "I...I was just...updating Mister Baxter's appointment book."

"And while you were doing that, you thought you may as well look into his financial records?" he said, raising his eyebrows.

"Listen, Jack, never mind what I was doing." She stood and composed herself. "We have to stop Baxter! He's meeting with a Solarian industrialist right now!"

"Is that so?" Jack pursed his lips. "Tisk, tisk."

"Don't you get it?" she exclaimed. "The rumors are true! The Solarians really are traitors, and Curtis Baxter is in a meeting with them selling us out!"

She tried to leave the room, but Nero blocked her exit.

"What is *the matter* with you?" she complained vehemently. "The entire sector could be overrun next week, and we're the only ones who know about this! We have to *stop* him!"

"Oh, really?" he patronized her, but did not budge.

"Look, we don't have time for this! If you don't believe me, just look at his computer. Either help me or get outta my way!"

"I don't think so. You're not going anywhere."

He shoved her violently, and she plopped down and rolled across the floor.

"So, what do you get out of this, a raise?" she spat.

"You could say that." He smiled wickedly as he moved over

toward her. "I'll get to be the Chief of Security for the Viceroy of the Earth. Has a nice ring to it, don't you think?"

"Ring this!" She lunged a fist up toward his crotch, but he caught it and yanked her to her feet with frightening strength.

"That wasn't very nice, Debbie," he growled.

She punched him with her free hand, but this had no effect. He spun her around and got her in a choke hold with one huge arm. He carried her out of the room while she kicked and screamed, and then he threw her into a closet-sized locker and quickly ordered the ship's computer to seal it through his wrist communicator. She beat on the door from the inside, but to no avail.

Meanwhile, down on the lower level of his small space ship, Curtis Baxter sat at the bar in his lounge, having a drink with a Solarian industrial analyst, Anhardos Senzi. He was a typical middle-aged, wealthy Solarian, meaning that he looked like a short, fat, blueish-gray Human wearing a very expensive suit. Mister Senzi was five feet tall, and he wore rather showy jewelry on his fingers and around his neck. Like all Solarians, he was a carbon dioxide-breather, and he used a small device on his belt which allowed his body to breathe the proper gas in this atmosphere.

"Have you heard the news?" Senzi asked nervously. "The Alamani, the Nephilim and the Heruli are all going to sign a treaty with the Tellopians."

"Not to worry, my friend," Baxter responded with a smug smile. "They will soon be busy on their own frontiers. The Strovats will come back to Epsilon Perseus with more ships than before. Our friends will handle them. Our business today regards the Tellopians. It's time to put an end to their farcical League."

"If they do not get us first," Senzi complained. "We have been under suspicion ever since Algenib."

"What did you expect?" Baxter shrugged. "Your government decided to make a secret deal with the Strovats on the eve of a major battle. If you helped the Sagobians, the Strovats would think you double-crossed them, but since you didn't help, the Tellopians now suspect treachery. Rather bad timing, old boy."

"We did not have a choice. The front runs through our space. The Strovats were breathing down our necks!"

"Yes, but now I'm afraid your government has angered the Amali and Burbesenys. Their failure to assist at Algenib has even aroused the suspicions of the Zuzims and the Nervii. Karnow has authorized Admiral Murko to spy on you fellows, so you should keep a low profile. You had better keep the Strovats away, unless they want to give you a hundred Bisas for protection."

"What can we do?" Senzi wiped his brow with a cloth. "We cannot cross the Strovats, and we will never find Murko's spy drones. We all fear the Burbesenys."

He leaned forward and whispered, "Tell me, are they preparing to attack us?"

"No, I think not." Baxter waved a hand. "Karnow will not allow them to do so without a full investigation. He'll make Murko submit so much paperwork first that you're more likely to die of old age than by his tentacles. Besides, once our plans are carried out, they'll no longer have the resources to attack Solari. They will all be too busy saving their own necks to worry about you and me."

"You are probably correct." Senzi heaved a sigh, sat back, and gulped down his drink.

"Now, let us get down to business." Baxter smiled and removed the small disk from his suit pocket.

Senzi's beady eyes lit up. He reached across the bar and tried to snatch it, but Baxter pulled it away.

"Ah, ah, ah." Baxter wagged a finger.

"Give it to me!" Senzi demanded. "We have already sent your payment."

"Not until I have the final part of the deal in my hands." Baxter grinned maliciously.

He held out his free hand. Senzi removed an old fashioned paper contract from his coat and handed it over. Baxter quickly thumbed through it.

"This appears to be in order." Baxter nodded, and then held out his hand again. "And now, my friend, the code disk, please."

"First give me the fleet disk."

"My dear Senzi, without the code disk I won't be able to communicate with the Strovat leaders. They'll see me as any other Human and kill me, and that rather defeats the purpose of my giving you the fleet disk, now doesn't it? Besides, how do I know that you even have it?"

"I have it." Senzi nodded and removed a similar small disk from his jacket. "But I was ordered not to give it to you without first obtaining the fleet disk."

"We are old acquaintances," Baxter said. "Can we not trust one another?"

"Very well," Senzi exhaled.

He handed Baxter the code disk. Baxter snatched it, and then handed Senzi the fleet disk. Baxter held the code disk up and laughed giddily, while Senzi heaved a sigh of relief and finally smiled.

"You must keep those codes with you at all times," he instructed. "They are your identification papers. With them you can get by any Strovat or Solarian military forces, for they will recognize who you are. Without them you are dead."

"These codes tell them who I am." Baxter no longer concealed the lust in his eyes. "They all will recognize me as the ruler of the Earth! At last, the age-old dream of world domination will be realized. Napoleon and Alexander could not do in their lifetimes what I will soon accomplish!"

"Yes, yes, it is all there in your contract," Senzi affirmed. "In exchange for this information, the Strovats will make you their Viceroy of the Earth, once they take it. The seal and the codes on the disk are from Prince Yaki, the Strovat overlord of the quadrant and son of the Third High Queen. All of the Strovats in this quadrant of the galaxy will recognize his mark."

"Most excellent!" Baxter snapped his fingers and put his new disk in his suit pocket. "And now that our business is concluded, may I invite you to stay and enjoy a fine meal with me?"

"No thank you," Senzi said. "I am in haste. I must return to Solari with this information as soon as possible. Our patrons are most anxious to receive it."

"Very well, my friend." Baxter rose and shook Senzi's hand. "I'll have Mister Nero show you out."

He summoned Jack, who escorted Mister Senzi out. Once the Solarian had boarded his own ship and flown away, Baxter invited Jack to sit and enjoy a few drinks with him in celebration of their upcoming administration.

"Mister Baxter," Nero said as he gulped down a shot of whiskey, "look...about Debbie, she didn't exactly take the rest of the day off."

"What do you mean?" Baxter sipped his champagne.

"She hacked into your computer and found your files," Nero replied. "All of them."

"Hmmm." Baxter set his drink down and frowned. "How naughty of her. Where is she now?"

"I sealed her in storage locker two." Nero poured himself another shot. "She's not going anywhere."

"Take me to her," Baxter ordered.

They walked through the ship to the little room where Debbie Parker was imprisoned. Baxter ordered the ship's computer to unseal the door, and they let her out. Beads of sweat rolled down her face, and she fell to her knees.

"Mister Baxter," she cried, "I'm so sorry! I...I can still work for you. I'll do whatever you want. Please, don't turn me in!"

"Turn you in?" Baxter gave Nero a crooked smile. "No, no, my dear, I have other plans for you."

"Other plans?" She gave him a quizzical look.

"Yes." He motioned for her to follow. "Walk with me a bit."

She stood and walked behind Baxter as he moved slowly down the corridor. He walked with his hands behind his back, all the while looking forward as he spoke. Jack Nero stayed behind, leering at her like a stalker.

"First of all, thank you for not insulting my intelligence by declaring your innocence," Baxter said.

"You're welcome." She looked nervously back at Nero. "I think."

"So, you saw what we're doing?" Baxter asked.

"I saw that you made a good deal with the Solarians," she admitted.

"And do you know what this means?" he pressed.

"The Strovats are behind it," she said, struggling to keep her cool. "They're going to attack us again."

"They will attack anyway, whether we act or not," Baxter pontificated. "The news media has been lying to everyone, Debbie. I have access to our intelligence reports and I know how strong the Strovats are. They are numberless. The Burbesenys destroyed tens of thousands of their ships, and tens of thousands more came. No one knows where the Strovats come from or how old they are. For all we know, they may already control most of the galaxy. The Tellopians stand no chance against them. They will inevitably fall."

They stopped in front of a heavy door leading to the outside, which was in fact the airlock to which Senzi's ship had formerly been attached. Baxter turned to face her. His eyes were lit with the fires of greed.

"But that doesn't mean that we must fall with them." He clenched a fist. "We Humans have an outstanding opportunity before us! The Strovats don't destroy all the planets they conquer. They need productive worlds to supply their expanding empire. The races who resist are punished, it is true, but the ones who submit, such as the Solarians, are treated well. Their lives continue as before, except under the rule of a Viceroy. Oh, there are a few who will be sacrificed, but that happens in any regime. A few will die so that many more may live.

"What the Strovats bring to the table is order! Their society is the most ordered one in the galaxy. They do not muck about with parliaments or committees. They get things done! They are the future of the quadrant, and we must become a part of this future, Debbie. Our survival as a race depends on it. What I have done this day is to ensure that the Human race will continue, and it will continue with order! I will bring peace and order to the Earth!"

At this point, Debbie stepped close to him. She smiled and ran her finger up and down the front of his shirt, as if what he had just said aroused her.

"I always knew you were special," she lied. "I really like a man in charge. I think I'm going to enjoy being a part of this, and I can make you enjoy it more, too. I think you will still find me to be...useful."

"Tempting." He smiled briefly. "But I'm afraid not."

His expression suddenly grew cold. He pushed her into Jack's arms.

"It was a mistake for me to bring you here, Debbie," he said. "And it was a bigger mistake for you not to take the vacation I offered you. Now, I must correct those mistakes. Computer, open airlock."

The inner hatchway opened.

"What?" Debbie's eyes grew wide. "No...*No! Wait!*"

"Goodbye, Debbie." Curtis Baxter waved.

Jack tossed her like a rag doll into the airlock. She tumbled over to the other side, and did not recover herself in time to prevent Baxter from closing the hatch behind her.

"*No! Please!*" She pounded on the hatch and screamed. "*I DON'T WANT TO DIE!*"

"I recommend that you exhale, Debbie," Baxter coldly stated

over the intercom. "It will go much more quickly for you if you exhale."

He keyed in a sequence on the pad by the hatchway, overriding the safety protocol, and the outer hatch opened. Debbie screamed and clawed frantically at the walls, desperately fighting a losing battle for her life as she was sucked out of the ship into the cold vacuum of space. A moment later she was gone, and Baxter closed the outer hatch of the airlock.

"Such a waste." He shook his head. "She had a good criminal mind and a great body. She had potential, that one."

"You sound like you're going to miss her." Nero smirked.

"No, I'm going to miss the sex, Jack. I could have had a robot do my secretarial work for me, but no robot could do what she could do."

"Glad to hear it. For a minute there, I thought you were getting soft on me."

"You know me better than that." Baxter smiled and slapped him on the back. "Now then, we need to get cracking. Did you refuel the ship yet?"

"Yeah, I put it on the credit card, just like you said to."

"Good man!" Baxter laughed. "Run those credit cards up. Max them all out. After all, the world's about to end. You and I will see to that."

"Yes, boss." Nero nodded and smiled wickedly.

"Oh, and see to Debbie's things." Baxter pointed to the airlock. "We no longer need them on board. Be sure to destroy anything that could identify her first. Not that anyone will ever find her body, but I like things to be done right."

"Yes, sir."

"Once that's taken care of, you and I are going to get ourselves out of this place. We need to disappear for a while. We'll keep a low profile until the Strovats are ready to deliver on their promise. So, we're going on a little vacation of our own."

"Where to?"

"Somewhere inconspicuous," Baxter replied.

☐

CHAPTER 10

Alaman Empire: Region 13, Rear Sector
1000 light years beyond the Orion Nebula

King Golar Hassiid sat in the command chair of his huge flagship, the Dreadnaught class battleship *Archangel*, with Admiral Karg seated on his right. On either side of his flagship, flying in a wedge formation, were two other Dreadnaughts. These oval-shaped vessels resembled giant, flattened eggs with delta wings, and were among the largest warships in the quadrant, surpassed only by the Burbeseny K class battleships and the Strovat Bisas. The Alamani possessed over two thousand Dreadnaughts of various design, at least half of which were older and somewhat smaller models, but these three represented the newest and best class.

The Alamani also possessed thousands of smaller warships, among which were their fast frigates. These were similar in design and speed as Jim and Franz's Nervii frigate, except that the Alamani did not use theirs for commerce raiding, as they deemed that type of warfare dishonorable. The Alamani used fast frigates much like light cavalry, for scouting and screening purposes. At this moment, a small fleet of them accompanied Golar Hassiid's Dreadnaughts, scouting out the area as they plodded forward. They appeared as a swarm of flies compared to the king's massive flagship.

They travelled through an area behind and below the great nebula that was littered with ruined planets from a civilization long extinct. Twelve days before, just a week after their declaration of war against the Strovats, their reconnaissance probes had picked up a massive power signal, the likes of which they had never seen. This mysterious vessel had been detected popping up here and there throughout this back sector. As no one could explain this, Golar Hassiid had consulted Orizah. After a day of meditation, the prophet returned with a message that the king should investigate it personally, rather than sending his military after it.

"I do not get out this way much," Golar Hassiid stated in a subdued tone.

"I am surprised Ator let you out of the palace," Karg remarked.

"He objected vigorously, but I reminded him that I am still the king," Golar Hassiid said. "Karg, these systems in this sector are all ruins, every one of them. One planet or two could be easily explained as lost colonies, but this entire sector was once inhabited and now it is a wasteland. I had heard tales of the ruined sector, but I had no idea that it was this extensive. You have been reading some of Talg's old books. What happened here?"

"My lord," Karg answered, "according to what I have read thus far, this is but one of many ruined sectors. This area is only a small part of the ruins of a once great empire, greater than our own. When you were a child, did your mother ever teach you a fairy tale called the Kwarizim?"

"Yes, I know that one. In fact, Radi teaches it to our children. The Kwarizim king was the richest in all the galaxy. He sat on a throne of bdellium, the rarest, most beautiful precious metal in the universe, and his castle was made of the most fabulous red crystal. His city was built out of gold, and lined with jewel-encrusted streets. To this day, adventurers seek out his fabled lost tomb and his mines in search of untold wealth. But, of course, they never find any of it. Kwarizim is a fairy tale. No such kingdom could ever have existed."

"Actually, in fact it once did," Karg said. "Though the ancient records do not speak of the bdellium and the red crystal palace, they clearly mention the Kwarizim kingdom as being a rich and powerful empire."

"So, once again fairy tales are based on reality. But why would we remember this fairy tale, and not the one about the Leviathan?" the king asked.

"One fairy tale is pleasant and the other is not, I suppose."

"Do the ancient books say where the fabulous Kwarizim kingdom was?"

"We see it before us." Karg pointed. "This ruined sector is a part of it, for the books say that our great nebula was the door to their kingdom. All of these ruined planets were once filled with life, until the Mentotians came. You see, my lord, according to the ancient tales the Kwarizim were as wicked as they were rich. Their cities were built upon the backs of slaves. They denied Alè, worshipping their sciences instead. Worst of all, they practiced inbreeding as a way to preserve their ancestral bloodlines."

"What a foolish thing to do," Golar Hassiid commented. "My ancestors avoided family intermarrying, because it is much more important to have strong, intelligent rulers than to keep all of the riches in the family. The practice of inbreeding serves only to eliminate costly dowries at the expense of weakening the family gene pool. It leads to weak-minded rulers and an entire list of hereditary diseases, including insanity. It seems to me that the Kwarizim may have destroyed themselves with such foolishness."

"According to the ancient chronicles that indeed is what happened, or rather they brought destruction down upon themselves," Karg reported. "The insanity of their emperors led to the persecution and death of several prophets. Finally, the annals state that the great God could no longer allow this to continue, and He called forth the Mentotians."

"Does it say that, or did Alè bring forth those Leviathans into the sector, and then the insane Kwarizim emperor attacked them?" Golar Hassiid asked. "It has always been taught to me that Alè allows us to suffer the benefits or consequences of our actions, and usually does not directly interfere. An arrogant or insane ruler who tried to eat more than his stomach could hold seems a more likely scenario. Any fool who starts a war with the monsters from my nightmares gets what he deserves."

"The chronicle which I read did not specify what caused the war, my lord," Karg admitted. "Only that God called forth the Leviathan, Mentotians from the Outer Rim of the galaxy, to punish the wicked kingdoms. But certainly, that is a good supposition and very likely what happened. In any event, we can see before us what happened to the Kwarizim. The science and technology which they so worshipped did not save them from the Leviathan.

"The chronicles also mention other great empires which were

destroyed at or about the same time. Kingdom after kingdom fell before the Mentotians. Their names are not familiar to us, but their tale is still worth telling. The Mentotians laid waste the Ystradi Empire. They killed the king of the Marcomanni and burned his planet. They smashed the Begrethians at a place called Camlann and slew their High Queen. They annihilated an army of five kings at a place called Dyrhm. The list goes on and on. Many more races such as these are listed, all of whom are long forgotten.

"I did some archeological research since our meeting with Orizah, my lord. These chronicles explain a lot about the ruined sectors. Other dead zones like this exist in the old Amali and Burbeseny sectors as well."

The king sat for a moment, silently digesting the information.

"It seems that we are caught in the web of history, my old friend," he finally spoke. "Let us be sure not to repeat our predecessors' mistakes."

As if on cue, as soon as he had finished speaking, the ship's power sensors went haywire. From out of nowhere, a ship appeared directly in front of them. Its power readings were incredible, greater than five Bisa supercruisers combined, yet the vessel itself was smaller than the Alamani flagship. Its shape resembled that of an old-style Earth delta wing jet aircraft, minus the nose. It was rounded with a slight bulge on the top, and what resembled a bridge superstructure ran along the spine of the bottom.

"All stop," Karg ordered.

"Shall we go to alert?" the first officer asked.

"No," the king answered. "Order all ships to stand down."

"All ships stand down," Karg ordered.

"So, they can cloak themselves after all," the king noted. "There is your invisible enemy from your dreams, Karg."

"I liked him better when I could not see him," Karg admitted.

☐

CHAPTER 11

Curtis Baxter was not present at the next Security Council meeting on Tellops. He did not call in nor report in any manner that he would not attend. When Karnow contacted his apartment, he was not at home, and his personal assistant also did not respond. Karnow could only reach their individual message centers.

"This is very strange," Admiral Murko commented. "The Human Baxter has always been reliable, and he is usually here before me. I will send a message to my liaison and have him check on Mister Baxter's whereabouts, in case there is a problem."

Juman thought to himself that this was a nice way of saying that Murko was going to send someone to spy on Baxter, but at least the Burbeseny admiral was not picky in whom he mistrusted.

Karnow began the meeting with good news, for once.

"The combined Nephilim-Heruli offensive at Epsilon Perseus has disrupted the Strovat offensive in that sector," he explained, using a holograph of the star systems in that area. "As you can plainly see, this has cut the enemy supply lines to Algenib. Our latest intelligence states they have diverted many of their forces there back to Epsilon Perseus. For the moment, this has given us a reprieve. We should discuss today whether or not a relief column to the surviving Sagobians at Algenib IV is viable."

"You are assuming the Nephilim will try to hold Epsilon Perseus, which is not likely," Murko stated. "They only hit the

119

Strovats with a few corps, and their attack resembled a larger version of General Blaaga's raids. They will likely withdraw if confronted with a major Strovat force. It could be a diversion to draw the enemy forces away from an Alamani strike farther to the rear, for Golar Hassiid has pulled many of his own elite corps out of our view. In any event, we are still vulnerable from attack even from Epsilon Perseus, if the Strovats so choose. Any counteroffensive to Algenib at this point is unadvisable."

"I must agree," Alatheus said. "With a third of our fleet out of service, we can barely defend the worlds that are on the frontier as it is. We would have to strip them of defenders in order to accomplish anything useful at Algenib. Instead I suggest that we use General Blaaga's special operation forces to aid and evacuate the Sagobians, while we do our best to bolster our defenses during this respite."

"Unfortunately," Blaaga responded, "at this time much of my force is unavailable. We will not be ready for any such operations for at least two months."

"Why is this?" Juman asked. "Are they on another mission?"

"No, they are on a much needed rest," Blaaga replied.

"General, we are at war," Juman lectured. "This is no time for a vacation. We need you to bring your forces back on line immediately."

"I will not," Blaaga retorted. "My soldiers have been on duty for several months behind enemy lines. It is easy for you, Juman, to sit in your office and issue orders. You are here every day, but my troops and I have been out there at the edge of the blade. It is now time for us to rest."

"I must agree with Blaaga," Alatheus politely argued. "Even the best soldiers require rotation. They cannot always stay at the front. To overuse some of our best troops now would be a mistake that would cost us dearly in the future."

"Yes, General Blaaga alone among us has had success against the Strovats," Murko said. "I will not have anyone here tamper with that. Leave him alone."

Both Juman and Karnow sat and silently fumed. Without the support of Alatheus, they were completely powerless to order Blaaga to do anything. Karnow wondered if Murko actually supported Blaaga, or if he simply used this as an opportunity to exercise control over Security Council decisions.

"Let us return to the Solarian question," Karnow said. "Our scout probes have indeed discovered a Strovat buildup at Alrami, the system next to Nunki. The number of Bisas there has jumped from thirty-seven to eighty. Also, the same number of enemy supertankers are also gathered in that system. So, it seems that the Solarians are justified in their fears."

"They are if they are still on our side," Xanthar said. "A fact which we have not yet been able to determine. Also, you failed to mention the utter lack of Strovat presence at Nunki, which the Solarians claimed."

"Eighty of their supertankers?" Rashaa wondered. "That does not sound like the normal Bisa-to-supertanker ratio."

"No, it is not," Juman stated. "There are twice as many supertankers at Alrami as normal. We do not know why this is."

"Eighty Bisas is significant," Murko admitted, "but not yet a threat to Solari, as half of them are there to garrison Alrami itself. Still, it cannot be ignored, especially because of the unusual number of the super-sized fuel ships. That is very odd."

"It sounds as if they are planning for a long space jump," Blaaga pointed out. "Whenever my forces go behind the lines we bring along twice as much fuel as normal, just in case we cannot steal enough from the enemy to get back."

"A long jump to where?" Mocor asked. "Any one of the populated worlds along our front are at normal range for them."

"Perhaps they are looking beyond the front, as we do," Blaaga replied. "I have seen your intelligence reports from this morning, Juman. There is also an unusual ratio of enemy supertankers at Algenib. I am wondering if the Strovats are planning for a long-range strike, perhaps at our repair base at Nihal, or even here at Tellops. We should take steps to reinforce the inner systems, particularly our repair base at Nihal."

"No," Murko dismissed. "If the Strovats are anything, they are consistent. Strovats are linear thinkers. They do not behave beyond the obvious, as you do Blaaga. They always attack frontally. We have been fighting them for a long time, and they have never, ever jumped over populated systems to get to targets behind the lines. It simply does not occur to them to do that."

"Murko is correct," Xanthar said. "I would say that the unusual number of fuel tankers has to do with the destruction of their fuel supply stations at both Rho Ophiuchus and Epsilon

Perseus, and not any unusual attack strategy on their part. If anything, the extra supertankers at Algenib are for use against the Nephilim at Epsilon Perseus. Nihal is in no danger."

"I do not agree," Blaaga argued, "and I do not think this is wise to underestimate our enemy's capacity for change. A third of our fleet is at Nihal, and not operational. If the Strovats somehow got lucky with one of their probes and found that repair base, then we would be in a lot of trouble. If the enemy hits us there, they would cripple our war effort in one blow. The reinforcements that we need to hold the line would be gone, and even more populated worlds would be wide open to attack. Then I fear the League would fall apart. We would have ten more worlds do just as the Solarians have done and call home their militaries. Therefore, I move that we reinforce Nihal at once."

Blaaga's motion was denied.

☐

CHAPTER 12

Franz and Tonya scheduled a rehearsal to take place three days before their wedding. Tonya's family arrived about 8:30 that morning at their church in Portsmouth. While they were waiting for the Zemmarichs to arrive, Tonya took the opportunity to try on her wedding dress, which she had just received from a mail order catalog. She tried it on in the women's dressing room with her mother, and then invited her father in for a look.

"Well, what do you think?" Tonya asked.

Adam coughed politely, taken aback by the amount of his daughter's cleavage exposure.

"It's umm..." He raised his eyebrows. "...very nice. But...isn't it a bit showy?"

"Dad, it's a wedding dress!" Tonya put one hand on her hip. "I'm not using it to apply for a job."

"If you did, you'd get the job," he murmured.

"I think you look absolutely beautiful, Honey," Violet said as she preened the back of the dress.

"Thanks, Mom." Tonya smiled at her.

Adam shook his head. "I don't remember it looking like that in the catalog."

"That's because those models in the bridal catalogs are all small women," Violet informed him. "Our daughter is much bigger than they are."

"My breasts are bigger," Tonya said. "It's not like I'm fat or anything."

"Your figure is fuller than those skinny models, dear," Violet said. "They need to eat more. You're just fine."

"Franz thinks so." Tonya looked in the mirror and smiled. "He thinks I'm perfect."

"Franz should," Violet said. "He's been in love with you since you were twelve."

"Wait till he sees me in this dress," Tonya giggled. "His eyes will pop out of his head."

A few minutes later, Franz and his family arrived. Tonya changed back into her black jeans and favorite purple shirt, and she and her mother carefully packed her wedding dress into a garment bag. They exited the dressing room into a hallway, where Franz awaited them dressed in his green fatigues. Tonya rushed over to him, and the young couple embraced and kissed.

"Ready for the rehearsal?" he asked.

"I'm ready for the wedding!" she growled and bit at one of the buttons on his shirt.

"Me too." He stroked her blond hair. "I have loved you since we were children."

"And I've loved you just as long," she said softly, and then kissed him again. "So, is everybody here?"

"Um..." Franz scratched his head nervously. "Sort of."

"Oh no, don't tell me." She exhaled in frustration. "Jim didn't get back yet."

"No."

"Is he at least on his way?"

"Not exactly." He shifted his eyes.

"Well, where is he, exactly?" She put her hand on her hip.

"He's still back at the ship," Franz said sheepishly.

"What?" Tonya griped. "He's not done yet? It's been five days!"

"So, what's going on with Jim?" Violet asked.

"Well, you know our ship's engineering is run by robots," Franz said.

"Yes," Violet replied.

"They also do our inspections while we're in port," Franz stated. "Five days ago, Engineer One reported a major problem with our hyperdrive, and one of us had to be there to help do the repairs."

"But the base is just up the road," Violet pointed out. "He couldn't take some time off and drive over here?"

"The docks are all full at the base," Franz replied. "And we have orders not to use the spaceport. So, we had to use one of the off-base facilities, which are all out on the moons of N Delta."

"Jim's two planets away?" Violet's jaw dropped.

"Fortunately, N Delta is lined up pretty close to our orbit right now, so he's only about twelve hours away," Franz explained.

"Oh, that's better." Tonya rolled her eyes. "How long have you known he wasn't going to be here?"

"Uh...well..." Franz looked about as if trying to escape. "He did send me a message yesterday."

"And you forgot to tell us," Tonya said.

"I got it right before dinner." He shrugged. "We saw the movie after that, and I just forgot. He promised to be here in time for the wedding."

"That's helpful," Tonya said. "Has he sent any more messages since last night?"

"Um...I don't really know," he admitted.

"Because you left your phone in your backpack at home, didn't you?"

He nodded.

"And you haven't even checked it since last night, have you?" she asked.

He shook his head.

"Franz, what's the point of giving you a phone if you never carry it around with you?" Tonya teased him.

"Because when I'm with you we always use your phone."

"Did you forget that my phone died last night?" Tonya asked. "Until I get a new one, you need to start checking your messages. You might miss some big event."

"Here on Planet Podunk?" Franz smirked. "I don't think so."

"Anyway, I thought you guys are supposed to be on vacation." She poked him.

"Our vacation will turn into AWOL if we don't fix our hyperdrive," Franz said as they walked down the hallway toward the chapel. "Our bosses frown on it when we don't show up for work on time."

"So, what's wrong with your ship?" Violet asked.

"There's some damage on the outer hull right above the fission reactor. The thorium drive core was leaking, and that's not good. If we try to slingshot out with a leaky core, we'll fry ourselves."

"So how did it get that way?" Violet asked.

"We probably hit some space junk on our way in," Franz responded. "There's all kinds of stuff floating around out there. Pieces of wrecked ships, dead probes, and even garbage."

"Wait a minute," Violet wondered. "Isn't it illegal to dump garbage in space?"

"Yeah, it is," Franz replied. "But people do it anyway, mostly because they don't want the cops finding illegal party items in their garbage at the spaceports. That's why we always do inspections every time we enter or leave a system."

"Yeah, space junk is a big problem," Tonya sighed. "Remember what happened to Jim's family?"

"I know they were killed in an accident, but no one ever told me the details," Violet replied.

"Space junk," Franz said. "The liner they were on hit an unreported dead satellite and crashed into Triton. They were coming out here to visit him on a routine flight, and in an instant he lost his mom, his brother, his sister and her little daughter."

"That's terrible." Violet shook her head.

"Well, I don't want you two frying yourselves," Tonya said. "So tonight, I want you to text him and let him know I'm not mad."

"He'll be glad to know that you're not going to kill him." Franz smiled. "Even though the best man doesn't do much."

"The best man is an important part of the ceremony," Tonya said.

"All he does is stand next to me and hand me the ring," Franz pointed out.

"He didn't take the ring with him, did he?" She stopped in her tracks. "You have the ring, right?"

"Yes, I have that." Franz nodded. "I kept it just in case Jim gets stuck out there."

"Good." She heaved a sigh of relief. "I'd hate to have to kill you before we're married."

They walked together into the chapel, where their families awaited them. Hugo Zemmarich was tall and stocky, with broad shoulders, brown eyes, and gray hair. His wife Maria was Tonya's size, with light hair and blue eyes. Tonya had always told Franz that he inherited his father's body and his mother's hair and eyes. She was very close to them, having spent half of her life in their house.

"I'm so happy that I'm finally going to be in your family!" Tonya cried as they embraced.

Maria smiled. "You have always been a member of our family."

Violet gave Franz a big hug, and Adam shook his hand and slapped him on the back. Their pastor entered the chapel from an office that was off to the right side of the pulpit. Bishop Green was middle-aged, tall, lanky, balding, bespectacled, and always seemed to be dressed in a dark suit, even during church picnics. He greeted each one of them with a warm smile and a friendly handshake. Franz shifted nervously as the pastor approached.

"Good to see you, Franz," Bishop Green said. "It's been a long time."

"Um...yeah." Franz scratched the back of his head. "I've been on active duty, you know."

"Wow, three straight years of active duty without a break," Bishop Green kidded. "Now, that's impressive. Tonya, how did you ever put up with that?"

"Because he comes home every few months." She elbowed Franz.

"Don't worry about him, son," Hugo responded in his heavy German accent. "He's just doing his job. He gave me a hard time, too."

"I certainly hope I'll see more of you after the wedding, Franz." Bishop Green smiled.

"Don't worry," Tonya replied. "You will."

Franz cringed at the mere thought of this.

At this exact moment, Franz's phone sat and vibrated furiously in his bag on his old bed, while Tonya's rested in her family recycle bin. With all of the family activities going on before the wedding, he had stayed the last few days at his parents' house. Franz had packed his phone away the night before, just in time to miss a frantic emergency message from Jim.

Eleven hours earlier, at the refueling station on one of the outer moons of Nihal IV, Jim sat in the cockpit of the Nervii frigate *Cherbourg* and pounded on the keys of his computer like a madman. Throughout the ship, robots furiously worked and darted back and forth.

"Jeez, I hope you guys get this!" He sweated. "C'mon, Franz

and Tonya, please check your phones again tonight!"

"Lieutenant Commander Washington," the chief engineer robot called him over the intercom, "please observe your sensors."

"I know!" he exclaimed. "I see them!"

"Shall we power up the ship for takeoff?" Engineer One dutifully inquired.

"NO!" Jim yelled into the intercom. "The only chance we have is to go silent! *Shut it down! Shut it all down, NOW!*"

CHAPTER 13

For some inexplicable reason, Burbeseny intelligence, which had heretofore been very reliable, had made a serious error. Their reconnaissance drones had counted the Strovat Bisas around Algenib IV. However, they had somehow missed, or didn't look for, a second much larger fleet of Bisas which had been accumulating behind Algenib VI. This planet, as opposed to Algenib VII, was at a point in its orbit where it faced the star Nihal. It was a long jump from Algenib to Nihal, but not an impossible one.

The Strovats began decelerating their fleet around Nihal IV at 9:24 PM Friday. The process took about three hours for all three hundred Bisas and their transports to come in, but the first sixty Bisas did not wait for the others. They immediately headed straight for Dragos.

At 9:32 PM Friday Lieutenant Commander Jim Washington sent a single warning message to the Dragosian High Command before he was forced to shut down. His message was received by a junior communications officer seventy minutes later, who immediately passed it to his superiors. They balked at first, for no one at the central government had sent the Dragosian High Command any warnings of any potential Strovat threat. The enemy was far away, and no one believed they would jump over the front to get to Dragos, of all places. However, after a while there could be no doubt as to the huge power signals coming in from N Delta.

The middle-management officers at High Command argued

among themselves, and their commanding generals were not around, nor did they answer their phones. Two hours passed before they ordered the junior communications officer to confirm the message, which he was unable to do because Jim had gone silent. After waiting another two and a half hours for Jim's non-response, someone finally thought to forward his warning to the secret repair base at Nihal III. However, the base commander there had figured out what was going on from his own sensors two hours previous, and he had already ordered an emergency evacuation.

The fleet based at Nihal III should have been in a better state of readiness. The fact that they were not was partly Curtis Baxter's doing. He had purposely sent conflicting orders about which ships to prioritize for repair, and he changed those orders every week. He also, unknown to Murko, had kept them on green alert as opposed to yellow alert. They were not expecting trouble, and when it came they simply did not have enough heavy warships ready to respond. Worse yet, most of the crews had been reassigned or were on leave. A third of the League's warships were at Nihal III, but only a fraction of them could fly out of the base. The rest were sitting ducks.

Meanwhile, sixty Strovat Bisas were bearing down on Dragos, and yet no emergency had been declared. A few junior officers at Central Command wished to contact the media, but the middle management refused to set off any alarms before contacting the top generals, who still were nowhere to be found.

Finally, at 5:45 AM Saturday a naval adjutant disobeyed orders and notified Admiral Takagi, second-in-command of the fleet, who was in the hospital on sick leave recovering from appendicitis. Takagi ordered the officers at Central Command to immediately mobilize all forces, including the reserves. He also ordered them to notify the media to put the entire planet on red alert.

The media had no power-sensing satellites, as these were strictly military, and thus had no idea a Strovat fleet was bearing down upon them. This initial warning was seven hours late, and sadly, by this time the Strovats were close enough to use their long-range jammers to disrupt most of the communications on Dragos. Only Samarkand, the largest city and the home of Central Command, and a few surrounding communities got the news. Communications were completely out in many other cities. Such was the case in Portsmouth.

At 6:22 AM Takagi arrived and took charge. He ordered a planetary evacuation, and put the army in charge of seizing all large commercial and private spacecraft. Unfortunately, he had to get his fleet off the ground to engage the incoming Strovats, and thus he was only at the command center for fifteen minutes.

Knowing they would be useless against the massive Bisas moving in, Takagi ordered his smaller warships to help with the evacuation. Just after 7 AM he took off with all his heavier warships, which consisted of twenty large Earth battleships and thirty smaller destroyers. He headed straight for the fleet of Bisas which was bearing down on Dragos.

Takagi stood like the rock of Gibraltar by his seat in the center of the bridge of his battleship. He was descended from a long line of naval officers that went back to the Imperial Japanese Navy. Takagi was the type of officer whose mere presence inspired his men.

"Sir," Gustav, his first officer, asked, "shouldn't we wait for Marshal Coriantumr? He has two hundred twenty-nine ships of the line he brought out of N Gamma."

"Two thirds of which are smaller Gutayid vessels," Takagi replied. "They are too far away to help us. We need to buy time for the evacuation of Dragos. Marshal Coriantumr has problems of his own. He has four times as many Bisas headed his way."

"God help them," Gustav said.

"These Strovats are in a hurry," Takagi said. "Neither group has formed into a true phalanx. If we concentrate our fire on the closest ones, we have a chance to do some damage and slow them down. Coriantumr has the same chance with his opponents."

A few moments later, the master chief technician pointed to his sensor array and said, "Admiral, sir, you should see this."

Both Takagi and Gustav moved over to him. Takagi cursed in Japanese.

"Those Gutayid dogs are deserting!" His face turned purple. "Cowards!"

"Marshal Coriantumr has no chance, now," Gustav said.

"General Lukan will hang for this!" Takagi spat.

As they drew close to the enemy, they finally realized what they were up against. Takagi had a competitive force in numbers only, for his fleet looked like insects going up against a flock of large birds.

"I think…" he said solemnly to his crew, "…that we should all take a moment to make our peace with God."

☐

CHAPTER 14

Admiral Takagi had left the organization of the evacuation of twenty million people in the hands of the same middle management officers who had taken seven hours just to wake him up. Because of the disrupted communications, they were reduced to sending soldiers and drones out to many of the other cities with the evacuation orders. Portsmouth, being in the opposite hemisphere from Samarkand, got no warning at all before drones arrived at 9:06 AM, and by that time the Strovats were almost on top of them.

Despite frequent testing, the computer controlling the civil defense system around the city of Portsmouth had completely crashed early Saturday morning. The third shift crew could not figure out the problem, but the district supervisor was not overly concerned. At 3 AM he told them not to worry about it, because he would be in with a full crew at eight. When the invasion news finally came in just after 9 AM, the sirens did not go off. The technicians worked frantically to bring them on line, but the damage had been done six hours earlier.

When phone service, radio, internet, and television services in and around Portsmouth all went out Saturday morning, everyone assumed it was just another outage, including Franz and Tonya. Their region was prone to major storms, and recently one in the area had caused a similar problem. Also, unfortunately for them, their church resided in a business section of town, which was mostly deserted on Saturday mornings. When the news finally reached Portsmouth, all military, police and emergency personnel concentrated on evacuating the residential areas and maintaining order at the spaceport.

Finally, when the Strovats were just minutes away, the civil defense system at Portsmouth came back on line. Sirens went off everywhere at once, which got everyone's attention inside the church.

"What's this?" Hugo asked. "It can't be a drill, not on a Saturday."

"It's probably a storm coming in," Bishop Green suggested. "We should check our phones."

"If they're working." Violet frowned as she tried her wrist phone. "Nope. Still out."

"Honey..." Tonya clutched Franz and gave him a worried look. "...all of a sudden I got a really bad feeling about this."

"Everything's going to be fine." He kissed her forehead.

Suddenly a Home Guard soldier burst through the front door. He was dressed in full combat gear, including infrared glasses, and he bore a heavy automatic rifle.

"You all need to get out of here! The Strovats are attacking!" he shouted.

"What?" Bishop Green responded with a look of shock. "Here?"

"Ohmygosh!" Tonya covered her mouth.

"Get to the spaceport!" the soldier ordered. "Evacuations are underway."

"Do you have a transport to get us there?" Bishop Green asked.

"I wish I did, but they're all in the residential areas," the soldier replied. "You have enough vehicles here to get everyone out, so get out as fast as you can. My unit is here to fight the Strovats!"

The soldier turned and disappeared. As if on cue, they heard explosions in the distance.

"We need to get out of here!" Bishop Green exclaimed.

"No, *wait!*" Hugo grabbed him by the arm. "Marry them, now!"

"I don't have the papers!" Green protested. "They're in my office!"

"Never mind the papers, man!" Hugo blustered. *"Just marry them!"*

"No." Bishop Green exhaled and composed himself. "We will do this the right way. Just give me a moment to get the marriage documents."

He removed Hugo's huge hand from his sleeve and ran into the office off to the right side of the pulpit. A close by explosion rocked the building. Everyone hit the deck, as plaster fell from the ceiling.

"That pedantic fool!" Hugo griped. "We do not have time for his papers!"

"Yeah," Tonya remarked, "I guess we'll just have to tell the Strovats that they can't eat us until after he's done with his paperwork."

"This is impossible!" Maria protested. "Why would they attack us? There is nothing here!"

"Yes, there is," Adam pounded the floor. *"Dammit!* They've found it! I don't know how they did, but they found it!"

"Found what?" Franz asked.

"The repair base on N Gamma," Adam said. "It was classified, but it doesn't matter now."

"Repair base?" Tonya squeaked. "We were told that was a big mining center!"

An explosion went off, much closer this time, breaking the windows in the back of the building. Everyone moved over and crouched down among the pews. Little Ben noticed how afraid everyone had become, and he cried.

"When the war started, the Tellopians weren't ready," Adam huffed. "A lot of their warships couldn't even fly. So, they set up that base and towed them here in secret."

"How many ships are we talking about?" Franz asked.

Adam gulped. "Two thousand."

"That's...almost half of the fleet!" Franz gasped. "Why isn't more of the active fleet here to protect that base?"

"I don't know." Adam hung his head. "Some top official decided they were needed more on the front, I guess. They were spread out so thin, you see, with so much of the fleet down. They had no reserves at all. It really hampered operations, and they were desperate to keep it a secret. That's why they put it here in the middle of nowhere, and that's why your corps has been so vital.

You guys have really been slowing the Strovats down and keeping their eyes on other places."

Another explosion rocked the church, breaking one of the stained glass windows.

"Wait a minute." Franz's eyes widened. "If we don't have any reserves, then all this time my corps had no backup."

"What do you mean?" Tonya asked.

"We were told that if we got stranded behind the lines, they had reserves that could come and rescue us." Franz shook his head. "But that was a lie?"

"Yes," Adam exhaled. "Your corps is considered expendable. I'm very sorry."

"Two missions ago we rescued several thousand Sagobians from a Strovat slave galley." Franz gritted his teeth. "They were in terrible conditions, but we didn't have enough room on our ships for most of them. The galley was crippled and we couldn't repair or tow it. We left them there and promised that our leaders would send a relief ship. Some of our own people stayed with them! We left them all there to die! Our leaders lied to us!"

"Or they were lied to as well." Adam put his hand on Franz's shoulder. "Those of us who are classified have little control over what we know. They don't always tell us the whole story, but we still have to follow orders. Blaaga probably knew about the shortage of ships, but he may not have known that there was no one to rescue your friends. I doubt if he would have allowed his own personnel to stay behind if he knew no relief vessels were coming."

Part of a cluster bomb landed next to the right side of the building. The men covered the women, and Violet covered little Ben. All of the remaining windows shattered and part of the right side wall and ceiling caved in, including the area around the side office.

"*Bishop Green!*" Maria cried out.

"*Ohmygosh, no!*" Tonya buried her face into Franz's chest. "Please...no!"

Both Adam and Hugo rose and climbed over the rubble to where the office used to be. They moved aside a small pile of plaster and wood and found Bishop Green. Hugo looked at Adam and shook his head.

"*No!*" Tonya screamed, and then dropped her face into her

hands and wept.

"Let's go!" Adam ordered. "We need to get out of here, while we still can!"

"We're not going to just leave him there, are we?" Maria pointed.

"There is nothing we can do for him." Hugo shook his head. "We don't have time. We have to go!"

Violet picked up Ben and nodded. Without saying a word, they all moved quickly around the rubble to the back door of the building, which was still intact. They exited to the back parking lot, where three hovercars sat amid chaos. All around them sirens wailed, and several buildings burned. Military aircraft from the Home Guard roared over their heads, and tanks rolled up the adjacent street. As they approached the hovercars, a missile screamed and exploded a thousand feet directly above their heads. They all fell to the ground, covering their ears as buildings all around them exploded. The bank on the opposite corner collapsed into the street.

"What was that?" Tonya asked Franz, who lay on top of her.

"A Strovat cluster bomb," Franz wheezed, and then called out, "Is everyone all right?"

They all answered to the affirmative.

"That thing went off right over us," Tonya puffed as they crawled to their vehicles. "Why aren't we dead?"

"Because it went off right over us," Franz explained. "Those type of missiles come in low and explode, throwing a cluster of bombs out like an umbrella. If it goes off over top of you like that one did, you're okay. If one goes off anywhere else near you, then you're dead."

"Well then, this must be our lucky day," Tonya huffed.

"It is, my love." Franz smiled halfway. "At least our hovercars are still here."

With all of the destruction around them, somehow both they and their hovercars had survived intact. Their vehicles sat undamaged in front of them, like a bed of flowers in the middle of a garbage dump.

"Franz," Adam said, taking him by the arm, "use your Ambulatory Directive and get Tonya out of here. Whatever happens, I know she'll be safe with you."

"I can't use the Ambulatory Escape Directive now!" Franz

protested. "All of my equipment is in my bag at Mom and Dad's house!"

"Take my hovercar," Hugo ordered. "Take Tonya and go back to the house. Get her out of here."

"No!" Franz argued. "We should stay together. Come with me, and I'll get us all out!"

"We already have a ship," Adam calmly replied. "If we split up, we double the odds of survival. If one doesn't make it, the other will. You're a military man. You know it's true."

Franz hung his head. He looked at Tonya and nodded.

"Daddy, no!" Tonya cried. "I don't want us to split up! Please come with us!"

"Don't argue!" Hugo pointed. *"Just go!"*

"Your father is right," Violet kept her composure and firmly addressed her daughter. "And we don't have time to argue about it."

Everyone hugged and said brief and tearful goodbyes. Tonya picked up her little brother Ben and held him tightly.

"See you on Earth." Adam smiled and shook Franz's hand. "Take care of Tonya."

"With my life." Franz nodded.

"Bye, Ben." Tonya handed him back to their mother and wiped away a tear. "I'll see you again. I promise!"

"Bye-bye." Little Ben waved while clinging to Violet.

Franz opened his parents' car with a voice command, and he and Tonya climbed in. He started it up, and they both gave their families a final wave. Then Franz lifted the hovercar into the air, turned it, and flew away swiftly in the direction of his father's house.

"What are their chances?" Maria asked.

"About the same as ours." Adam motioned with his hand. "Come on, we need to go!"

☐

CHAPTER 15

The cab of the hovercar possessed four seats in the front, and four in the back. Tonya buckled herself next to Franz and gripped her armrests tightly as he raced the vehicle out of the city. She looked down at the burning buildings as they flew over them. She saw tanks and troops moving toward the north, where off to the horizon could be seen the flashes of battle. A flotilla of jets flew overhead in that direction.

"Fighter bombers," Franz noted. "Our home forces will give them more than they bargained for."

"Do they have a chance?" Tonya asked.

"We always fight harder than most of the other beings," Franz replied. "We'll inflict heavy losses on them, and that will be a nasty surprise. The problem is the enemy must be here in overwhelming force to take out that base on N Gamma."

"Great," she sighed.

"I just don't understand what's going on here." He shook his head. "The Strovats never go behind lines, and they never do hit and run. They always attack us head on."

"What makes you think this is a hit and run? If they take this system they'll have a base behind the lines, and then they could do us even more damage."

"I love your tactical mind, but that won't work in this case. You see, we're so far back that they had to cut their supply line just to get here. The Strovats need food and fuel as much as we do, and there's not enough here to indefinitely sustain a large fleet of Bisas. They can't sit here out of supply for very long, especially with the Heruli right next door. That's just asking to get blown up. No, this must be a hit and run, and it's a totally new trick for the Strovats."

"At least that would be some good news if they don't stay here and harvest us all like wheat." Tonya exhaled.

"Not necessarily." He frowned.

"What do you mean?"

"When we hit and run, we try not to leave anything behind for the enemy. We nuke everything in sight."

Their conversation was cut short because they quickly encountered chaos around them as hovercars, air trucks, and helicopters flooded the air in pell-mell fashion. Two jets suddenly collided and exploded directly in front of them. Their hovercar shuddered as Franz pulled it up and then arced sharply to the right to avoid a head-on collision with a jet cycle. They rode on a wild rollercoaster in the air as Franz bobbed, weaved, dived, and climbed suddenly to avoid other collisions. Tonya clutched a ceiling handle with one hand and covered her eyes with the other. After two minutes of this, which seemed like an eternity to her, they broke through the anarchy and entered the countryside. Franz finally levelled off the hovercar and accelerated full-throttle toward home.

"You can open your pretty eyes now." He smirked.

"Whew!" She wiped her brow with one hand while still clutching the ceiling handle with the other. "I thought we were gonna die back there. My life flashed before my eyes, and it was too short!"

"Oh, we are going to die," he said. "Just not today."

"Well, you're just Mister Sunshine, aren't you?" she commented.

At full speed, they reached their parents' houses six minutes later.

"No sign of looters," he noted as they came in for a landing. "That's good."

"We live in the country," she pointed out. "Not a lot of people out here to loot."

He parked the vehicle on the grass between the two houses and shut it off. He reached across Tonya and opened the glove compartment, where he had stashed his .45 caliber pistol before the wedding rehearsal.

"Stay behind me," he instructed as they exited the car. "Just in case."

Franz gripped his handgun, with Tonya right behind him, as they crept up to his parents' house. He opened the door and looked around, but all was quiet. He heaved a sigh of relief and handed the pistol to Tonya.

"Keep an eye out while I get my stuff together," he said.

They went into his old room, where he had left his duffel bag and an oversized, black trombone case. He threw the case on his bed and opened it.

"Yikes!" Tonya's eyes nearly popped out of her head. "Was that coming with us on our honeymoon?"

"I always keep it close," he said. "In case of emergency."

Inside the trombone case was a .308 caliber assault rifle, five fifty-round clips, a bandolier loaded with .45 caliber bullets, three grenades, and a metal canister. He removed the rifle, slapped one ammo clip into it, and checked the chamber. He donned the bandolier around his waist and put the remaining fifty-round clips and the grenades in his bag, which he slung over one shoulder.

"Now we go to your house." He nodded.

They headed cautiously across the yard to the West home, with Franz in front brandishing his assault rifle and Tonya behind him watching the rear with his pistol. When they arrived, Tonya slowly opened the side door. Once again, there was no sign of activity, and nothing was out of place.

"Only pack the things which are most important to you and that you can carry," he told her.

For a moment she stood and stared at the wall full of family pictures in the living room. The feeling of it all overwhelmed her, and she covered her eyes with one hand and cried.

"Tonya," Franz said softly, putting his hands on her shoulders, "I'm sorry, but we don't have a lot of time, my love."

"I...I'm okay." She took a deep breath and wiped away her tears. "This is all just so hard!"

"I know." He pulled her into his arms and held her tightly. "I'm sorry that we had to separate, but your father was right."

"I know." She closed her eyes and clutched him. "But at least we're together now. All those times before, when you were gone...I was afraid I'd never see you again! Thank you for bringing me with you!"

"I'm glad you're with me now," he said.

"Don't you leave me! You better not leave me alone on some

safe planet while you go off to fight!'"

"No more separation. Whatever happens from this point on, we'll go through it together. We'll just have to get you a job on our ship as a volunteer."

"Thank you!" she sniffed. "I love you so much!"

"I love you just as much!" He stroked her hair.

They kissed, and then with a sigh resumed what they had come to do. Tonya picked up a small electronic photo album from a living room table, and then she led Franz by the hand into her bedroom. She removed a large duffel bag and a suitcase from her closet, and packed the suitcase full of clothes. She grabbed her hand computer and stuck it into her pocket. She placed the photo album and a small teddy bear that her father had given to her when she was three into the duffel bag. She removed the diamond and gold pendant necklace which Franz had recently given her from around her neck, placed it into its small box, and put it in the suitcase. Then she emptied her jewelry box and another box of silver coins into the duffel bag.

She removed her new magnetic pistol from its case. Franz helped her load it and also helped to put the holster belt around her waist. He put the extra boxes of its shells into her duffel bag as she holstered her weapon on her hip.

"Ready to go?" he asked.

"No." She shook her head. "Not just yet."

He followed her out to her father's computer. She pulled the hard drive out of a slot in the back and then smashed the rest of it on the floor. She asked Franz to help her place the hard drive and all of his papers into the fireplace and burn them. She informed him that she was following her father's instructions to do this if he couldn't, for his files were all classified.

As the fire burned, she entered her parents' bedroom. She packed the gold from her mother's jewelry box into her bag, and then removed a metal strongbox from underneath their bed. She opened it with an old fashioned metal key which her father had given her, revealing a few memory chips and several rolls of gold coins.

"Wow." Franz eyed the family stash.

"Dad said this stuff would help," she said. "He told me to take it if we ever had to evacuate, but I don't know why. We can't eat it, so it's pretty much useless until we get to Earth."

"No, we can use it," Franz said. "Other races won't trade with Earth money, but they will take our gold and silver, and our diamonds, rubies, and other precious gems. Word is the Alamani really like our blue sapphires."

She packed the contents of the strongbox into her duffel bag and sealed it. Then she picked both it and her suitcase up.

"I'm ready," she exhaled.

"Let's go." He motioned with his head.

They exited the house, and for a moment Tonya stopped and took a last look at it. Suddenly, a blinding flash of light exploded behind them, coming from the direction of the city. Franz didn't turn to look, knowing what it was.

"Damn it!" he exclaimed.

"What was that?" she asked.

"No, don't look!" He quickly grabbed her and prevented her from turning around.

"What's going on?" she demanded.

"They just nuked the city," he replied.

Tonya wrested her arm away from his grasp and turned to behold a huge red and black mushroom cloud towering over Portsmouth.

"NO!" she screamed.

She fell to her knees and wept. Franz knelt next to her and cradled her in his arms. He gently lifted her by the chin and looked into her blue eyes.

"Tonya," he said. "Tonya!"

"Yes?" she sniffled.

"Can you see me?" he asked.

"Yeah." She composed herself. "I can see just fine."

"So can I." He heaved a sigh of relief. "We're lucky we were looking the other way when that bomb went off, or we'd both be blind right now."

"What about the radiation?" She bit her lip. "Do you have any anti-rad pills?"

"Yes, in my first aid kit," he answered. "We won't get radiation sickness, but anti-rad pills don't cure blindness. Look, right now we need to get into my parents' shelter. We've got maybe a minute before the outbound winds hit us."

"Right." She nodded.

They grabbed their luggage and ran behind the Zemmarich

home to a metal door which lay flat on the ground and was secured with a heavy-duty combination padlock. Before Franz could do anything, the padlock began to shake, followed by the ground. The loudest clap of thunder they had ever heard rolled over, forcing them to cover their ears. The boom rattled windows and vibrated everything around like a minor earthquake. Once this had passed, they heard a distant whistle. Tonya looked behind them and saw what looked like a huge dust storm. The outbound winds from the great explosion were fast approaching as Franz fiddled with the combination.

"Um, Franz…" She tugged on his sleeve.

"I've almost got it," he said.

He pulled on it but it didn't open. Tonya saw the dust cloud coming up on the neighbor's house, just half a mile up the road. The whistle of the approaching wind ascended to a roar.

"Don't you remember the combination?" she yelled.

"The numbers, yes. Not the order," he shouted. *"Give me a second."*

She looked back again and saw the neighbor's house explode. As the windstorm bore down on them, she saw a cow flying in the midst of it.

"Franz!"

He drew his pistol and shot the lock off. She ripped open the door, and they jumped inside with their luggage. He slammed the door shut just as the giant dust cloud engulfed them. Once inside, she could not see her hand in front of her face, while outside it sounded like a train wreck, up close and personal.

He pulled a small, battery-powered light from his bag, which lit up the area around them. They stood in a large room lined with shelves full of canned food, and with water barrels in the corners. A table and chairs sat in the middle, and a doorway on the back wall opened up to another room, where Tonya knew the Zemmarichs had more storage and a bathroom.

The storm outside subsided after only a few seconds. Tonya attempted to go up the stairs and take a look outside, but Franz stopped her.

"It's not over, yet," he said. "The winds will come back to fill in the blast vacuum."

He placed the light on the table, dug into his duffel bag, and removed a small vial of pills. She grabbed some bottled water from a shelf, and they each downed two anti-radiation pills. No sooner had they done this, then the storm outside returned from the opposite direction. Within seconds it had passed.

He exhaled. "It's safe to go outside, now."

They climbed up to the outside, and Tonya covered her mouth. Franz sighed and shook his head. The roofs of both houses had been blown off, and every window was shattered. Only the walls remained, and the yard was strewn with glass, wood, furniture, and personal belongings. Tonya picked up Ben's favorite toy truck and began to weep.

Franz held her close, resting her head on his chest. Now that the immediate danger had passed, he gave her a few moments to vent her feelings. She cried for a minute or two, but then snapped out of it when she noticed their hovercar, which had flipped over and now sat in Hugo and Maria's front yard. It rested on its side, and its roof and windows were all smashed in.

"Great," she sniffed. "Now what do we do?"

"We'll be all right," he replied.

"Do you think they got out in time?" she asked.

"If they got to the spaceport in time, then they're fine," he said. "That place is bomb proof. The trick is getting off the planet. The Strovats might not like the idea of people leaving."

"So, how do we get out of here?" She wiped her face with her sleeve. "We don't even have a ship."

"Then we'll have to get a ship. One that the Strovats won't shoot down."

"How?"

He sifted through his bag and removed a red hand computer.

"The Ambulatory Directive," he said as he typed on it. "We're going to steal a ship. A Strovat ship."

"We're going to steal a Strovat ship?" She folded her arms and gave him a doubtful look. "Getting a little ambitious, aren't we? Don't you think the Strovats will mind us using one of their ships?"

"If this works, they won't know the difference," he said. "There, the signal is sent. That was part one."

"What's part two?" she asked.

He pulled a grenade out of his bag.

"We blow up the hovercar," he replied.

"What?" Her eyes nearly popped out of her head. "Are you crazy? Exactly what kind of pills did you just take?"

145

"I'll explain everything in a minute." He pointed. "Take the gear and get back behind the house."

Tonya nodded and did as she was instructed. Once she was in a safe spot, Franz activated the grenade and tossed it inside the hovercar. He ran and dived behind his parents' house, where Tonya lay covering her ears. Hugo's hovercar exploded, showering the area with metal and glass. It burned furiously, creating a large plume of black smoke which rose high into the air.

Franz tossed the hand computer over toward the hovercar, and it landed six feet from the burning wreck. He moved Tonya over under the partially collapsed roof of his parents' back porch.

"Okay, this is good cover," he said. "We're within range, but out of sight."

"So, how does this Ambulatory Directive work?" she asked.

"It was devised as a way to get soldiers that were caught behind the lines safely back to their units," he explained. "That little computer over there is specifically designed for this. You see, Strovats have a hive mentality, and that's their weakness. They're a lot more susceptible to breakdown of command and control than the rest of us.

"Most Humans have the same capabilities. Any one of us has a chance to become a leader in our society, but Strovats aren't like that. They have a caste system, where they're bred to be either royalty, leaders, or drones. Their workers and soldiers are all drones, and they have zero chance of advancement because they can't think for themselves. So if you kill the leaders, then the drone soldiers get confused and wander around like lost ants. Kill enough Strovat leaders and you can disable an army of millions.

"The bottom line is that the Strovats don't care how many drones we kill, but they really don't like it when we kill their leaders. They especially don't like it when we capture their leaders, and they'll go out of their way to keep us from doing it. If they know one of their lieutenants is isolated or injured, they'll send out an ambulance to rescue it, pronto."

"An ambulance?" Tonya wondered. "They have those?"

"That's what we call it," Franz replied. "It's a small, very fast rescue ship. Anyway, at the beginning of the war we captured a few of their smaller ships and used them to break some of their computer codes. Now either they're really stupid, or they don't care, because they've never bothered to change these codes. We still can't hack into their warships, but we can signal them, and we can also use the codes we have to fly their smaller ships."

"So, you used that little computer over there to signal the Strovats and tell them we've captured one of their leaders?"

"I used it to send out a false distress signal to the Strovat fleet, telling them that one of their mid-level lieutenants has crashed his jet hovercraft and he's injured. Then I set it to repeat the distress call over and over so they'll home in on it."

"So they think he's about to be captured, and they're gonna send an ambulance here to rescue him."

"And we're going to kill those bugs and steal their ship."

"And because you have their codes, we can fly out of here and they won't shoot at us." Tonya smirked and snapped her fingers. "That's brilliant! All we need to do is whack a couple of Strovats, and we are outta here!"

"Uh…yes, and no," Franz said as he removed a pair of infrared binoculars from his bag.

"What do you mean?" Her smile disappeared. "They're only sending rescue personnel, right?"

"Well…" he replied, "…not exactly. We might have to deal with more than just a couple of Strovats, you know."

"No, I don't know." She gave him a hard stare. "What do you mean by more than a couple?"

"Well, they've got plenty of drones to spare, so they always send out a few extra. But we do have the element of surprise on our side."

"Franz, exactly how many Strovats do you think we're going to have to fight?"

"I told them a mid-level lieutenant was down here." He scanned the skies with his binoculars. "So, they should only send one ambulance. Your typical Strovat ambulance has a compliment of twelve: four paramedics, six fighter drones, a pilot, and a low-level lieutenant in command. None of them can operate effectively without their commander, including the pilot."

"A dozen." She gulped. "Franz, this directive…it was designed to get more than two people out, wasn't it?"

"Technically, yes," he admitted. "But that's why I said a mid-level lieutenant. If I'd said a high lieutenant, they might send a hundred down. If I'd reported a missing Strovat noble, they'd send a light cruiser with five thousand drones to get him. So, twelve is much better odds for us."

"Oh, my gosh!" Tonya covered her eyes. "We're gonna die!"

"Yes, we will." He put down his spyglasses and lifted her chin. "But not today."

"Oh yeah, six to one. Those are good odds." She rolled her eyes.

"Honey, we'll be fine. It doesn't matter if they send twelve or a hundred. If we take out the leader first, the rest will be like shooting fish in a barrel."

"Maybe for you, but I've never been in real combat before. What do I do?"

"Well, the first thing you need to do is activate your weapon. Stay low, take aim, make your shots count, and whatever you do, don't panic. Panicking will get us both killed. Now, at least four of them will be unarmed medical workers, so shoot at the ones carrying the laser rifles first. Once they leave the ambulance we need to move, because we have to get in between them and their ship. If they get back to their ship and take off, it's over. If you see a red one carrying a big plasma rifle, that's the leader. Take his head off and we win the game."

"Anything else?"

"Yeah, whatever happens, do not let any of them get close. They have long, straw-like tongues that are very sharp. If you're not wearing armor, one of them can pick you up and punch holes in you with his tongue. They can hold you with their claws while they suck out your blood, your heart, or your brains. I've seen what they can do, and it's ghastly. Also, no matter what, even if I go down, don't surrender. Prisoners usually end up as frozen dinners. It would be better for us to go down fighting, even if we have to save the last two bullets for ourselves."

"This is not making me feel any better!" she complained.

He put his hands on her cheeks and looked into her eyes.

"Tonya," he said, "you've always been clairvoyant. What does your heart tell you?"

She looked down for a moment, took a deep breath, and resumed eye contact.

She exhaled. "I feel like we're going to be fine."

"That's my girl." He put his hand on her shoulder. "We're going to make it."

"Right." She nodded and activated her gun.

"One more thing." He held up a finger. "We need to count them as we take them out. We can't lose track or miss any. If we lose track of just one, especially the leader, it could be a fatal mistake."

"Got it."

He kissed her and resumed scanning the skies with his binoculars. She put her hand over her brow and also searched. After twenty minutes or so, she thought she saw something on the horizon behind them, and she tugged on his shirt.

"What's that?" She pointed.

"That..." He turned around and focused on a tiny black dot. "...is our ambulance. Good eyes, my love. We make a good team."

The dot very quickly grew larger until it was easily distinguishable. It resembled a military style jet hovercraft, except it was larger and had a bigger engine in the back. The front was oval shaped and the back rectangular, with small delta wings protruding from its sides and a fin on the top of the rear. The front had one bubble-like window which revealed half of the cockpit and its occupants. Tonya could plainly see a white Strovat drone sitting at the controls.

The small space ship kicked up a large cloud of dust as it came in for a landing on the road in front of their houses. It came to rest with the front of the vessel pointed down the road, as if it was going to drive to town, with the main hatchway on the left side facing the smoking hovercar.

Franz removed the small metal canister from his bag and put it in his pocket. He fixed a grenade to the end of his rifle and motioned for Tonya to stay low and follow him. They crept around the other side of his former house and positioned themselves in a patch of high grass on the shoulder of the road, a few feet to the rear of the Strovat vessel. She trembled in fear, and noticed beads of sweat forming on Franz's brow and running down his face.

"I'm scared," she whispered, clinging close to him.

"So am I," he quietly responded. "Just don't let the enemy know it."

The main hatch opened, and several Strovats bounded out. They were a strange sight to behold, resembling huge ants that walked upright on three bandy, spider-like legs. Each drone was white, with four arms, antennae, pincers, and bulbous insect eyes which made them seem like creatures out of a low-budget horror movie. Tonya had seen images of them, and had shot several target Strovat statues, but to see them up close in real life gave her the creeps. Four smaller unarmed drones moved up to the burning hovercar, while two drones armed with black laser rifles accompanied them. Four other armed drones positioned themselves on the ground in front of the hatchway. A red leader was nowhere in sight.

Nonetheless, Franz knew that he could wait no longer, because soon the enemy would figure out what was going on. He raised his rifle and fired the grenade. It landed square in the middle of the four guarding the ship, blowing two of them to bits and taking off the head of a third. The fourth one was knocked off balance. He returned fire, but his laser bolt shot wildly over their heads. Franz took aim and coolly decapitated him with his assault rifle.

The remaining two armed drones now returned fire, as the four unarmed ones turned around and headed back for their ship. The ground in front of the two young lovers ripped apart with laser fire from one, while the other one fired over their heads. Tonya hit the deck and got off four rounds, but not being used to firing from a prone position, she missed everything. Franz loaded and fired his last grenade with deadly precision. It landed exactly in between the two remaining armed drones and shredded them.

Franz now stood and charged the hatchway, attempting to cut off the four medical drones. As he ran he fired his assault rifle from the hip, emptying his magazine and cutting three of them down in the process. As the last one approached the hatchway, Franz dropped his rifle, pulled out his pistol, and shot it in the head at close range.

Tonya ran up behind him and picked up his rifle. They both pressed their backs to the side of the alien ship, within reach of the open hatchway. She handed him the .308, and he removed the empty clip and applied a fresh one while Tonya pointed her gun at the downed Strovats to make sure none of them sprang back to life.

"Well," he huffed, "that was easier than I thought it would be. Good thing I brought those grenades."

"Franz," she wheezed, "I'm only counting ten here, and I don't see any red ones."

"You have good eyes," he exhaled. "That means their leader

and another one are still inside."

"Why haven't they closed the hatch and tried to take off yet?" she asked as she loaded four replacement rounds into her pistol. "That's what I'd be doing right now."

"Hard to tell," Franz answered. "Maybe we got lucky and took out the pilot, or maybe they can't leave without orders from their mother ship. Either way, it's good news for us."

He removed the small metal canister from his pocket.

"It's time to smoke these cockroaches out." He gritted his teeth.

He twisted the top of the can and tossed it inside the alien ship. Before long, white smoke poured out of the hatchway, as if it was a smokestack.

"Is that mustard gas?" Tonya asked, covering her mouth and nose with her shirt.

"No," Franz replied while raising his rifle. "We only use that stuff when we have protective suits. This is just ordinary smoke. It won't hurt us, but they can't stand it."

"And you think I can?" she coughed and waved her hand in front of her face.

A few seconds later, a white drone stumbled out and fell on the ground. Before it could regain itself, Franz shot off its head. They waited for a red lieutenant to appear, but no other Strovats came out of the ship. Eventually, the smoke grenade spent itself and the smoke dissipated. Franz scooted along the side of the ship and peeked through the hatchway. Nothing stirred inside.

"That's odd," he said. "Eleven drones without a lieutenant?"

"Maybe he's still hiding in there." She pointed.

"No way." Franz shook his head. "No bug can stand that much smoke. They really hate that stuff."

"Franz," Tonya said as she put her hand on his arm, "please, be careful!"

Franz stepped in front of the open hatch and fired a short burst. The bullets ricocheted around but did not shake anything loose. All was silent inside the ship. Franz slowly walked up the short ramp with his rifle at the ready. Tonya placed herself two steps behind him, holding her pistol at the ready with both of her hands.

The second Franz stepped into the alien ship, the missing red lieutenant revealed himself. It had pressed itself against the inside wall next to the door, and somehow had managed to withstand the smoke. The large, bug-like alien clutched the end of Franz's rifle with its claws and tore it out of his hands. Before he could draw his pistol, it grabbed both of his arms. The hideous alien pinned Franz's arms to his sides with two of its arms and held him a foot off the floor with the other two. Franz struggled and kicked, but to no avail. He wrenched his head back as far as it could go to avoid getting it crushed in the creature's huge pincers. The alien looked at him with its compound eyes and then opened its mouth, revealing its deadly spear of a tongue. All Franz could do was to close his eyes and brace himself. He knew his heart was about to be ripped from his body.

Tonya leaped into the ship like a bolt of lightning, landing next to the giant red insect and firing her .70 caliber handgun at point blank range. Her first shot took the top of the alien's head off, and it dropped Franz and staggered sideways. She stepped forward and emptied her gun's magazine, shattering the creature's thorax and blasting its body to pieces.

For a moment she stood motionless, still holding down the trigger even though her gun was empty and its chamber open. Franz recovered himself and stood. He moved over to Tonya and helped her put the gun down. She looked at him with tear-filled eyes.

"Thanks!" He exhaled in relief. "I owe you one."

"Franz..." She trembled. "...I...I was afraid...that thing was going to kill you! I couldn't let him do it! You're all I have left!"

"And you're all I have left." He wiped away her tears and then kissed her.

He held her in his arms and let her cry on his shoulder. Eventually she composed herself and looked up at him.

"Are you hurt at all?" he asked.

"I'm all right," she said. "Are you okay?"

"Just a couple of bruised arms. Hey, you really did good for your first battle."

"I'm not so good at this. I missed everything out there."

"No, you were great. The idea of cover fire is not to hit the enemy so much, but to make him move so he misses your partner. You did that enough for me to use the grenades on them, and in here...well, you just saved my life."

She sniffed. "I'm not going to let anything take you away from me."

"Well," he said, "you just did better than a lot of trained soldiers do in their first battle. Now, you need to reload. We're not out of here yet."

Once they reloaded their weapons, they carefully inspected the inside of the small ship. Finding no more of the enemy, they went outside to retrieve the rest of their gear.

"We make a good team," he said as they carried their luggage into the ambulance. "But, we, umm...have one more thing to do, unless you want him to go with us."

He pointed at the dead Strovat.

Tonya shivered. "No, I don't want that creepy thing looking at me. It can stay here with its friends."

Franz removed two pairs of rubber gloves from his bag and they tossed the larger remains of their squished enemy outside. The smaller pieces would have to be vacuumed up, so they left those laying in the ooze.

"Ew." she protested as she handled the gooey pieces. "This is so gross! I like the ones at the shooting range better."

Once they finished this undesirable job, Franz hit a button on the side wall which closed the hatch, and then they picked up their gear and entered the bulbous cockpit. Inside they saw four very large, black, bat-like seats arrayed in semi-circular fashion, the one on the middle left being the pilot seat. The seats had back rests to support the Strovats, as they had to deal with G-force like every other race. However, Tonya noticed they also had holes in the back for the Strovats' third, rearward legs. Positioned in front of the pilot's seat was a computer console with alien alphabet buttons. Situated on the floor directly in front of this seat were two pedals, and just to the right rested an old-fashioned stick shift. The entire front of the cockpit was made of titanium glass, which was as hard as the hull and gave the passengers a one-hundred-eighty-degree view of the outside.

They placed their bags in the two outer seats. Franz sat in the driver's seat, and Tonya plopped into the seat to his right. He removed a small book from his duffel bag and thumbed through it. Meanwhile, she searched the floor around her.

"Um, Franz, I don't see any seat belts. How do I strap myself in?"

"Er, hang on..." He flipped through the pages. "...It says here that the arms of the chair will automatically fold in to fit our bodies when we start to move."

He grew silent and continued to scan through the book. Tonya studied him for a few moments, wondering if he knew what he was doing.

After an uncomfortable minute, she asked, "is everything okay?"

"Yes," he replied without taking his nose out of the book. "I have to find the correct starting sequence, that's all."

"This is a non-classified ship, right? Why can't you just hotwire this thing?"

"Because all Strovat ships have anti-hijack programs. This thing is booby-trapped. If I try to hotwire it, or put in the wrong launch sequence, then we'll be just as dead as Abraham Lincoln."

"Oh." She blinked. "Well, then...take your time."

"Ach, this is meschugge!" he complained. "It's like reading stereo instructions, and I can't find some of these symbols on this console."

"Oh, how sneaky of the Strovats not to have their controls written in German so you could read them." She folded her arms. "Franz, how many times have you actually done this Ambulatory Directive thing?"

"Counting today?"

"Yes."

"Once," he admitted, "but it's gone well so far, don't you think?"

"Oh, my gosh!" Tonya covered her face with one hand. "We're gonna die!"

"I wish you'd stop saying that," he said as he resumed his search.

He glanced back and forth between the book and the controls in front of him, and then snapped his fingers.

"I found it." He typed on the alien keys. "Let's try...this."

The ambulance sprang to life. The operating screen came on, and the ship powered up. The wings of their bat-like seats folded over their waists and locked into place.

"Wow, this isn't too bad," Tonya said as she checked out the unorthodox safety restraints.

"They have sensors that adjust to your beautiful body." He smiled at her. "Now, hold on. Here we go."

He gently pulled back on the stick shift while adjusting the foot pedals. The ship rose into the air and then turned. Unfortunately, he did not have a good feel for the rather weird Strovat control system, and the ship spun around in circles several times before he was able to stop it. In doing so, he nearly slammed them into the ground.

"Whoa!" she exclaimed, clutching her seat with one hand while holding the other outward. "Watch it!"

Franz instinctively pulled back hard on the stick to avoid hitting the ground. The ship responded in an irrational manner and shot a thousand feet straight up into the air. First Tonya was crushed into her seat, and then she nearly lost her eyeballs when Franz suddenly halted the ambulance at its new altitude.

"Dammit!" She gave him an angry look. "Don't do that!"

"Sorry!" He grimaced.

The ship tipped and wobbled a thousand feet in the air as he tried to get a feel for the controls.

"Franz!" she protested, while gripping her seat.

"I got it. I got it," he reassured her. "The controls are very sensitive, that's all. I can do this."

Finally, he managed to stabilize the ship. They both relaxed in their seats and let out a sigh of relief. Franz reached over and took Tonya by the hand.

"Are you ready to start our new life together?" he asked.

"Yes." She nodded. "Together."

He tilted the ship upward and they took off toward outer space.

CHAPTER 16

"Boy, this thing is fast!" Franz grinned.

As he pulled back on the stick shift, Tonya felt the effects of G-force. A giant, invisible hand pressed her into the seat as they shot through the stratosphere of Dragos. She knew the feeling, having travelled into space before, but not to this degree. This hand was oppressive, crushing down upon her and making it difficult to move and even to breathe. She glanced at Franz, who gritted his teeth. She watched him strain his powerful body to remain in control of the alien vessel.

Within seconds, they were out of the atmosphere and into the darkness of space. The oppressive hand relaxed as the resistance of the planet's gravity disappeared. They headed out away from Nihal, so the darkness was that of midnight. Tonya could see thousands of tiny bright pinpricks of light in front of them, with the largest one directly in their path. This was in fact Nihal IV, the last planet in the system, where Jim waited on board the *Cherbourg*. She noticed that even though they were in space, their bags did not float away from their resting places.

"This ship has a gravity generator?" she wondered. "I thought it was too small for that."

"It's more expensive to put them on small ships, but it can be done." Franz shrugged. "It wouldn't be a very good ambulance if the patients floated away, now would it?"

"Where's the Strovat fleet?" she asked.

"Right in front of us." Franz pointed to his computer

monitor, which revealed several orange blobs in their vicinity.

"How come I can't see them?" She pointed to the window.

Franz chuckled. "This isn't TV or a movie, where all the space ships are lit up like light bulbs. The only way you can see them with your eyes out here is if they want you to, like if they turn on all of their lights, or if light from a star is reflecting off them. Now, with something as big as a Bisa, you can sometimes see its shadow, because it's so big it blocks out the stars behind it. Anyway, we never look for them with our eyes. We track their power readings on our computers."

"What if they mask their power signal?" she asked.

"You mean cloaking?" Franz shook his head. "No, the really big ships put out too much juice to do that. Even when they power down, we can still see their reactors. The smaller ships, like ours, can power down to the point where no one can see them. Jim is probably doing that right now, because that's our directive when we face overwhelming odds and we can't get away. We call that running silent, but it's not really cloaking. No one can actually mask their power signals."

"We're coming up next to one of those Bisa supercruisers now." He pointed to the window in front of them. "If you look closely enough, you can see its shadow as we pass."

"Can they see us?"

"Yes, but we're not the only ambulance out here. Hopefully, by the time they figure out this one's no longer on their program, we'll be well out of range."

"Hopefully?"

"Like I said, this is the first time I've done this."

Franz bated his breath, and Tonya said a silent prayer. Seconds passed like minutes as they watched a dark mass move in from the right side of the window and engulf most of the stars. As they passed by it, the stars reappeared.

"That was huge," she gulped.

"So far, so good." He exhaled in relief.

"If they do figure this charade out, can they catch us?" She bit her lip.

"Not once we're past their fleet," he replied. "This is their fastest type of ship. They may come after us anyway, because this is a non-starship and eventually we'll run out of gas."

"What do you mean this isn't a starship? It's a space ship, isn't it?"

"Yeah, it can go to N Delta, but it can't go out of the system. We can't take this to Earth."

"Okay, yeah, I get it." She nodded. "We're not using it for that anyway."

"Right." He smirked. "We're only borrowing it for a while. They can have it back once we get to the *Cherbourg*."

"Seriously?"

"No, we'll probably blow it up."

"Good."

After half an hour, they finally cleared the seemingly endless Strovat fleet and they broke into open space. The computer console beeped for a few seconds, and once again Franz referenced his little Strovat manual. He typed in another sequence and the beeping stopped.

"What was that?" she asked. "What did you just do?"

"Manual override." He exhaled. "They didn't like it when we flew past them, so Strovat central just tried to bring us back by controlling our computer. I cut off their signal and changed the code so they can't try it again. They told us this would happen in training."

"And what if it didn't work?"

"In half an hour, we'd have been peopleburgers."

She cringed at this, but Franz reached out and squeezed her hand.

"It did work, and they can't catch us." He smiled reassuringly and reached into his bag. "We're going to be fine. You should sit back and try to relax."

He removed a bottle of pills and handed it to her, along with his canteen.

"Here, take one of these muscle relaxers," he instructed. "It'll help you get some sleep. Even as fast as this thing can go, it will be at least ten hours before we get to Jim."

"Shouldn't we send him a message?" she asked before gulping down a pill.

"Yeah, we'd better." He raised his eyebrows. "Good thinking."

He pulled his phone out of his bag and activated it. Once it booted up, he finally saw Jim's message from the previous day.

"He's there all right." Franz nodded. "He sent me a message

yesterday. He's going by the book."

"The book has something for when a planet gets blown up?" Tonya gave him a funny look. "Wow, I'm impressed."

"No, it's in case we get stranded or separated. He's running silent to keep the Strovats away, and he's waiting seventy-two hours for me to reply to his message."

"And if you didn't call him back in three days?"

"He'd figure I'm dead, and then he'd have to program one of the robots to help him fly the ship out of here. That's if he fixed the fission reactor before he had to shut everything down. If not, he'll be there for a while anyway. It really doesn't matter either way. We're going to get to him long before the seventy-two hours is up."

He sent Jim a text message, and then placed his phone in between their seats. Tonya curled her legs up on the seat and turned on her side facing him.

"You really need to check your phone more often," she murmured as she closed her eyes.

She awakened to the ringing of his phone's alarm. For a moment, she thought she was in her bedroom and that maybe she was waking up from a bad dream. She looked herself over and saw the bat-like seat restraints still upon her, which held her in her seat but remained just loose enough for her to shift about and stay somewhat comfortable. She glanced to her left to see Franz sit up, stretch, and then shut off the alarm

"Hi, Honey." He leaned over and kissed her.

"Hi," she reciprocated. "How long have we been asleep?"

"You've been out for seven hours, believe it or not," he replied. "Four hours ago, we got past the last asteroid between us and Jim, so I decided to put this baby on auto-pilot and get some sleep myself."

"Well, I'm glad you're so confident, considering this is the first time you've ever stolen a Strovat ship."

"Hey, I got everything under control. We're alive, aren't we?"

"If we weren't, I wouldn't speak to you for a long time. How far are we from N Delta?"

"Look." He pointed to a very bright point of light directly in front of them. "That's it, dead ahead. We'll be there in about ninety minutes. This thing is even faster than I expected. There's no way they could catch us from behind."

"I guess we pulled it off." She heaved a sigh of relief.

"Let's just say that in ninety minutes we will be out of the frying pan." He pointed to his monitor. "But if we stay on that moon station too long, we'll be back in the fire. We've got company coming in from N Gamma."

"What is it?" Tonya looked at it and saw an orange dot off to their left.

"That is a Strovat light cruiser, and it's on a beeline for Jim." Franz frowned. "They must have tracked where we're headed, or maybe they picked up his signal. He's powered up our ship by the looks of it."

"That doesn't sound too bad. You guys have a Nervii frigate, right?"

"Light cruiser is a relative term," Franz informed her. "The key word here isn't 'light', it's 'Strovat'. Their light cruisers are almost the size of our battleships. That guy over there is fifty times bigger than us."

"That's…overkill." She swallowed. "We're going to beat that thing to Jim, right?"

"Oh, yeah, we'll get there ahead of it with time to spare, but it's a good thing we left when we did, or Jim would've had to move out without us."

"With that Strovat fleet parked around Dragos, I think if we waited any longer we would've been toast anyway."

"That was nothing compared to what's over at N Gamma." Franz shook his head. "There's got to be two hundred Bisas over there. I've never seen anything like that."

"And the repair base?" She bit her lip.

"No activity on our part. I'd say it's fried."

"Do you think that our families got out?"

"Anything's possible. The Strovats usually go after the big ships first, so a lot of times the little ones can get away, and my dad's a really good pilot. I sent a text to his phone, but he hasn't answered, so I don't even know where he is. They could be hiding behind an asteroid, a moon, or on the other side of Nihal for all we know. Even if they're okay, we may not find out until we get back to our base in the Errai System."

Franz grew silent. He could see in his mind his mother and father, with the city burning and crumbling all around them. This was his last memory of them, and he struggled to hold back his tears. He glanced over to see Tonya wiping away her own. He reached over, took her by the hand, and squeezed.

"It'll be all right," he said. "We'll see them again."

CHAPTER 17

The base where the *Cherbourg* rested was small and well hidden. It lay in the south polar region of the third largest moon of Nihal IV, a gas giant similar to Saturn. It was strictly military, designed for small to medium-sized ships, and possessed but four docks, with two on each side. The base came complete with living quarters, food and water stores, a fuel station, and a maintenance facility. It was a self-serve installation, and no personnel resided there.

Franz parked the stolen ambulance at the dock opposite to the *Cherbourg*, which was the only other ship present. Tonya had seen photos of their ship, but this was the first time she beheld it close. The *Cherbourg* was shaped like a bumpy cigar with a large, spherical head and three huge jet-like exhaust ports arrayed in triangle fashion at the tail. As she expected, the bottom was flat for easy landing. However, it was larger than she had imagined, being thirty-five feet in height and longer than a football field. Still, she thought it was a gnat compared to that Bisa which they had passed.

Franz connected the airlock and powered down the ambulance. They grabbed their gear and exited through the hatch into the main warehouse of the station, where Jim awaited them. He immediately gave Tonya a hug.

"Hey Babe." He smiled halfway. "Franz messaged me that you got your first bug today."

"Yeah," she sighed and thumbed toward the ambulance. "What's left of it's in there."

Jim entered the ambulance and briefly inspected the remains. When he came back out he gently patted her on the shoulder.

"Wow, good job," he said. "You got an LT for your first kill. One of the big boys. Blaaga's going to be impressed. He gives out commendations for those."

"Whatever," she said unenthusiastically. "I didn't have a choice. I wasn't going to let that thing kill Franz."

"Oh, you had a choice all right," Jim pointed out. "You could've froze and got both of yourselves killed, which is exactly what most civilians do. Those bugs are different in real life, aren't they? Not quite like the ones at the target range."

"The ones at the target range don't shoot back," she grumbled. "And they don't try to eat you!"

"Well, at least we know that gun of yours works," Jim said. "Now, I'd love to stay and talk all day, but as Franz has already told you, we got company. We need to move on outta here."

Franz and Tonya followed Jim through a warehouse packed with skid loads of food, water, and supplies. They walked toward the dock where the *Cherbourg* was stationed.

"I'm sure glad you guys got my message," Jim said as they walked. "Until I got Franz's reply, which was late I might add, I was afraid they turned you all into microwaved strudel when they nuked the cities."

"We almost were," Franz stated. "Those dummkopfs at the civil defense didn't warn us until the bombs were dropping on our heads."

"Really?" Jim raised his eyebrows.

"That, and Franz never checks his phone," Tonya murmured.

"We'll go over all that when we do the reports," Jim said. "What happened to your families?"

"We separated," Tonya replied in a subdued tone. "They had their own ship, and Dad said we'd double our chances for survival if we split up."

"You know our fathers," Franz exhaled. "If they buy something, then they have to use it."

"Well, your dad was right, Tonya," Jim quietly responded. "I'm real sorry that you got separated, though. You know, your family is like my family, too. I'm glad you came with Franz. At least I know you're okay."

Tonya silently nodded.

"Did you see what happened?" Franz asked.

"I saw everything." Jim frowned. "Even a really big naval base that wasn't supposed to be there. Well, it used to be there, anyway. We can talk about it later when we sit down to do the report."

They entered the *Cherbourg* through the side airlock, which was located in the middle of the ship. The inside consisted of one long corridor which ran the length of the vessel. On either side of the corridor near the front, where the cockpit lay, were ten small rooms. Just past the airlock, going toward the rear of the vessel, the corridor opened up into the mess, which contained a small kitchen and a medium-sized table with ten chairs. A door behind the kitchen led into the cargo area, the back of which had a large double door which opened to the outside for loading purposes. Along the walls were four doors which led to hidden walkways, crawl spaces, and ladders that led up and down throughout the skin of the ship for service and repair purposes. A hole in the floor with a downward circular ladder led to the engineering section below deck.

The cargo hold not only contained weapons and spare parts for repairs, but it was also laden with enough food and water to sustain two dozen people for several months in space. This included packs of personal supplies, blankets, and clothing, which were all there for rescue operations.

Upon entering the ship, Tonya bumped into one of the engineer robots. The crew of the *Cherbourg*, beside Jim and Franz, consisted of four engineer robots, six security robots, and one navigator robot. The engineers were each five-and-a-half feet tall, with cylindrical bodies, flattened round heads, and three arms. They all possessed magnetized tracks, so that they could climb walls and work sideways or even upside down. They were equipped with small thrusters and stabilizers to operate in zero gravity, and also to allow them to go up and down ladders.

The security robots were built in much the same way, except that they were larger and armored. They each had four arms and built-in weapons such as lasers, light machine guns, and grenade launchers. Their chasses were collapsible, giving them the ability to crouch down low or stand up straight during combat.

The navigator robot was smaller and spherical, and it moved about completely via grav thrusters. Navigator had no head and only possessed two arms. It mostly stayed in the cockpit and monitored the ship's controls while Franz and Jim rested. Navigator, along with Engineer One, could command the other robots, do inspections and repairs, and pilot the ship if necessary. To prevent hijacking, the ship's computer purposely did not possess enough artificial intelligence to run the entire vessel. Without Franz or Jim, no one could utilize the *Cherbourg*, unless they could control the robots.

Jim told them that the minute he got Franz's message he had begun his preparations. He powered up the ship and the base so that he could refuel. He did a final check on the repaired fission reactor, and then had the robots do system checks and load a few extra supplies. This way the ship would be ready for launch by the time the couple arrived.

"Franz, go warm up the engines," Jim instructed. "I'll make sure everything's battened down. Tonya, pick a cabin and just throw your stuff in the wall drawers for now. That'll keep it from getting damaged when we take off."

Franz led Tonya by the hand to his cabin, which was on the left behind the cockpit and directly across from Jim's room. Tonya smiled at her fiancé, shook her head, and then chose the cabin next door.

"Nice try," she said.

"It was worth a shot." He shrugged. "Put your things away and come into the cockpit. We should be ready to go in about five minutes."

The spacious cockpit contained six comfortable, black seats; two in front and four behind. Franz entered and sat in the pilot's seat on the front left and donned a wireless headset. He flipped a few switches on the control panel and booted up the computer console in front of his seat. He typed in one sequence and the engines roared to life. He typed in another and the metal cover over their front titanium glass window withdrew, giving the cockpit a full forward view. He glanced over at Jim's console to see where the enemy was.

"Commander," he spoke into his headset, "looks like we need to get a move on."

At this moment, Tonya walked into the cockpit, sat behind Franz, and buckled her seat belt.

"I hear you," Jim replied loud enough for Tonya to hear. "I'll be up there in one minute. Make sure Tonya's up there and buckled in."

"Where's that enemy cruiser?" she asked.

"There." Franz pointed to a red spot on Jim's screen. "It's coming in down and off to the left, behind moon number six."

"Looks like he's still pretty far out."

"They don't have to get that close. They just have to get us in maximum effective range of their missiles before we can outrun them."

"Oh."

"We're okay. This moon has almost no gravity, which means we can go full-bore pretty quick. Out here we can go from zero to maximum sub-FTL in less than ten minutes."

He handed her a headset.

"Put this on," he said. "You'll need it to talk to us, and it will also protect your ears. The engines get pretty loud."

Forty-five seconds later, Jim buckled himself into his seat and donned his own headset. The engines hummed and vibrated the ship, as the two men did a last-minute checklist.

"They're too close for us to try to slingshot out of here," Jim grumbled. "They'll pick us off before we can reach jump speed. Plot a course four o'clock, negative sixty. Take us down below."

"Roger." Franz nodded.

"Down below?" Tonya asked.

"We go down below the system." Jim pointed to the floor. "We'll go out there and run silent for a few days. We have enough fuel and supplies to hide for a long time, and they're not gonna waste time and energy looking for a small ship out in deep space."

Franz released the ship from its mooring and lifted it off the surface of the moon. He gripped and turned the small steering apparatus below his console, and the ship pointed in the desired direction. He reached for the speed control lever which protruded from the control panel on his right side. He pushed the lever upwards with one hand, and the ship blasted off.

Tonya felt a nasty jolt, strong enough to have knocked her for a loop if she had not been strapped into her seat. Because of the lack of gravity resistance, she was not forced into her seat as she had been when they left Dragos, but found that she could move her arms and legs freely. She could also tell that the ship was already moving very, very fast. The *Cherbourg* shuddered as if it was in an earthquake, and the engines roared like a space shuttle.

166

"Wow, this thing really moves," she said while adjusting her earphones.

"You have no idea, Babe." Jim glanced back at her. "We're not even close to top sub-FTL speed yet."

She watched the red dot approach the base which they had just left behind. At the moment, it was gaining ground on them. Five minutes after they launched, the green dot which represented the base blinked red and disappeared.

"What happened?" Tonya asked.

"They just nuked our base," Jim replied.

"Can they get us, too?" she asked.

"No, we're already out of range," Jim said.

"But, their gaining on us!" she complained. "How are they doing that?"

"Because they're already at their maximum speed, and we're still accelerating from a stop," Franz explained. "We had a window of time to leave before they could catch up to us, and we left in time."

"Yeah, you guys timed your entrance just right," Jim said. "Don't worry about the monitor, Tonya. We've done this before."

Tonya could not help but worry about Jim's monitor. It was right in front of her, and by the looks of it, the enemy light cruiser was slowly catching up to them. Seconds seemed like minutes as she watched the enemy ship close the distance between them, slowing gradually as they picked up speed. After three more minutes of this torture, the enemy dot stopped its advance and began to crawl backward, as the *Cherbourg* now outpaced it. However, before she could relax, two smaller red dots appeared in front of the enemy ship. These new dots moved much faster, and they were gaining ground.

"Two nukes inbound," Jim reported, as if nothing was out of the ordinary.

"Nukes?" Tonya asked.

"Looks like they didn't like us taking one of their ships." Franz smirked. "But we're out of range. They can't lock onto us. Just watch."

Franz turned the steering wheel slightly and altered their course. The two missiles curved away from their green dot in the center of Jim's monitor.

"Watch, when they reach maximum range they'll detonate,"

Jim said.

Two minutes later, a flash of light lit up the space behind them. Tonya sat back in her seat and heaved a sigh of relief.

"Not even close." Jim grinned. "What'd we tell you? We do this all the time during rescue operations."

"Remind me not to apply for your jobs," she said as she wiped her brow.

"What do you think?" Franz asked Jim. "Should we let loose some junk mines? That would give them a nasty surprise."

"Naw, they'll probably break off in about ten minutes anyway." Jim shook his head.

"What are junk mines?" Tonya wondered out loud.

"They're magnetic explosives disguised as space junk," Franz replied. "When a ship gets close, they attach themselves to the hull and activate. They can punch holes in smaller ships, and damage sensors and weapons on larger ones. The trouble is they have a mind of their own. Once you release them, they attack the next ship that comes close, even if it's your own."

"Which is why we only use them in enemy systems," Jim pointed out. "And whenever we do use them, we have to file reports listing exactly where they are. We don't want to accidentally take out any friendly ships six months from now."

"I don't think that will be an issue here," Franz disagreed. "This system wasn't a tourist trap before. It's no man's land now."

"Yeah, well, tell that to the Heruli," Jim retorted. "Trust me, the Stosstrupen will be here in three days to kick some Strovat ass."

"They're breaking off anyway," Franz said.

He pulled down on the accelerator lever. The roar of the engines dropped to a loud hum, and they could talk without the use of headsets.

"What are Stosstrupen?" Tonya asked.

"They're the Heruli elite Special Forces," Jim answered. "They're controlled by the ruling baron. They keep the other clans in line, and they can also beat anything anyone else has got. They're top of the line, grade A, nasty mother..."

"They have the best equipment," Franz interrupted, "and possess some of the hardest striking power in the quadrant. They're first rate corps, and they're as good as anything that even the Alamani have."

"How about the Nephilim Argolath Guards?" she asked.

"They're first rate corps, too," Jim replied, "but not as good as the Stosstrupen. When the Alamani had their last big war with the Burbesenys, it was the Heruli Stosstrupen who did the most damage. Even the Burbesenys fear those cats."

"The Nephilim situation is different," Franz explained. "They're a monarchy, and the Argolath Guards are the king's house troops. Unlike the Stosstrupen, the Argolath Guards are personally loyal to their monarch and his family. King Zoar was born with absolute power. The Heruli are ruled by clans, with the Stosstrupen as enforcers. They can make or break Heruli emperors. If the ruling clan lord is strong enough, then he can hold absolute power, but if he's too weak the Stosstrupen will remove him."

"And you think the Stosstrupen will come here?" Tonya asked Jim.

"I think the Heruli can't ignore this new Strovat presence on their flank," Jim said. "And I also don't think Baron Hareseth will pass up an opportunity to grab a system with a terraformed world and good mining resources. If anything, the Strovats just gave him an excuse to take Nihal."

"Great." Tonya frowned. "So, we're stuck out here in the void. Meanwhile the Strovats and Heruli are going to fight each other over my former home. We're screwed."

"We're alive, and we aren't stuck in the void," Franz defended. "We're following normal procedure, Honey. Whenever we can't safely slingshot out of a system, we run silent until one of the outer planets opens up."

"Right," Jim added. "Neither side has enough fuel to put large warships around both the third and fourth planets indefinitely. After a while, they'll leave one of them alone long enough for us to move back up and slingshot outta here."

"So, how long could this take?" she asked.

"Usually, a few days." Jim shrugged. "Sometimes it takes a week or more, but like I said, the Heruli will likely show up at some point. The Stosstrupen will move the Strovats out pretty quick."

"I don't see how that's an improvement," Tonya griped. "Like the Heruli are going to just let us go? Frankly, I'd just as soon avoid them as much as the Strovats."

"They only make gladiators out of their enemies," Jim explained. "We're their allies, now. I doubt if they'd kill or imprison us."

"Really?" She folded her arms and gave him a funny look. "What do you think they'll do, treat us to brunch?"

"They need us to help fight the Strovats, Tonya," Jim replied.

"Do you really want to take that chance?" Franz gave him a serious look. "Allies or not, the Heruli aren't known for their hospitality. Out here they could kill us just for the sport of it, and no one would ever know."

Jim thought about this for a moment, and then he exhaled and nodded.

"You're right," he conceded. "We'd better avoid the Heruli for the time being."

He stretched and looked up at the navigator robot, which had magnetically attached itself to the roof of the cockpit before they left. It had been so quiet that Tonya did not even notice it.

"I don't know about you guys," Jim said with a yawn, "but I haven't had much sleep the last two days. Now that we're in the clear we can get some shuteye. Navigator."

"Yes, Lieutenant Commander Washington?" The robot suddenly came to life, and nearly made Tonya jump out of her seat.

"Jeez, don't do that!" She winced. "I didn't see you up there, Navigator."

The robot detached itself from the ceiling and hovered over to Jim. It had its back to Tonya and it completely disregarded her. Since robots were an essential part of everyday life, she was used to being around them, but she was not used to being ignored by them.

"Hel-lo, Navigator." She waved at it. "I'm right over here. Anybody home?"

She knocked on its back as if it was a door, but it still did not acknowledge her existence. She put her hands on her hips and gave Franz an annoyed look. Franz, who was thoroughly enjoying this, smiled and shook his head.

"Our robots won't listen to you," he said. "For security reasons, they will only respond to the voice prints of their commanding officers, or whoever we give clearance to. Commander, since we have to live with Tonya now, it might be a good idea to protocol her."

"Right." Jim smirked and then looked at the round robot. "Navigator, the Human female behind us is Tonya West. She is a new volunteer. You are to follow her in the chain of command with the rank of ensign. She is the new ship's medical officer."

"Medical officer?" Tonya choked. *"What?"*

"Voice print copied," Navigator stated.

"Did you go space happy while you were out here by yourself?" She poked Jim.

"You're the only one of us that has any kind of medical training," he replied.

"Medical training?" She laughed. "I'm a dental hygienist! If you get shot, I can clean your teeth for you."

"At least you know CPR," Jim countered. "Look, eventually we're going to have to report back. When General Blaaga asks me what my new civilian volunteer's duties are, I can't just tell him you're the ship's babe. He's flexible, but stuff around here still has to at least appear regulation."

"I get that." She motioned with her hand. "We all have to work to survive out here. I know I have to do my part, but medical officer, really?"

"Yeah, really," Jim affirmed.

"You guys are in trouble," she chuckled and shook her head. "All I know is CPR and some first aid. There's no way I could do surgery, especially in combat."

"No, but you can learn how to diagnose issues, and put patients that you can't help in suspended animation," Franz pointed out. "We have a ton of medical software on board, as well as medical, diagnostic, and pharmaceutical manuals."

"Yeah, and one thing we have plenty of in space is time," Jim added. "You'll have plenty of time to go over that stuff while we're waiting for a planet to open up, and then again during the four-day trip to Errai."

"Whatever." She leaned back in her seat.

"Anyway, as I was saying, I need a few hours' sleep," Jim said. "Navigator, we're going to rest. Afterward we'll be busy. I want you to hold this course for the next seven hours and then run silent. Once we reach those coordinates, if any ships get within a quarter of a gigamile of us, you let me know. Got it?"

"Yes, Lieutenant Commander Washington," came the robot's reply.

"A gigamile?" Tonya asked.

"We use gigamiles and teramiles to measure distances out here," Franz explained. "The old English mile is so out of style that we use it as a kind of code, you see."

"A gigamile is a thousand million miles," Jim stated. "It's a little more than the distance from Earth to Saturn when they're lined up. You guys did about three quarters of a gig getting here from Dragos, and we're going about half of a gig outside the system to sit and wait for an opening."

"So, a teramile is a thousand gigamiles?" she deduced.

"Yes, and that's almost a sixth of a light year," Franz answered. "Earth is about seventeen hundred teramiles away. That's why it takes six days to get there."

"You two get settled in, get some grub, and get some rest," Jim ordered. "When I get up we have reports to do. It won't be a lot of fun talking about the last thirty-six hours, but we have to do it."

☐

CHAPTER 18

Once the control of the ship was safely in the hands of the navigator robot, they were finally able to take a break. Though Franz and Tonya had already managed to get some sleep, neither of them had eaten anything since breakfast, almost fifteen hours previous. They did not notice their hunger until after they were finally out of danger, and then it hit them all at once.

Franz quickly grabbed a stack of MREs from the pantry, sat at the mess table, and chowed down. Tonya opened an MRE, sniffed it, and curled her nose.

"Ugh!" she complained. "How do you eat this stuff?"

"You have to pick the ones you like," he answered as he munched on a brown hot dog. "They're not so bad once you get used to the taste."

"I'll take your word for it," she said while rummaging through the pantry. "What else have you got in here? All I see is freeze-dried stuff and MREs."

"Go back into the cargo hold." Franz pointed. "There's a lot of different stuff in there. We keep frozen meat and bread in a couple of the cryogenic suspension modules in the back."

She emerged from the back with a pack of bagels and a small ham hock. She thawed them both in the microwave, and then made a batch of lemonade from the freeze-dried stock. She poured them both a glass before she sat down to eat.

"This is really good," he complimented, after he had guzzled half of his share.

"There's a lot of good food in the hold," she noted as she ate a bagel sandwich. "Why in the world do you eat those salty MREs?"

"They're quick and easy." Franz shrugged. "No cooking involved. They're like our version of fast food."

"Fast food tastes good, and at least it looks right." She pointed to his hot dog. "That thing doesn't look natural, and it smells like it's older than me."

Franz sniffed it and said, "yeah, it might be," before finishing it and starting on another.

"How do you live like this?" She looked around at their messy kitchen. "Between those 1980s surplus MREs and all these dirty dishes, I'm surprised you haven't both died of the Bubonic Plague by now."

"We don't exactly have a cook. The job's open, if you want it."

"No, I'm the medical officer, remember?"

"Oh, yeah. Well, we're men, and we only get inspected about three times a year. You expected the kitchen to be clean?"

"You have a point. Well, I won't live like this. I refuse to eat and drink from dirty dishes."

"We have dirty laundry, too."

"Forget it."

Franz helped her clean the kitchen. Afterward she went to her room, gathered some clean clothes, and then asked him about their showers. He led her to one of the rooms in the corridor that was next to the kitchen. He pointed to the room directly across the hallway from the shower and informed her that that was the latrine.

"Is it recycled water?" she asked with a look of distaste. "My dad told me about the water on these ships. You all use the same water over and over. You just run it through filters."

"Not the drinking water," Franz denied. "We have plenty of that stored in barrels in the hold. We would only recycle that if we ran out of supplies, which we've never done."

"I didn't ask about the drinking water." She put her hand on her hip. "I asked about the shower."

"Yes," Franz admitted, as if he was a criminal being cross-examined, "the shower and the faucet water are all recycled through filters. But you don't have to worry about it being mixed with the toilet water. That's separate from everything, because it has to go through our sewage treatment system."

"Thank God for that," Tonya exhaled. "Where are the towels?"

Franz opened a locker and provided her with two towels, and then he waited outside the room for his turn. She didn't take long, because she knew that they had a limited amount of hot water. The trick, her father had taught her, was to get into the shower first. She emerged fully dressed, much to Franz's disappointment, but with wet hair.

"I don't suppose you have any hair dryers on board?" she asked as she toweled her head.

"No," Franz chuckled. "Jim and I barely have any hair."

"I guess I'll have to cut my hair then, or it'll be constantly wet," she sighed.

"No!" Franz protested. "Your hair is a treasure. There are many places in the galaxy that would pay a fortune for it."

"Really?" she wondered.

"Yes, many things which we take for granted are worth a fortune in other parts of the galaxy," he explained as he stroked her wet locks. "Even so, I love your hair, and I wouldn't sell it for a ship full of gold. I'll have the engineer robots build you something that you can dry it with."

"You are so sweet." She smiled and put her arms around his neck. "I love you!"

"I love you, too." He kissed her. "Does this mean that the next time I can shower with you?"

"Only if you marry me first." She gave him a coy smile. "We can do a lot of things after that."

She ran her tongue down his neck.

"We...um..." he said as beads of sweat formed on his face, "...need either a...chaplain or... a captain for that...hey! This isn't fair!"

"Poor baby." She kissed him on the cheek. "I need to go finish unpacking. When we got here I just threw everything in those wall drawers."

"Yeah, me too." He sighed and nodded.

Franz had his belongings put away in five minutes, so he decided to give Tonya a hand with her stuff. He found her seated on her bed, clutching a picture of her little brother. Tears streamed down her cheeks, and he sat next to her and held her close. She buried her head into his shoulder and wept.

Eventually, they laid on her bed and went to sleep. Six hours later, Jim found them cuddled together and he gently awakened them. He had already showered and was dressed in his fatigues.

"Time to do that report," he said.

The three of them walked to the mess, where Jim had just finished his breakfast consisting of freeze-dried bacon and eggs.

"Gross!" Tonya stuck her tongue out.

"It's not bad, compared to the freeze-dried vegetables." Jim shrugged and placed his dish in the sink. "And it's a lot better than rations."

Jim grabbed his notebook computer from the counter. He sat across from the young couple, placed his computer in the center of the table, booted it up, and inserted a small thumb drive.

"I know this is going to be hard for you, Tonya," he began, "but we need to record your escape from Dragos, and I need you both to be specific. Start with the moment you were under attack, and go until we met at the station. I want you both to speak freely, and we can take a break if you want. I'll start the report by relating what I saw out here again."

"Again?" she asked.

"I sent out a probe with a report on the battle before I got Franz's call," Jim stated. "I hadn't heard from you guys, and I didn't know how things were going to go. So, I sent a report to our headquarters at Nerva. That could be why they sent a light cruiser out here after you. They might have picked up the trail of my probe, and between that and an unresponsive ambulance headed this way, they figured something was up. Anyway, now I want to do a full report with all of us. I'll send it out on another probe, so Blaaga will know we're still alive."

"What happened at N Gamma?" Tonya swallowed. "Dad said there was a base..."

"Wait a minute." Jim held up a finger. "We have to do this officially."

Jim hit the Enter key, activating the recorder program. He began by stating the date and time, and their names and ranks. He introduced Tonya as a civilian volunteer and their new medical officer. Then he proceeded with what he witnessed, first as the Strovat fleet came into the Nihal system by braking around the fourth planet, and then as their massive fleet assembled practically right over top of him. He did manage to send out a warning signal before he had to shut everything down. Jim stated that he had counted a total of three hundred Strovat Bisa supercruisers.

"Oh, my gosh!" Tonya gasped and covered her mouth.

Franz said nothing. He took a deep breath and shook his head.

"Sixty of the Bisas broke off and headed for Dragos," Jim narrated. "The remaining enemy fleet headed straight for Nihal III. We didn't know that was a naval base there, but they sure did. When that base went on alert, it lit up like a Christmas tree. I couldn't believe the number of ships' power readings I got."

"My father said that it was a massive naval repair facility," Tonya broke in. "He told us that there were two thousand ships there. He also said it was supposed to be top secret."

"Apparently, it was only a secret to us," Franz murmured.

"That would explain why the Strovats came here, of all places," Jim said. "Two thousand ships would be over a third of the League's fleet."

The three of them sat in silence for a moment, contemplating the ramifications of the last statement.

"What I'm about to describe," Jim said, taking a deep breath, "is nothing less than a disastrous defeat of our forces by the Strovats. There was a lot of confusion on our part. I know the Dragosian High Command got my message, because they radioed me back to confirm. Even with sixty Bisas bearing down on them, which they had to see coming, the Dragos Defense Force didn't respond for several hours. I monitored and recorded all signals, and they're attached to this report. The signals I got from the planet sounded like no one could find any of the top generals, and no one wanted to operate without orders. Fortunately, Admiral Takagi eventually took charge of that right away by commandeering all of the public and corporate liners and transports.

"At the base, they looked like they were in a panic," he continued. "Ships came out of that place like a bunch of angry hornets. The problem was, I didn't see any of our really heavy ships. I counted twenty-two Tellopian battle cruisers, and fifty-seven of their light cruisers. I also saw sixty Gutayid cruisers, and ninety Gutayid corsairs. These were the only ships of the line that came out of there, and they were under command of the Tellopian

Marshal Coriantumr. There were about two hundred smaller ships, and another hundred transports, but these ships all evacuated the system, so I assume most of the personnel of that base got out.

"Coriantumr's battle cruisers are the same size as our battleships, and their light cruisers are only half that size. The Gutayids' largest warships are their cruisers, which are only half the size of our battleships, and their corsairs are about the size of our destroyers. Admiral Takagi commanded twenty of our battleships and thirty of our destroyers, which are each only about a third the size of a battleship. So, combined, our forces had two hundred seventy-nine ships of the line facing three hundred Strovat Bisas, each of which being about fifty times the size of one of our battleships. To give you an idea of the odds tonnage-wise, Tagaki and Coriantumr were outnumbered over a hundred to one."

"Wait a minute." Tonya bit her lip. "I know Admiral Takagi. He's one of my dad's friends. Why are you speaking of him in the past tense?"

"Takagi moved his fifty ships out against sixty Bisas," Jim explained with a sad expression. "He was trying to buy time for the evacuations, you see. He ordered all of his smaller warships, over a hundred frigates and gunships, to help get people out of Dragos. Coriantumr was cut off from helping Takagi by the rest of the Strovat fleet heading his own way.

"The Strovats only brought a hundred light cruisers with them, and they're using most of these to protect four hundred huge transports. I'm guessing because they had to jump so far behind the front to get to this base, that most of these are fuel transports so they can get back. There's no way they're all staying at Nihal. There simply aren't enough resources on Dragos to support a fleet of this size indefinitely.

"Anyway, because they didn't have to deal with any enemy light cruisers, they did manage to inflict heavy damage on the enemy. The Earth forces nuked sixteen Bisas before they went down. Takagi and his fleet died to a man defending the evacuations."

"No!" Tonya turned her head into Franz's shoulder. "All of our friends are dead! Our families are missing, and our world is destroyed!"

Jim paused the computer for a few moments to allow Tonya to grieve. After a couple of minutes she composed herself, and he resumed the report.

"Coriantumr did no better." Jim shook his head. "He moved his fleet right out at the Strovats coming for his base. Like Takagi, he was trying to buy time to get as many of those ships off that repair base and out of here. Unfortunately, General Lukan, the Gutayid commander, had other ideas. Before Coriantumr could get in front of the Strovats, Lukan cut and ran, and all of the Gutayid ships deserted. They headed for the first planet, which is on the other side of Nihal, and they've since slingshot out from there."

"They...ran away?" Tonya dropped her jaw.

"Schweinhundts!" Franz frowned. "The Gutayids have always been unreliable. They should be kicked out of the League."

"Yeah, I agree." Jim nodded. "I'm sure the Security Council won't be happy when they get this report. They left Coriantumr in the lurch. It was a suicide mission anyway, but they could've helped him buy some time. With two thirds of his fleet deserting him, he didn't have a prayer going up against two hundred and forty Bisas. I think his own people lost their heart when the Gutayids left. They only took out nine Bisas, and once Coriantumr's ship blew up, the rest of the Tellopians broke formation. The Strovats blew right through them after that. Only two of their battle cruisers and five of their light cruisers made it out."

Jim paused to take a drink of water, took a deep breath, and continued.

"The Strovats moved over that base and blew it to Kingdom Come. Before that happened, I counted four hundred twenty transports and small warships that got out of there. The only ships of the line that got out were the useless Gutayids and the seven Tellopian cruisers. If your dad was right, then that means over fifteen hundred of our ships never got off their docks."

Tonya gasped and put her hand over her mouth. Franz hung his head.

"Counting Takagi's fleet," Jim droned, "we lost one hundred twenty ships of the line, plus whatever didn't get off the ground at Nihal III, which could have been another fifteen hundred. Enemy losses were sixty-two Bisas between our navy, the ground defenses on Dragos, and the base ground defenses. For what it's worth, we Humans gave a good accounting of ourselves. Between Takagi and the Dragosian Defense Forces, we took out forty Bisas and sixty landing transports, despite being heavily outnumbered.

"The people on Dragos didn't have much time to get out of there, but thanks to the actions of Admiral Takagi, I estimate that almost one million were evacuated in time. After that, the enemy surrounded Dragos and nuked all of the larger cities."

"One million," Tonya quietly lamented. "There are over twenty million people on Dragos, and most of them are homesteaders who are too poor to own space ships. They would've had no way to get out."

"Well, with all of those transports, my guess is they aren't planning to stay long anyway," Jim stated. "And if they were looking for a quick harvest, they got a nasty surprise. They found out that we Humans don't go down as easy as some of these other races. Our resistance was obviously tougher than they expected. We were literally decimating the small fleet they sent to try and take Dragos. Their options at that point were to either withdraw and come back later with reinforcements from Nihal III, or blast us from space. That's probably why they were so quick on the nuclear trigger."

They took a short break, during which all three got themselves something to drink. When they resumed the report, Jim asked the two young lovers to recant their narrow escape from Dragos. Franz started from the beginning at the wedding rehearsal. He explained about the media blackout, and Tonya reported that the civil defense sirens didn't go off until right before the bombs began to fall. Jim then informed them of the Strovat long-range jamming of Dragosian communications.

"I monitored the transmissions that did get out while I sat out here in the dark," he said. "There's no good way to say it. The High Command on Dragos got caught with their pants down. I think some of their top guys were on vacation with their phones off, because no one could find them, and their subordinates froze. Those missing generals never did show, by the way."

"I think 'caught with their pants down' is probably right," Tonya complained. "I'll bet they were off somewhere porking their secretaries."

"If they're still alive, and they have any brains at all, they'll stay missing," Franz said with a frown. "And any surviving Portsmouth city leaders should be hanged for not setting off the sirens until we were already under attack."

Franz and Tonya resumed the telling of their tale. When Franz got to the point when Tonya killed the Strovat lieutenant, Jim stopped him and asked her a few questions. Franz than explained that the Ambulatory Directive went by the book, except that the smoke grenade did not affect the Strovat lieutenant.

"At least we know that directive works," Jim said. "I recommend we switch from using the normal smoke to tear gas when we flush them out. That'll make it unpleasant inside until the air can be refreshed, but it will remove any hidden enemy lieutenants. I'm also recommending commendations for both Lieutenant Franz Zemmarich and Ensign Volunteer Tonya West. Lieutenant Zemmarich successfully executed the Ambulatory Directive and safely evacuated a civilian in the process. Tonya West exhibited courage under fire by killing a Strovat lieutenant at point blank range. This ends the report."

Jim removed the thumb drive, and then put away his computer. Franz hung his head.

"We didn't get anyone else out," he sighed. "Our families didn't come with us."

"That was their choice," Jim said. "They had their own ship, so it's not an issue. It's also not your fault that no one else was around when you initiated the Ambulatory Directive. You followed your orders and you two got out, in the nick of time I might add. When the enemy nuked the cities, they knocked out most of the heavy surface-to-air resistance, so they were able to move their Bisas in close. Once they did that, they were able to fry almost every ship that left the atmosphere. Even in an enemy ambulance you would have been in a shooting gallery. God was with you two yesterday."

"I know," Tonya sniffed and wiped away a tear. "I know that He was helping us, or we would never have made it out."

"Whatever," Franz droned.

"Well, I had to stay powered down most of the time back there," Jim said. "When I finally did get the power on, I had to gas the ship up. So, I only had time to do a few quick checks before you got here. Today Franz and I are going to run diagnostics on all the ship's systems. Tonya, I want you to start studying all the medical info we have. We do a lot of Evac-Rescue, and sometimes we pick up sick and wounded people. I suggest you start with the first and second aid software. We also have manuals that you need to familiarize yourself with, in case the computer equipment gets damaged or fails."

"Yes, sir," she sighed.

"Any word from your families yet?" he asked.

"No," Franz quietly replied.

CHAPTER 19

"So how are you going to send this report?" Tonya asked. "My dad takes his reports to the base so they can go out on a ship, but we're already on a ship, and we're not going anywhere."

"Obviously, we can't do it that way," Jim said. "Since you need to know how to do this anyway, let me show you how we send reports from the field."

She followed the men into the cargo hold, where she noticed one awake engineer robot and five sleeping security robots. Jim introduced her to Engineer One in the same way he had done with the Navigator, and it also copied her voice print.

"Are we going to do this routine with all of your robots?" she asked.

"No," Franz replied. "This robot has already communicated your voice print to the other Engineers. The same will go for the security bots."

They climbed down the ladder which led to the engineering section below. They were immediately greeted by an active security robot, which pointed a built-in machine gun at Tonya.

"Yikes!" She jumped behind Franz.

Jim ordered it to stand down, and then he had it copy her voice print.

"Now you can operate every robot on this ship," Jim said.

She smacked the robot on the head as they walked past.

"That was rude!" she griped at it.

"Yes madam," it dutifully replied.

They entered a circular room lined with computers and electronic equipment. Three engineer robots worked and monitored the controls.

"This is our engineering section," Franz said. "Everything runs through here. If the bridge gets knocked out, we can fly the ship from this room. If we get injured, the robots can fly her."

They walked up to a closed metal door that had a keypad over the handle. Jim punched in a code and opened the door, revealing a corridor that extended for about thirty feet. Its walls were lined from the floor to the ceiling with seven-foot-long, coffin-sized drawers. He pulled and twisted one of the handles, and slid open a drawer which was full of six-foot-long missiles; each of which had a shiny, red, metal bowling ball with a keypad for a head.

"The missiles in this row contain drones," Jim said. "The ones in the other rows have warheads. Once I insert this drive into one of these drones, it'll automatically be ready for launch."

He keyed in a sequence and a small door opened in the drone's head. Jim plugged the thumb drive into a slot inside, and the door shut.

"Why do you have to use a thumb drive?" Tonya asked. "Why not just program it from your computer?"

"This way prevents smart-ass college geeks from hacking and stealing military drones," Jim explained. "Imagine what could happen if someone stole one of these. That person could disrupt military operations in an entire sector with false reports, or even create a world-wide panic somewhere with fake news of an invasion, and then clean up on the stock market."

"Our thumb drives are all numbered and coded," Franz added. "You can't use any one of them without the right key code. The same goes for these drones. Even if the enemy manages to capture one, if he tries to open it without the right code he'll nuke himself."

"Nuke?" She backed away. "That thing's atomic?"

"They all are." Jim smirked. "Practically everything in this room is. The other missiles all have either nuke or bunker-buster heads, and these drones have small thorium drives so they can travel between systems just like any starship. We'll send this one here back to N Delta, where it'll slingshot into FTL speed and head for our headquarters at Errai. Even if the enemy is parked at N Delta, these things are so small and fast that they almost never get shot down."

"And they can also make us glow in the dark," Tonya remarked. "Remind me to take another anti-rad pill when we go topside."

Jim and Franz took most of that day doing ship diagnostics, with each man taking an engineer robot with him and looking over a different section of the ship. Tonya gathered up all the ship's medical books, manuals, and software and took them to her room. Very quickly she realized that the software would eat up all the spare memory on her little hand computer, and then some. So, she decided to look through the cargo hold for a spare computer. She found a black notebook stashed behind one of the clothing boxes.

"Wow, this is convenient," she said as she looked it over. "I wonder if it's any good."

Once she got it back to her room and booted it up, she realized why it had been hidden away in the cargo hold. It was loaded with nothing but porn.

"Oh, you gotta be kidding me!" she griped. "Even out here I can't get away from this crap?"

She played classic rock on her own computer while she worked. First, she formatted the black notebook, and then spent the better part of the morning and early afternoon configuring it as her new medical computer. At 14:00, the videocom on the wall next to her bed buzzed. Tonya clicked it on and Jim's face appeared.

"Hey, we're gonna to break for lunch," he said. "You wanna join us?"

"Sure," she replied.

The three of them met in the mess room, where they each prepared their own meals. Tonya kissed Franz and sat next to him.

"How's your research going?" Jim asked.

"Oh, great." She smiled and drank some lemonade. "I found something that'll be a big help to me doing my new job."

"Cool," Jim said as he munched on a food bar. "What is it?"

"A black notebook," she replied with a stare that would have made a Heruli uncomfortable.

Jim spat out a chunk of his granola. Franz almost choked on his brown MRE hot dog.

"It has lots of memory, and it's perfect for what I need," she continued mercilessly. "I had to format it first, though. It was all clogged up."

She lowered her deadly stare upon Franz, who held up his hands as if he was surrendering.

"It wasn't mine," he quickly denied.

"What exactly wasn't yours?" she cross-examined.

"Whatever was on that thing," he said and pointed. "It was his."

"Thanks a lot," Jim said to Franz like a man who had just been thrown under a bus. "By the way Tonya, your boyfriend here keeps some memory chips in his top drawer that you might want to look at."

"Do I have to?" She burned Franz with her eyes.

"No," he sighed. "I'll get rid of them."

"Smart man," she said.

"You could give them to me," Jim griped. "I just lost a bunch of very good classic porn, and I'm not engaged to anyone. Do you have any idea how hard it is to get the good stuff out here in the middle of nowhere?"

"Fine, but if you want to play that crap around me, then I got two words for you: Sexual harassment," she warned.

"Understood," Jim said.

When they resumed work, Franz asked for permission to put some music on to work by. Jim agreed, and he showed Tonya how to play music throughout the ship by plugging her hand computer into her videocom. At first, Jim, a cool jazz fan, did not appreciate Tonya's taste in classical music. But eventually, as he worked close by in the cockpit, a song came on which he actually enjoyed.

"Hey, that's a flute. Is that Mozart?" he called out.

"No," she answered. "It's called *Bouree,* by Jethro Tull."

"Not bad," Jim commented. "It's a lot better than that other stuff you were playing."

"You don't like Ozzy Osbourne?" she asked.

"For future reference, no," he responded.

Franz poked his head into her cabin and grinned.

"If he likes Tull, maybe he'll like Led Zeppelin," he said.

"Or Pink Floyd," she said with a shrug.

She worked on her new computer until 18:30, when she came down with a headache. She called it a day, took two aspirin, and laid on her bed. What seemed like a moment later, she was awakened by a smiling Franz, who sat next to her.

"Hi, Honey," he said.

"Hi." She smiled, sat up and stretched. "What time is it?"

"19:30. Did you have anything to eat for dinner?"

"No."

"Good, because I brought dinner with me."

He put a small bag on the desk in her room and pulled it over to her bed. He removed a candle, four cans of food, and two cans of soda from the bag.

"What's this?" she asked.

"I dug out a few special treats for us tonight," he said. "I brought canned ham, sweet rolls, and yams."

"Ooooooo!" She held her stomach. "Where did you get the soda? I didn't see anything like this in the cargo."

"We keep some stuff stashed away for special occasions," he explained. "Like when we win a battle or complete a successful mission. We have a cooler down below in engineering, where no one else will look."

They sat on her bed and ate the best meal that they'd had in days. Jim knocked on the door just as they finished.

"Hey, you two," he said, poking his head inside. "Don't do anything tonight that I can't do right now."

"Don't worry," Tonya responded. "As your new medical officer, the last thing I want to do is deliver my own baby."

"I wasn't worried about that," Jim said. "I don't have a girlfriend on board, and I don't want to hear any noise outta you two. I'd feel deprived."

"Good night." Tonya waved.

After Jim closed the door, she put on some light music.

"Would you like to dance?" she asked.

"I'd love to." Franz kissed her.

They danced slowly and she held him tightly, resting her head on his chest.

"Do you have to stay in your cabin tonight?" she asked.

"Didn't you just tell Jim that we weren't going to…"

"Yeah, but I don't want to sleep alone, either. Remember when we were teenagers, and we would stay up all night in my dad's living room and watch movies?"

"Yes, we would curl up on the couch together under a

blanket, and you would fall asleep in my arms."

"My dad would wake us up!" she laughed. "I think it drove him nuts. If it was anyone but you there, he would've gone on a killing spree."

"Yes, I remember." He smiled.

"Why don't we do that tonight?" she asked. "I have movies in my computer."

"When the most beautiful woman in the galaxy asks me to stay with her, how can I refuse?" he replied.

They curled up on her bed and watched movies until they fell asleep in each other's arms.

CHAPTER 20

The next morning, Tonya didn't want to get out of bed. She pleaded with Franz for five more minutes in his arms, and he couldn't refuse her. Twenty minutes later, Jim knocked on the cabin door. He entered to find Tonya crying on Franz's shoulder. Franz's eyes were also misty and red. Jim pulled up her desk chair and sat in reverse fashion, facing them.

"We've heard nothing from them." Franz hung his head.

"I'll be okay." She sat up and sniffed. "I...just needed a good cry."

"It's okay," Jim exhaled. "Take as long as you need. I know how it is."

"I know you do." Tonya wiped the tears from her cheeks. "That was a really rotten thing that happened to your family."

"Yeah, and it still hurts," Jim said quietly. "It never really goes away. A wise man once said that dying is easy, it's living that's hard. That's what we have to do, to live on. I know how much faith you have, Tonya. You know there's a purpose for this life, and a better place beyond it. God got me through losing my family, and I know He'll get you through this.

"Now, I'm not saying your families are gone. Phone contact out here is iffy at best. Unless you know the general area where to aim, your family might never get your messages. Or they could've got them and replied when we were behind N Delta."

"I didn't think of that," Franz said.

"Thanks." Tonya tried to smile. "That really helps. It still sucks that we don't know what happened to them."

"And you may not know for a long time," Jim pointed out. "The best thing to do is to get on with life, but never give up hope. You still have each other. That's a miracle in itself. Most people never find what you two have."

"I know," she said. "I thank God every day for Franz. I've also been thinking a lot about how we got out of that mess on Dragos. I didn't realize how bad it was until we did that report. You were right, Jim. God was really with us."

"Um, I think my piloting had a little bit to do with that," Franz objected. "So did our AD equipment."

"Yeah, but it didn't go the way you planned it," Tonya said. "The smoke didn't work on that big red one. What were the odds we both survive that?"

"We were lucky," Franz admitted. "And you did your part. Give yourself some credit. You'll probably get a medal for that."

"Franz, I can't believe we were just lucky," she said. "Would it kill you to admit for once that God was looking out for us?"

"Did He look out for our families, too?" Franz folded his arms. "What about everyone else on Dragos? I might be more likely to believe in a God that isn't so selective about who He helps."

"The standard Agnostic argument." Jim shrugged. "What do you want us to say to that, Franz? God didn't kill those people on Dragos any more than he killed my family. It rains on the just and the unjust. If He saves everyone, then where's our free will?"

"Right," Tonya added. "And I remember reading something about faith as well. There has to be opposition, or we can't prove our faith. Any suffering we go through in this life is not the point, Franz. The point is how we deal with it. The promise of happiness isn't in this life, it's in the next."

"For you that's fine," Franz stated. "And for our children. I've already agreed to this. But for me, I believe what I see."

Weary of arguing, they resumed their duties from the day before. By noon, the men had finished all of the ship diagnostics. At 12:30 Franz poked his head into Tonya's room and found her reading a medical manual.

"Hey, Honey," he asked. "You want to take a break?"

"Sure," she said, putting down the tome. "I've studied so much that my eyes are about to fall out of my head."

"Come on." He motioned with his head.

"By the way, when are we getting out of here?"

"That depends on how long the enemy stays between us and our way out. We check the sensors every four hours, and at 12:00 he was still too close to N Delta for us to safely head back."

"So how long do you think he'll be there?"

"Honestly, I have no idea. He could leave tonight, or he could sit there for another week. Depends on his fuel, and how pissed off he is at us for stealing one of their ships."

"So, in the meantime what do we do to keep from going space happy?" she asked as they walked into the mess.

"Today, we play cards." Jim grinned at them as he sat at the table and shuffled a deck.

"At least you guys aren't taskmasters," Tonya said as she pulled up a chair.

They played cards until the next sensor check at 16:00. Much to their relief, the Strovat light cruiser which had pursued them was heading in a different direction, and far enough away that Jim said it was okay for them to go back.

Even though it was an eight hour trip, Tania wished to sit in the cockpit. She had always wanted to travel in space, and despite their circumstances she was going to make the best of her situation. She brought her hand computer with her, and using her astronomy program mapped out the stars while the men piloted the ship. Jim and Franz showed her which stars had planets, and also which system belonged to which race or empire. She was fascinated by their view of the Great Orion Nebula. Though it was twelve hundred light years away, it was clearly visible from their vantage point in space.

"Wow, it's so beautiful!" She stared. "From the ground, it just looks like a small white cloud at night, even with binoculars. I've seen the pictures, but this is something else."

"You wanna see it up close?" Jim asked.

Tonya nodded, and Jim typed in a sequence. He reached up and tapped the windshield, which magnified the nebula in 3D fashion to the size of a basketball in front of her. Both her eyes and her smile grew wide as she studied it.

"This is so cool!" she said. "Can you do that with the other stars, too?"

"Sure." Franz nodded. "We can magnify whatever you want

to see."

For the duration of the trip, Tonya was a kid in a candy store as Franz and Jim enlarged one star after another right in front of her. She viewed the red giant Betelgeuse, and Rigel, the home of the Alamani. Among all the different star systems, it was Sigma Orion which fascinated her the most. This was a star cluster consisting of one larger star next to a binary star, with another triple star close by. To Tonya, it looked like a giant blue planet with stars for moons.

Before she knew it, they were back within range of Nihal IV. Jim scanned the area as Franz plotted a course to slingshot the *Cherbourg* around the gas giant into FTL speed, and then launch toward Errai.

"Now, that's funny," Jim noted. "That light cruiser that was chasing us didn't go back to their main fleet."

Franz took notice. "Where's it at?"

"Are they after us?" Tonya asked with trepidation.

"No, that's the thing," Jim replied. "They've joined up with another light cruiser at nine o'clock minus sixty, about three hours out, but they're not heading for us. They're bearing mark twelve plus twenty; up and over to the left for some reason."

"That's good news for us," Franz stated as he typed.

"Where's the main Strovat fleet?" Tonya asked. "Are they at Dragos?"

"Some of them are," Jim said. "About thirty Bisas are there, but about two hundred are still at N Gamma with most of their transports. There's one on its way over here, but it's at least eighteen hours away."

"We must have really ticked them off to send a Bisa after us," Tonya commented.

"I doubt if he's after us." Jim shook his head. "I'd say they saw a bigger fish out this way, like a Heruli scout or something."

"That ought to be a good fight between the Strovats and those Stosstrupen guys," Tonya said.

"Yeah, but we're not going to be here to see it," Franz retorted. "Give me another minute, and we are outta here."

"Now, hang on for a minute." Jim held up a finger. "Tonya, we've got some muscle relaxers in that med cabinet back in storage. You should probably take one. The slingshot into FTL is always rough."

"It can't be any worse than pulling ten Gs in that Strovat ambulance." She folded her arms. "If that little ship didn't make me throw up, this big one won't."

"All right," Jim warned, "but we have a rule around here. If you chuck it up, you clean it up."

"Which means I don't have to clean up after you two," Tonya replied. "Good."

Just before Franz keyed in the final sequence for their escape, Jim's console beeped several times. It sounded like the same message, over and over, three long beeps followed by three short beeps.

"Aw, you gotta be kidding me!" Jim griped. "Not now!"

"What is it?" Tonya asked.

"A distress signal," Franz exhaled. "Someone out there is calling for help."

"Engineer One, full stop!" Jim barked into his headset. "Franz, bring her around so I can pinpoint where that message is coming from."

Jim looked at his controls, and then sat back and uttered a word which made Tonya's jaw drop.

"Well, this doesn't sound good," she commented.

"We got a small ship, mark twelve, plus thirty." Jim frowned. "Right in the path of those two light cruisers."

"Figures." Franz smirked and shook his head. "It's never easy, is it?"

"We're not going to leave them to the Strovats, are we?" Tonya asked.

"No way," Jim answered. "If we can get to them in time, we'll get them outta there. That's what we do for a living. Franz, I'm keying in the coordinates. Take us there, full throttle."

The ship jolted and shuddered, and once again the engines roared so loudly that they had to put on their headsets.

"Will we get to them in time?" Tonya asked.

"It's gonna be close," Jim replied. "They're just over ninety minutes away, but I figure we should get to them with about a half hour to spare. The Strovats have further to go."

"How many do you think we'll be picking up?" she persisted.

"The scanner says it's a class D van, which puts it at about a quarter the size of this ship," Jim replied. "Any starship that small is mostly engines and fuel. Shouldn't be more than twenty or so on board."

"With the panic we saw on Dragos, I wouldn't assume anything," Franz cautioned. "There could be a hundred people on board that van."

"Oh, my gosh!" Tonya worried out loud. "Where would we put them all?"

"In the cargo hold," Jim stated. "It's okay. We do this all the time, and we've picked up more than a hundred before."

"Hopefully they didn't bring any spiders with them," Tonya murmured.

"How are they even still here?" Franz wondered. "They should've either been long gone, or turned into peopleburgers by now."

"Well, whatever their story is, they must've run silent until we showed up," Jim said as he typed. "As soon as they started their SOS, the Strovats must've seen them...There, I've locked on. Now we can talk to them, whoever they are. I'm sending a text identifying ourselves and asking for a reply."

Thirty seconds later Jim repeated the message.

"Why don't they answer?" Tonya asked.

"They haven't got it yet," Franz answered. "We're still about four light minutes away, which means we won't get a reply for eight minutes."

"Such wonderful 19th century technology," she murmured. "We may as well be using Marconi's wireless telegraph."

Almost exactly eight minutes later, someone from the beleaguered van responded, but not in text form. A frantic male Human voice came over their headphones.

"Jeez!" Jim gave the computer a funny look. "What language is that?"

"I have no idea." Franz shook his head.

"Sounds like either Arabic or Turkish to me," Tonya said. "Hey, why didn't our computer auto-translate that?"

"Because they're talking directly into their radio," Jim said as he typed another message. "He can read what I sent him, but he doesn't seem to know how to work his ship's computer."

"Well, no wonder they're stuck." Tonya raised her eyebrows. "Some pilot they got there."

"I'd say their pilot's down," Franz said.

"We're gonna find out in eighty minutes," Jim said. "I'm

sending another message, and a program which will auto-link our computers. That way they can talk all they want into their radio and our computer will translate it into text."

Eight minutes later the reply came in text form, translated by the computer.

"That was Arabic," Jim said. "Very good, Tonya."

"We get all kinds at a dentist's office." She shrugged.

"Can you speak it?" Franz asked.

"No!" she laughed. "We used a robot for translation like everyone else, except apparently you guys."

"Well, isn't that special?" Jim said as he read the message. "Their pilot is dead, and their engineer is unconscious. They also have ten people in cryogenic suspension, and no one to thaw them out."

"I can do that." Tonya pointed. "That's the first thing I studied up on."

"We won't have time." Jim shook his head. "We'll get there thirty minutes ahead of the Strovats, but we'll have to slow down in order to dock with that van. The enemy will be going full bore the entire time, and we'll have to get back up to full speed before they catch us. I figure we'll have maybe ten or fifteen minutes to evacuate them. That's not enough time to fool with thawing people out. I'm telling them to prepare for evac immediately upon our arrival."

"So, we're just gonna leave them to be frozen dinners?" Tonya gave him a stunned look.

"No," Jim said. "If we can't save them, we booby-trap their ship. When the Strovats try to get them, they blow up."

"You use them as bait." Tonya folded her arms and frowned. "Nice. Remind me never to try cryogenic suspension."

"War has casualties," Franz exhaled. "Fifteen minutes gives us two choices; either we save who we can and get out, or we all die trying to save ten more. The ones in cryo won't know what happens to them, which is better than letting the Strovats wake them up."

"You've had to do this before." Tonya put her hand on his shoulder. "I'm sorry."

"We've had to leave people behind who were still awake." He closed his eyes and shook his head.

"Tonya, let's trade seats," Jim instructed. "I need to go in the back and configure a nuke for a timed blow, which'll take some time. I want you to help Franz up here."

Tonya sat in his seat and eyed his computer console and the mass of controls and sensors around it. She suddenly felt like a remedial math student who had been sent to calculus class.

"You've got to be kidding me!" She gave Jim a look of disbelief.

"All you have to worry about is that number there, and that clock ticking on my computer screen," he explained while pointing to the controls. "Franz will be asking you about those. I've set everything else on auto. Oh, and if those people message us again, you're the one who'll respond."

"What do those numbers on your screen mean?" she asked.

"That's how long we'll take to get there, and the other one is how much time we'll have to evac them before the enemy can catch us. Right now, we're sitting on twenty-seven minutes, but it'll drop when we have to slow down. If that number goes below ten, call me."

After Jim left, Franz smiled. "Not quite like your car, is it?"

She looked at him, wide-eyed, and shook her head.

Thirty-five minutes later, Jim returned and relieved her of his seat.

"Should I tell him?" she asked.

"You took the call," Franz said.

"What?" Jim asked.

"Our future passengers sent us a text." Tonya bit her lip. "There's more than twenty people in that van."

"So? I told you we can handle a lot more than that," Jim responded.

"Well...it's not so much that there's thirty-eight of them," Tonya said. "It's that thirty of them are kids."

"Thirty kids?" Jim complained. "What is that ship, the Kindergarten Express?"

"They're orphans, mostly," she replied. "The ship is owned by Hassan Ben-Hadad."

"Where have I heard that name before?" Jim asked.

"He's the big-time energy baron who came here from Earth a few years ago," Franz said.

"Oh, yeah." Jim nodded. "He owns most of the mining

operations on Dragos. That guy's the richest man on the planet. He should be on his own luxury liner on his way back to Earth by now. What's he doing in a broken-down van with thirty kids?"

"Sounds kind of bogus to me," Franz said.

"It could be a trap," Tonya added. "I mean, an energy baron and bunch of orphans? Seriously? Maybe some pirates are trying to play on both our greed and our heartstrings."

"I seriously doubt any pirates would be sticking around to try and hijack a much heavier warship while the Strovats are coming at them from the other side," Jim stated. "But one thing I've learned is that anything's possible in outer space. When we get there, we'll send in Engineer Four first. If he doesn't see an Arab Sheikh and a bunch of kids, then we blow the airlock and send them spinning."

"Why not send in one of those big security bots?" Tonya asked.

"Engineer Four is expendable," Franz replied. "And its more user friendly than the warbots. It has a cutting laser that can take your pretty head off, but it won't accidentally shoot anyone. And if any bad guys get past it, then they'll get cut to pieces by our security bots."

"At least it won't scare those kids," she noted. "If that guy was telling the truth, that is."

"I know this is going to sound bad," Jim exhaled, "but I kinda hope it is a trap. The thought of having thirty screaming kids on board scares me more than any pirates."

Tonya laughed out loud.

"Men!" She shook her head.

Five minutes later, Franz cut the engine power to stop the ship's acceleration. Fifteen minutes afterward, he initiated reverse thrusters to begin the braking process. Tonya noticed that the evac time on Jim's computer immediately began to drop.

At this point, they were close enough to make radio contact without major delays, and Jim did so. A man with a deep voice responded in Arabic.

"Sir," Jim interrupted, "this will be a lot easier if we can talk to each other without the computers. Do you speak English?"

"English? Yes."

"Very good. We will be docking with you in about ten minutes. We need you to get everyone there ready to go, and gather all of the food and water that you have to bring with you."

"Yes, sir."

"Call me Jim."

"Yes, Jim. My name is Hassan. We have one adult who is unconscious, and ten people in cryogenic suspension."

"At least he speaks good English," Tonya said.

"Yeah," Franz agreed. "We don't get that very often."

"Hassan, we have two enemy ships coming in fast," Jim instructed. "We'll only have about fifteen minutes to get you all off safely. I'm sorry, but we won't be able to save your people in suspension, but I don't want you to unplug the cryogenic units. Leave them on. Do you understand?"

"Yes, I understand," Hassan replied in a subdued tone. "Why not shut them down?"

"I'll explain when we get there."

"Very well. We will be ready to evacuate when you get here, my friend. Thank you."

"I think that really is Hassan Ben-Hadad out there," Tonya said.

"Me too," Franz added. "You know her feelings are always right."

"Great." Jim covered his face with one hand. "Thirty screaming kids. I need some aspirin."

☐

CHAPTER 21

When they finally arrived at the disabled van, Franz was relieved to discover that it was stationary.

"At least their pilot had the decency to stabilize his ship before he died," he said. "It's a lot easier to link when the other ship isn't spinning."

"Spinning?" Tonya gaped.

"Yeah, we get that sometimes," Jim said. "If we can't hack into their computer to stabilize a spinning ship, then we have to use rocketed grappling cables and yank it into place. Talk about whiplash."

"Ugh!" She stuck out her tongue and held her stomach. "That's awful! A ship full of people throwing up."

"Yeah, it's not very pleasant," Franz stated. "If they spin for too long, like days before anyone gets to them, then unless they're in cryogenic suspension it's usually fatal."

"I can see how someone like that could lose their will to live," she commented. "Yuck!"

The docking sequence went quick and easy, and Franz sealed the airlock.

"Let's go," Jim said as he unbuckled. "We have to blow the airlock in fourteen minutes, or this rescue means nothing."

They grabbed their weapons and moved down the corridor to the airlock in the middle of the ship. Jim had already parked three robots in front of the airlock, with Engineer Four in front and two larger warbots behind. Franz, Jim and Tonya hung back, just around the corner in the corridor. Jim cocked his modern, air-cooled Tommy gun, Franz brandished his .308, and Tonya clutched her pistol with both hands.

"Ready?" Jim asked.

"Ready." Franz nodded.

Jim clicked on his headset.

"Hassan, this is Jim. Please step back from the doorway and let our robot through. This is normal procedure, and it will only take a moment."

"I understand," Hassan replied.

"Engineer Four, move forward and scout," Jim ordered.

As the robot moved into the van, Jim watched the video relay on his hand computer. What he saw tugged at his heart.

"All robots stand down," he heaved a sigh. "Code yellow. C'mon guys, let's get to work."

"What's code yellow?" Tonya whispered to Franz.

"The engineer bot is now in rescue mode," he quietly responded. "The warbots are in security mode, and will not fire unless fired upon. Stay behind me until we get inside, my love."

They entered into the cargo bay of the broken-down van and were greeted by a very large, muscular Arab man who wore a very expensive, tailored dark suit and a white kaffiyeh upon his head. Two men dressed in black with plaid kaffiyehs stood by his side, brandishing assault rifles. Behind them knelt five women, four of whom wore blue and gray plaid jilbabs and black scarves over their hair. The fifth woman was younger than the others, wore a casual, long-sleeved shirt, designer jeans, and a purple scarf over her head. On the floor behind the women sat several very frightened looking children.

"I am Hassan Ben-Hadad." The huge man smiled and enthusiastically shook Jim's hand. "These men are my personal guards, Akbar and Mahmud. The women behind me are my wives, Lela and Zarifa, the wives of my men, and my sister Yasmeen."

Jim thought that Yasmeen looked like a supermodel, with long dark hair, a perfect terra cotta complexion, and gorgeous brown eyes. She smiled at him, and he froze in his tracks. For a moment, all he could do was gaze at her beautiful face and her slender, perfect body.

"Commander, I don't mean to be rude, but we don't really have time for introductions," Franz spoke up from behind. "We only have twelve minutes left."

"Right." Jim snapped out of his trance. "Hassan, get the women and these kids on board our ship, and then we'll load your food and belongings. We have to move fast, and it's going to be a rough ride at first, but we have safety straps all over the ship. The women can strap the kids and themselves in, while the men load your stuff. Franz and Tonya will show everyone where to go."

"Thank you, my friend." Hassan nodded, and then turned and gave instructions in Arabic to the others.

Franz and Tonya led the women and children into a safe area in the back of the cargo hold of the *Cherbourg* which was specifically designed for refugees, having a cushioned floor and enough safety straps on the walls for fifty people. They quickly showed the women and older children how to safely buckle in.

"Put the boxes and your belongings in this room," Franz instructed the men, pointing to one of the extra cabins. "We don't have time to secure it in the cargo hold, but at least in there it won't bounce around and hit anyone. You can sort it out later."

Back inside Hassan's ship, Jim called Engineer Two on his headset and ordered it to bring out the bomb.

"Bomb?" Hassan did a double take.

"The Strovats will probably search your ship for the people in the cryogenic suspension," Jim stated. "We're going to leave a time bomb on your ship. This way the enemy won't get to the people in cryo, and if we're lucky we'll take out one of their ships in the process."

"This is why you told me not to shut off the cryogenic units?" Hassan asked.

"Yes," Jim replied. "The Strovats will see the power is still on, and they don't usually pass up free meals. I'm sorry, but there's nothing else we can do for your friends in suspension. We don't have time."

"It was written," Hassan exhaled. "It is better this way. They are people who worked for me. I am glad they will not be eaten by those filthy bugs."

Franz and a few of the older children entered to help with the loading. Behind him Engineer Two rolled up carrying a six-foot-long black missile. Tonya followed right behind, carrying a small black medical bag.

"What are you doing here?" Franz griped. "You should be back on our ship helping the others."

"I'm the medical officer, remember?" she retorted. "Hassan said his engineer is unconscious. I'm going to check him out."

"Oh, no you're not." Franz pointed. "We've only got six minutes left. You're supposed to be..."

"I showed Yasmeen and the others what to do, and they're taking care of the kids." Tonya put her hand on her hip. "Shouldn't you be getting our ship ready for launch?"

"No time to argue, my friends," Hassan interrupted.

"He's right." Jim motioned with his head. "Franz, go get the ship ready. Tonya, you have two minutes, and that's it."

Hassan said something to the oldest teenage girl, who nodded.

"This is Talia," he said. "She will take you to our engineer."

Two minutes later, as the others were loading the last of the supplies, Tonya and Talia returned. Tonya looked at Hassan and shook her head.

"I'm sorry, but your engineer's dead," she said. "Insulin shock, according to my diagnostic sensor. I checked the pilot too. Looks like he died of a heart attack."

"The fools." Hassan shook his head. "They did not tell me. I would have taken care of them."

"Severe diabetics aren't allowed to fly, or do any essential duties onboard a space ship," Jim explained as they lugged boxes of food and water onto the *Cherbourg*. "People with heart problems aren't supposed to fly either, because they could do exactly what your pilot and engineer just did to you. They must have lied to get their licenses."

"No, they were friends who needed jobs," Hassan admitted. "It is my fault. I did not know this."

"Two minutes!" Franz announced over the intercom.

Everyone heard the roar of the *Cherbourg*'s engines, as he fired them up.

"Time to go!" Jim ordered.

Hassan's two bodyguards grabbed the last item, a large chest, and they carried it into the ship behind everyone else.

"Do you have all of the kids on board?" Tonya asked Yasmeen, who was buckling herself to the corridor wall near the cockpit.

"Yes." She nodded. "I counted them myself."

She reached up and clasped Tonya's hand. *"Thank you!"*

"Everything's going to be all right now," Tonya said.

Jim hit a button on the wall and closed the airlock door, then he, Hassan, and Tonya rushed into the cockpit and buckled themselves in. Franz blew the airlock with thirty seconds to spare, and Hassan's ship drifted away. Franz turned the *Cherbourg* back in the direction from which they came and blasted off, full throttle. Everyone in the ship got a nasty jolt, and a few of the children screamed. The women calmed them down fairly quickly, and after a minute or so only a couple of toddlers were crying. Hassan, who sat directly behind Jim, closed his eyes and repeated a prayer in Arabic. Tonya could barely hear him over the roar of the engines.

"That was close." Franz exhaled in relief.

Hassan opened his eyes and watched Jim's monitor. He noticed the two red dots gaining on them.

"Can they catch us?" he asked with a worried look.

Tonya handed him a headset and told him to ask again.

"No, we can outrun them now," Jim replied. "They'll get close before we get to full velocity, but not close enough to fire at us. But one more minute back there, and we might have been toast."

"You have risked your lives to save myself and my family," Hassan said gratefully. "I cannot thank you enough, my friends. I am a man of some influence in the League, and I will see that you are rewarded. The entire League will hear of your bravery."

"Thanks," Franz said. "For what it's worth, we appreciate it."

"I do not understand what you mean." Hassan gave him a puzzled look.

"Guys, I don't think he knows," Tonya said.

"Hassan, there was another battle at the third planet of this system," Jim stated. "We had a huge naval base there."

"A naval base?" Hassan wondered. "I have been supplying fuel for the building of a large agricultural and mining center at N Gamma. I know of no naval base there."

"Did you ever see this mining center?" Tonya asked.

"No." Hassan shook his head. "The place was restricted, even to me. The contract was through the central government, and there were government administrators who we worked through."

"You didn't notice how much fuel they were using?" Franz asked.

"The government buys my resources in bulk quantities, and then ships it where they need it. Yes, they buy an immense amount of fuel, but there are different types for different uses. We sell oil, uranium, plutonium, curium, thorium, and cryogenic gases among others. The government does not inform me where it all goes to."

"Well, a lot of it must've gone to N Gamma," Jim stated, "because we had over two thousand ships there."

"*Two thousand?*" Hassan gasped. "What kind of base was that, and why was it *here* of all places?"

"It was some sort of huge repair facility," Franz replied. "It must've been top secret, too, because none of us knew about it, except Tonya's dad."

"My dad works in intelligence," Tonya added. "He's the one who told us about it."

"That's what makes this all the worse," Jim said. "The Strovats went right for it. There must be a major security leak at League central."

"How many of our ships got out?" Hassan asked.

"Most of them didn't." Jim shook his head. "We lost at least a third of the fleet. Takagi and Coriantumr are both gone."

"I know about Takagi," Hassan said sadly. "He sacrificed himself so that many of us could escape. But, I did not know of the other battle. Not long after we got to here, our pilot died, and the engineer turned the power down so that the enemy would not see us. Then he became sick as well. We did not know how to use the ship's controls."

"You mean you all just sat there in the dark for two days?" Tonya gasped.

"Yes, it was very frightening, especially for the children," Hassan replied. "We all prayed for deliverance, but we could only see enemy ships on our radar device. Then, just an hour ago, we saw your ship and radioed for help. Praise God that you are here now! But how did this come to be? Where did you come from?"

"Hold that thought," Jim interrupted. "Those two Strovats are coming close to your ship. Thirty seconds to detonation. Cross your fingers, everyone."

He pointed to his monitor, which showed images of the enemy light cruisers approaching Hassan's van.

"They're maintaining full speed." Franz shook his head. "They're not going for the bait."

The two enemy vessels passed Hassan's ship and continued their course toward the *Cherbourg*. The van detonated behind them.

"That's unusual," Franz noted. "Those bugs normally don't pass up any scrap of food. We should've got at least one of them."

"Between this and nuking our cities, they're acting like they're mad about something," Tonya added.

"Well, it was worth a shot," Jim exhaled. "Those Strovats are too close now for us to slingshot out. Franz, take us below."

Jim explained to Hassan that they had to go hide outside the system for a few days until it was clear enough around the fourth planet for them to safely speed-orbit into FTL.

"To answer your earlier question, Hassan," Franz said, "we barely got away from those bugs ourselves, and just like now we didn't have enough time to go into FTL. We were sitting out in deep space until about eight hours ago."

"And now we get to go back," Tonya murmured. "Whee."

Suddenly, one of the Strovat light cruisers disappeared from Jim's monitor.

"What the..." Jim wondered.

The second light cruiser faded out.

"What's going on?" Franz asked.

"Those bugs' lights just went out." Jim typed in a sequence.

An outside camera shot appeared on the windshield in front of them. Jim zoomed it in on their enemy's coordinates and found nothing but dust and a few sparking chunks of metal.

"They've...blown up." He raised his eyebrows.

"How?" Franz asked. "There are no other ships in the area, are there?"

"Uh...no." Jim looked at the power reading monitor and did a sensor sweep. "Nothing...Whoa!"

A red dot appeared on his monitor, and the power readings shot to the top of the scale.

"What the hell is that?" Franz pointed to it.

As soon as he said this, the dot disappeared and the power readings went back to zero.

"This is nuts," Jim griped. "Franz, take us down to quarter speed."

The roar of their engines diminished to a whisper.

"Okay, what's going on?" Tonya asked.

"I would like to know as well," Hassan said. "Whatever that

was, your computer did not like it very much."

"Uh..." Jim fumbled about with his instruments. "According to our sensors, the two ships that were chasing us are now space junk, and another ship appeared and then disappeared."

Franz gave him a doubtful look. "A single ship? That's impossible. The sensors were reporting a power level equal to five Bisas."

"Yeah, I know." Jim tapped an instrument with his finger. "It's gotta be a malfunction."

"What about the Strovats?" Tonya asked. "Is that a malfunction, too?"

"Naw, they're fried." Jim pointed to the windshield. "Look for yourself. That's what we call visual confirmation."

"So, maybe it's not a malfunction," Tonya deduced. "Maybe there's another ship out there. Seems to me that anybody with power ratings like that could make mincemeat out of a couple of medium-sized Strovat ships."

"And us," Hassan pointed out. "Perhaps we should not have slowed down."

"Yeah, except nobody has power readings like that," Jim responded.

"So, what happened to the two Strovat light cruisers?" she asked. "Did our bomb get them?"

"No, they were out of range," Franz said. "Maybe one had a reactor meltdown, and when it blew it damaged the other one."

"Yeah...maybe." Jim continued to search for answers in his equipment.

"Or maybe it was another, really powerful ship." Tonya shrugged.

"So, where is it?" Jim asked. "I'm getting nothing on my sensors right now. Ships don't just disappear, Tonya."

"Perhaps it is cloaked," Hassan pointed out.

"There's no such thing as cloaking." Franz shook his head. "This isn't TV. With that much juice, even if they powered down to run silent we'd still see their reactor. No one can mask their signals out here, particularly not one that had power readings like that."

"No one that we know of," Tonya argued. "That doesn't mean they don't exist. The last time I checked, outer space was chock-full of aliens."

"And what I have learned in the last three hours is that anything is possible in space," Hassan added.

"Yes, many unexplained things happen in space," Franz retorted. "We call them anomalies."

"Yeah, that's definitely what this looks like," Jim agreed. "I can't find any logical reason why two enemy ships just disintegrated. It's not like we were in an asteroid field, or we used our junk mines and got lucky. This is just plain weird."

"Except for that massive power signal that you're ignoring," Tonya reminded him.

"That was a malfunction," Jim insisted.

"But a powerful alien ship would explain everything..." she persisted.

"Tonya," Jim interrupted, his voice strained, "when I fill out my report to General Blaaga, I can't just tell him that we think the Klingons blew up two Strovat light cruisers that were chasing us. Now, while we don't know why the enemy ships blew up, because of that false power reading we have to assume, for safety reasons, that our sensors are malfunctioning. Franz, resume course and take us below at half speed."

"Yes, sir."

"Hmmph!" Tonya folded her arms and frowned.

"So, we are not jumping out of the system, even though it is now clear to do so?" Hassan asked.

"Our primary objective is your safety," Franz explained. "If there's any problem with the ship, it's better to find it and fix it before we jump. The slingshot has to be precise, or we could throw ourselves into a moon or an asteroid field."

"We have enough food, fuel and water to hide out in deep space for months, if we have to," Jim said. "I'd rather spend a few days checking the ship out, rather than risking your family's lives."

"Yes." Hassan nodded. "That is agreeable."

"By the way, how did you end up in a dinky little van with all of those children?" Jim asked. "Don't you own a luxury liner?"

"Of course I do, but I sent it to the city to help with the evacuations. The children are from an orphanage which belongs to my sister Yasmeen."

"She runs an orphanage?" Tonya asked.

"It is what she does in her spare time," Hassan replied. "She is a model."

"I thought I'd seen her before." Tonya snapped her fingers. "Franz, she modeled some of the wedding dresses from that catalog I had."

"Yes." Hassan frowned. "She owns her own agency. I did not approve her modeling dresses, but she is very strong-minded. I tell her she needs to get married, but she does not like anyone I have introduced to her.

"Yasmeen loves children. This is why she founded an orphanage, and she hired all of the teachers herself. She was at the orphanage when news of the attack came. When she called, I had already sent the liner to the city, so I went and got her and the children. By the time we arrived back at our house, the city was in a panic and everything was jammed. I did not want to risk getting stuck trying to get to the spaceport. That van was my personal limousine, and it was designed for interstellar travel. So, I decided that it would be best for us to use it to get out."

"What you did was a wonderful thing, Hassan," Tonya said.

"There were too few ships, and too many people." He shrugged. "We knew that those children would be left behind if we did not take them. There was never a question in our minds."

"I noticed that you all had plenty of supplies on board," she said. "That was smart."

"Yeah, I can't tell you how many times we pick up people who didn't think of carrying extra food, and especially water," Jim said. "We've found ships where half the people inside were dead."

"And a few where they were all dead," Franz murmured. "No one ever seems to think that they just might get stuck somewhere."

"My people do not take the necessities of life for granted," Hassan replied. "We had put the supplies in that ship beforehand, in case of an emergency like this. Unfortunately, I was not aware of my two friends' health problems."

"Well, I'm sorry there wasn't anything I could do for them," Tonya sighed.

"It was written," Hassan quietly stated.

"Anyway," she asked, "are all of these kids orphans?"

"No, five of them are mine," Hassan answered. "Two from Lela, and three from Zarifa."

"No offense, but I don't get the polygamy thing." Jim looked back at Hassan as if he had sprouted tentacles. "Why do you have to have two wives?"

Tonya cringed, and Franz put one hand over his eyes.

"Why not?" Hassan asked. "It is perfectly legal, and my women consented to it. Plural marriage is a common practice among all of the races of the galaxy. Tellopian law encourages it, for those who can afford to do so, as a means to more quickly populate the League, particularly terraformed worlds such as Dragos. You should know this."

"I'm sorry, Hassan," Tonya said. "He didn't mean to be so rude…"

"Rude?" Jim interrupted, looking at Tonya as if she had just usurped command.

"He's from a fundamentalist Christian family in the US Southeast," she continued unabated. "He didn't grow up around plural marriage like Franz and I did."

"Yeah, well they don't really do that much back on Earth," Jim countered.

"Ah yes, but they do," Hassan politely argued. "I am also from Earth, but not from your American culture. The American and European cultures do not practice polygamy. Those cultures sprang from earlier cultures who based their laws on the ancient Roman system. The Romans practiced monogamy, but not all cultures on Earth sprang out of Rome. In fact, many ancient European cultures practiced polygamy before they became Romanized…"

Tonya watched Hassan as he told the story and dynamics of his family. He was very large and muscular, with the same skin complexion as Yasmeen. He was clean-shaven, with a well-groomed mustache. Tonya looked into his dark eyes and, despite his intimidating appearance, saw a kind man who would risk all of his wealth to save lost and forgotten children.

He asked about the details of what happened to them during the fall of Dragos. He listened intently in particular to Franz and Tonya's part of the story, and grinned when Franz told him what Tonya had done.

"So, you got one of the bugs." Hassan slapped his meaty hand on Franz's back, which made him wince. "She is fiery. You are very lucky to have a strong woman such as this."

"I have no idea how we got out of there, only that God helped us," Tonya commented.

"God was with us all." Hassan pointed upward. "He heard

our prayers this day."

"Here we go again," Franz murmured.

"What do you mean?" Hassan asked.

"Don't pay attention to him." Tonya pointed. "He's an infidel."

"What?" Franz turned around and gave her a funny look.

"It is all right," Hassan said. "We will convert him."

Chapter 22

News of the crushing defeat at Nihal had scarcely reached the Earth when Curtis Baxter arrived, escorted by a fleet of two hundred Bisa supercruisers and over a thousand city-sized Strovat transports; each of which carried a quarter million drones. This armada was so large that it took a day and a half for it to decelerate and assemble at Neptune. Prince Yaki, the Strovat overlord of the sector, had given this horde to Curtis Baxter along with a new title: Viceroy of the Earth.

Most of the Earth fleet was scattered about the League, because the Solar system was too far behind the front to be considered a priority by the Tellopian Central Command. Thus, the meager home defense force consisted of a mixture of twenty-four old battleships and fifteen old cruisers. Rather than waste his small fleet in a useless stand in open space, Admiral Konev pulled his ships in close to the atmosphere, inside the range of the Earth's ground-based defenses.

The Strovats saw the Earth and lusted after it, for it was better than even Curtis Baxter had described. They beheld a world teeming with life and full of water. Besides being one of the most heavily populated worlds in the quadrant, the Earth was filled with livestock, raw materials, and industrial mechanization. This was better than any world they had taken from either the Amali or Burbesenys. The Strovats had not seen a planet as rich as the Earth in decades.

As the Strovat armada moved in close, the Earth's defenses opened up a terrific bombardment of both missiles and ground-based laser cannon. At the same time, Admiral Konev did an end run around the planet, bypassing the main Strovat battle phalanx, and attacked the transports. Before they knew it, the enemy had lost twenty Bisas to ground fire, and twenty-five transports to Konev.

Stunned by the ferocity of the Human assault, the Strovat commodore backed his fleet up. He also dispatched thirty Bisas to protect his transports, but Konev blew up another forty before being forced to retire. Curtis Baxter encouraged the commodore to attack the Earth's land-based defenses and to nuke several of the larger cities.

However, the Strovat commodore was hesitant to resume the attack. The last thing they wanted to do was to nuke the cities and turn large portions of this rich planet into a radioactive wasteland. They were also concerned about the massive amount of batteries the Humans had and their will to resist, which was much stronger than even they had anticipated. The commodore feared the possibility of losing so many ships and drones in capturing the Earth by conventional means that he would never be able to hold it.

Baxter, who cared little for Strovat losses, reminded the commodore that the Crown Prince had made him the overlord of this system. He ordered the Strovats to reduce the Earth's defenses with conventional weapons. The Bisa phalanx spread out around the earth and released twenty thousand fighter bombers. The Earthlings put up a terrific fight, destroying thousands of these and another sixty-two Bisas. However, Baxter's intricate knowledge of the location of the Earth's defense systems eventually took its toll. After two days, the silos and heavy batteries on the ground finally fell silent.

At this point, the Strovat commodore halted the attack. As far as the Strovat commanders were concerned, they had softened the Earthlings up, and now it was Baxter's turn to do his part. They expected him to either convince the leaders of the Earth to lay down their arms, or to convince the Earth armed forces to change sides, as had been done on other worlds.

On the large, oval-shaped bridge of the Strovat flagship, red lieutenants bustled about at their instruments, while their huge, black commodore sat in the center in his bat-like chair. Baxter sat in a custom-made chair next to the commodore, looking like an aphid amid army ants.

"This battle has not gone according to plan," the commodore buzzed through his translator at Baxter. "The Humans have put up much resistance. We have already lost too many capital ships and used an inordinate amount of supplies. We cannot sustain a siege."

"The Humans have over a hundred million trained soldiers, according to your records," a red adjutant complained. "They have even more para-military, and four of the six inhabited continents have armed populaces. These Earthlings are very warlike. It could take our forces months to subject them, if we can do it at all. We may have to simply exterminate."

"Extermination is out of the question," the commodore balked. "There are too many of them. If we exterminate the Humans, we will also destroy most of the planet's resources in the process. That defeats the purpose of our coming here."

"My friends, you must trust me," Baxter calmly replied. "I know the Earth leaders. None of them have military backgrounds. They all got where they are at by promising social reforms. These people do not have the backbone to stand and fight a protracted battle."

The wily politician hadn't been idle during the time before the attack, and he still had a trick up his sleeve. Having formerly been a powerful member of the Earth's government, and having travelled all over the globe, Baxter had many old and trusted friends in both politics and the military. He had previously contacted all of the ones who had an ax to grind with the current Earth leadership, and together they made plans for his new regime. Furthermore, being on the Security Council gave Baxter access to classified security drones. No one questioned his appropriation of several of these, supposedly for use at the Nihal III repair base.

From the moment the Strovat fleet had appeared at Neptune, Baxter's people on Earth took control of three major networks and flooded the media with false information. These rumors were soon confirmed to the Ruling Council by incoming security drones. These drones were coded as being from the Tellopian Central Security Council, and thus could not be ignored, even though what they reported was unbelievable.

The drones told the Earth leaders of huge Strovat offensives, and of the collapse of the League. Solari, Kirhara, Tellops, Zuz, and Nerva had all been overrun. Most of the Earth fleet had perished with the Nervii, and the Amali and Burbesenys had been badly mauled and had retreated into Alamani space. The Earth was next on the Strovat hit list, and there was no one left to help them.

Of course, none of this was true, but the President of the Earth and his Ruling Council had no way of knowing it. The probes were from the Central Security Council, and the codes were confirmed. No one else could have possibly sent them other than a member of that council. The president simply could not dismiss them. Nor could he ignore what was happening to his world. All things considered, he had two choices; either go down fighting and watch these numberless insectoids keep coming and coming until the entire Earth was utterly wasted, or to come to some sort of agreement with the enemy. The first choice was unthinkable, and the second wasn't much better.

Baxter finally coaxed the Strovat commodore to use nuclear weapons, stating that it would break the resolve of the Earth leaders. He chose to destroy three population centers which had specific cultural significance to them; Los Angeles, Hong Kong, and Paris (he had never liked the French much anyway). He very much wanted to destroy New York City, where his ex-wife resided, but the Strovats simply refused to fry the third largest population center on the planet.

Once the deed was done, he had the commodore send a message to the Earth leaders requesting to negotiate an honorable surrender. If the Humans would lay down their arms, their world would be spared. They would be subject to a Strovat appointed Viceroy, who would govern them fairly, and they would be required to pay tribute. They could otherwise keep their properties and could continue their lives as before. The Earth leaders were reminded to think of their mates and their young, who did not need to perish. They had three hours to consider, or the bombardment would resume. Every three hours another three cities would be destroyed.

Two and a half hours later, the Earth Ruling Council backed down. Baxter had been correct; they had no stomach for a fight to the death when they believed there would be no hope of reinforcements from Tellops. Several of the Earth's military leaders would not agree to the cease fire, and these for the most part went underground. Admiral Konev, who hadn't received any news from Admiral Clarke, didn't believe a word of those coded messages. He gathered the remainder of his fleet and headed for the Errai system.

What they didn't know was that the Baxter's string had nearly run out. The Strovats had no intention of destroying any more of these beautiful cities, which seemed like gigantic food orchards to them. Had the Ruling Council refused, or delayed for just thirty-one more minutes, the Strovats would have executed Baxter and retreated out of the system.

A truce was called and a meeting arranged. A shuttle was sent to Berlin, where the president had his seat of government, and the entire Ruling Council was brought to the Strovat flagship. President Schickel intended to oversee the change in government, and to offer the services of the council to the new Viceroy.

The staff members were led into a side room, but the members of the council were taken to a large white room with no furniture. The group of twelve men and two women stood in what seemed like a cavernous tomb lined with Strovat guards. To their utter dismay and horror, Curtis Baxter entered from the other side, dressed in a purple robe. He grinned at them maliciously, announced that their services were no longer required, and that they were to be detained.

All of the members of the Earth Ruling Council, with the exception of the president, begged Baxter for forgiveness and mercy. One by one, Baxter had the men dragged away, weeping and pleading, to the ship's storage unit, where certain, horrible death awaited them. This went on until all that were left were the president and the two women; one of whom was young, and the other old and wrinkled.

"Please, I have children!" Luciana, the younger one, begged in her Italian accent. "I came here a month ago. I had nothing to do with any of this! Spare me for the sake of my children!"

She removed pictures from her small purse to show Baxter. He looked over Luciana, who was very attractive, with dark hair and blue eyes. He scanned her family photos and nodded.

"I admit, I do not know you," he said.

"She was one of the undersecretaries!" accused Madame Brumaire, the much older woman. "She knew all about it. I was the one who tried to stop them from banishing you!"

"*No!*" Luciana fell to her knees and cried. "Check the records!

Check the records! *I had nothing to do with this!"*

Baxter smiled at Luciana and said, "I believe you. You may go home to your family."

Luciana thanked him, over and over. He had her escorted into the room with the staff, who were all informed by their captors that they would be spared. Baxter had always had empathy for the working class, and didn't wish to persecute the people who were just doing their jobs. Even the Strovats had agreed that they would be useful in the government changeover.

"You, Madame, are a liar!" Baxter pointed at the older woman.

"No!" Brumaire dropped to her knees. "I defended you!"

"You knew my ex-wife," he accused. "You helped her destroy my career, Madame. Now it's my turn."

"Take this one to the kitchens immediately." Baxter motioned to a Strovat guard. "There is no need for her to wait!"

The guard dragged the old lady out, kicking and screaming, to her horrible execution. Baxter turned to the defrocked president and grinned, but Hans Schickel refused to give him the satisfaction of begging for his life. Baxter did not have him hauled off like the others, but instead had him bound and gagged for the trip back to Earth. He wished to question Schickel later, but for now the former president would have a front row seat of Curtis Baxter's glorious return.

Baxter parked a hundred Bisas in space above the hundred largest cities on Earth. At the same time, his forces on Earth staged a coup and unseated the British governor in London. Once this was accomplished, Baxter rode in triumph in his yacht through the skies over London, escorted by three Strovat light cruisers and a huge transport. Baxter landed at Heathrow, but no cheering crowds greeted him, only a few of his associates who had taken part in the coup. The people of London stayed indoors as a Strovat Bisa supercruiser and three light cruisers hovered menacingly overhead.

The massive transport landed nearby at the Northolt military spaceport, where Baxter's personal army disembarked, complete with armored hovercraft and tracked, armored personnel carriers. These quickly dispersed throughout London and the midlands, gaining control of the major industrial and population centers. Four more transports landed near Portsmouth, York, Glasgow, and Dublin. All over the globe this routine repeated itself as the remaining nine hundred thirty transports invaded all the major populated regions of the world. There was little resistance, for the government's order to stand down, along with the threat of the Bisas hovering over the major cities, quelled the Earth's remaining military.

Baxter took up residence in Buckingham Palace, after the Strovats had disposed of its unhappy inhabitants. The new Viceroy immediately declared world-wide martial law, with the order that everyone continue to work. All strikers, looters, and protestors would simply be handed over to the Strovats.

Over the next few days he purged the military, replacing top officials with his cronies. He dissolved the Earth Supreme Senate and had all of its members locked up for security reasons. He disposed of the world's two hundred seventy-five district governors and replaced them with his own supporters, and they in turn dissolved their respective district parliaments.

Massive protests broke out. In Washington DC, thousands of citizens were shot down by Strovats. The ringleaders and their families were quickly rounded up, never to be heard from again. Other protests in Cairo, Sao Paulo, and Manila were also brutally suppressed. The members of the press who openly objected to the massacres were handed over to the Strovats, and then replaced by those who were more compliant. All other media members who dared to even question the new Viceroy were quickly given the same treatment. The new media people were forced to ignore further protests and massacres, and focus on the new government's upcoming positive reforms.

Baxter set up a committee to organize world-wide supply. Everyone was to have enough food to eat and medical care, so long as they were productive members of society. He founded organizations that would improve working conditions in the poorer districts of the world, and he went to Asia and Africa to personally hand out food and medical packets to the impoverished while the cameras rolled. His goal was to keep the working class satisfied, and the media was required to portray him as a man of the people. Not that he actually cared, but he needed to keep the people working to meet his tribute requirements.

Behind the scenes, he gave all of the members of the former government who had previously opposed him to the Strovats. The remainder were ordered to either swear an oath of allegiance or die.

He wanted very much to feed his ex-wife to the Strovats. However, she was in Paris when he blew it up, and he had carelessly executed all of those who knew this. Of course, she never turned up, and this really got under his skin.

Baxter streamlined the world judicial process, doing away with the grand jury process and most of the appellate courts. Each district would keep its local judges and courts, but now would only have a single High Court for appeals. The judges on these High Courts were all appointed by Baxter's cronies. In addition, the world's prisons were emptied to help fulfill the first month's tribute. Afterward, all convicted felons, whether murderers, or thieves, or town drunks, would share the same death sentence. Only women of child-bearing age would be spared, if a man would take her as his concubine. The polygamy that the other races of the galaxy promoted now came to all regions of the Earth, but not for the same reasons. Baxter needed the population to flourish for future quotas.

To cut medical costs, and to complete tribute requirements, all nursing homes were closed. All non-essential people over the age of 78 were "retired" to internment camps, which were nothing more than processing centers for the Strovats. The severely disabled and the terminally ill met the same fate. The medical personnel from these facilities were transferred to areas where they were needed. Most of them were sent, unwillingly, to work in the poorer districts.

Baxter was so busy during the first month of his reign that he had virtually no personal time. Finally, once his government was set in motion and his people took over their responsibilities, he was able to tend to his personal life. The first thing on his list was to choose a number of pretty young women for his harem. The next thing to do was to finally deal with the former president, Hans Schickel. He prepared something special for his old political adversary, and then he had Schickel cleaned up and brought to him in shackles.

Hans Schickel was led into the Viceroy's spacious main office in Buckingham Palace by Baxter's old friend Henry Jeffries, who was now the Master Chief of Police. Accompanying them was Jack Nero, who wore a decked-out field marshal's uniform. Nero was now the Master Chief of Security, and head of all the Earth's armed forces. Schickel looked about at the paintings and tapestries on the walls, all of which were ancient masterpieces that Baxter had recently "appropriated".

"Hermann Goering would be proud," he muttered in his native tongue.

Baxter himself sat at a large table and enjoyed a fine seven-course meal with two lovely young girls. Baxter excused his concubines, and Chief Jeffries led them out. He poured Hans a glass of wine and invited him to sit across from him. When Hans declined, Nero knocked his legs out from underneath him, and he flopped to the floor with a groan. Nero picked the former President of the Earth up, plopped him into the desired chair, and then Baxter motioned with his head for the field marshal to leave.

"So, what do you think of my consorts?" Baxter asked while he ate.

"Very nice," Hans wheezed. "How many members of their families did you kidnap to get them to be with you?"

"None at all," Baxter replied. "They were lowly strippers under your regime. Now they are queens. Those are but two of many."

"And they are all your slaves?"

"No, I see no need to force beautiful women to be with me. I've discovered that many of them find wealth and power attractive. My women are all here voluntarily. You see, they applied for their positions, and I had my choice of literally thousands of gorgeous applicants. My queens get to live in the lap of luxury, and their children will be my children and will have a royal heritage."

"Yes, and also the heritage of a traitor," Hans scoffed.

"I beg your pardon." Baxter sipped his wine. "I am a capitalist, and I merely capitalized on the inevitable."

"You were on the Central Security Council," Hans seethed. "You were behind the defeat at Nihal. You led them right to us! Tell me, you schwienhundt, who else on the central committees were in on this?"

"Very perceptive of you, Hans. You're more intelligent than your other friends. Too bad. A mind is a terrible thing to waste."

"I'm to assume that my friends did not survive their interviews?"

"Oh, they survived the interviews. I'm afraid it was the executions afterward which did them in."

"History will remember you for what you are," Hans accused.

"A murderer and a traitor!"

"History is written by the victors, my friend." Baxter raised his wine glass.

"Answer my question," Hans fumed. "Who else was in this with you?"

"My, but you're demanding." Baxter raised his eyebrows. "Considering where you find yourself at the moment."

"Consider it a last request," Hans sneered. "I presume this is to be my last meal."

"Very well." Baxter put down his drink and leaned back. "No one else on the Security Council was involved, though I did have a few friends in the Solarian government. Most of my help actually came from here, right under your nose. You've already met Mister Jeffries. Other old friends of mine who helped include Admiral Donahue, General William Howe..."

"Howe?" Hans gave Baxter a look of utter shock. "But...he was on the Joint Chiefs of Staff!"

"Yes." Baxter smiled wickedly. "There were many high-ranking military officials who were rather disgruntled with your cuts in their spending to fund your socialist programs. Many captains of industry as well. Quite a few of them were eager to get rid of you."

"Did they know that the Strovats were part of this deal of yours?"

"Many of them did, the rest quickly fell into line. Unlike you and your socialist dreamers, my people are all realists."

"You and your people are all traitors to mankind!" Hans spat. "You sold us all out to line your pockets, and for what? Only to be slaves to the Strovats. You will bring ruin upon this world that you wish to rule!"

"Oh, come off it, Hans," Baxter retorted. "We saved the world. The Tellopian League is weak. I know better than anyone, for I have seen how divided they are. I've seen the numbers myself. They cannot possibly defeat the Strovats. They will keep coming and coming until we're all destroyed. What's happening here now was going to happen within the next ten years anyway. We had two choices, either watch our people be slaughtered and our planet destroyed like the Sagobians, or flee and become refugees like the Burbesenys.

"But there was a third choice, one that only the strongest

among us would consider: To make a deal now and save our race from extinction. You and your people were too weak to make such a decision. You would discuss everything in committees until the Strovats were on your doorstep, and then it would be too late."

"No." Hans shook his head. "We would have fought them to the last."

"Just like you did before I arrived?" Baxter scoffed. "No, you submitted because to do otherwise would have destroyed the Human race, and that is precisely my point, Hans. I have saved it! I have done what you and your cronies could never do. I have saved mankind, and now I will bring them *order!*"

"It seems that we Germans have heard that speech before," Hans commented.

"You're very bold for a condemned man," Baxter said with a frown.

"If you were expecting me to beg like the others, then you will be disappointed." Hans smiled and finally gulped his glass of wine. "I wish you luck with your new world. Even with the Tellopians helping us, it is still a mess. Your new order will have to deal with droughts, floods, hurricanes, earthquakes, famines and pestilence everywhere. Crime is rampant, the infrastructure is crumbling, the medical system inadequate, and the taxation system is a bureaucratic nightmare. Also, you'll be glad to know that after all these years, there are still plenty of religious zealots who are willing to strap bombs to themselves and blow up just about anything."

"Alas, the more things change, the more they stay the same." Baxter's evil smile returned. "Let me explain how an autocrat handles things. I am not as squeamish as you and your liberal friends. Through pragmatic measures, we are already well on the way to solving world-wide crime. Not having to spend money on condemned felons will drastically cut our costs. There will be more food to go around, and no one will miss the criminals. The reduced crime will create more productivity, and the money we save by closing most of the prisons will be used to fund massive state-run livestock farms. Soon there will be plenty of food for both us and the Strovats."

"You will never satisfy the Strovats." Hans shook his head. "The more you produce, the more they will demand. You have made a deal with the devil to try and become another Alexander the Great, but you will find that you are nothing more than a slave."

"I have done what Alexander could not do," Baxter said with a fire in his eyes. "I have the entire world at my feet!"

"I grow tired of this," Hans sighed. "Let us proceed. I assume the charge against me is sedition?"

"Officially, yes." Baxter gulped down the last of his wine. "However, in your case, I will consider commuting your sentence in exchange for some information."

"What could you possibly want that would curb your personal vendetta toward me?"

"Someone I want more. Thus far, Rhonda has somehow managed to elude me. We cannot find her anywhere. Would you happen to know where she's hiding?"

"Your ex-wife?" Hans laughed. "Of all the people that can cause you trouble now, and you're looking for her?"

"I don't see why you find this so amusing," Baxter growled. "I will give you one last chance. Where is Rhonda?"

"How should I know?" Hans shrugged. "She has a brother, doesn't she? Why not torture your ex bother-in-law?"

"I've already done that," Baxter replied with disgust. "He wouldn't stop talking, and blubbering. My people peeled him like a banana. If he knew anything he would have told us."

"And your son?"

"I have not had contact with my son since the divorce. He's serving somewhere in the outer fleet under Sir Nigel Clarke. I asked because you were Rhonda's friend."

"I have not had any contact with her in over a year." Hans shook his head. "You may torture me if you like, but I cannot help you. May I suggest Ian Fenwick, or Lord Chase?"

"They're dead," Baxter exhaled. "They're all dead. You are the last of my old enemies, other than Rhonda."

"It seems that you killed Madame Brumaire too soon!" Hans chuckled. "She could have told you everything you want to know."

Baxter frowned and snapped his fingers. Four Strovat guards appeared out of the shadows. As Baxter stood, one of them picked Hans up like a sack of groceries.

"This interview is over," Baxter stated in an icy tone. "It's time to watch you die."

The Viceroy had prepared a special room for executions on the other side of the palace, and this is where they carried the former President of the Earth. They marched down several corridors until finally coming to a closed door at the end of a hallway. A horrible stench wreaked from behind the door, along with an unusual noise. It sounded as if a hundred soldiers were marching around the room on a floor of croutons.

Curtis Baxter opened the door with a skeleton key, revealing Hans Schickel's fate. The roof had been removed, and they could see the gray sky above. Below the floor fell away, and the walkway extended forward eight feet to a drop off. Several feet below, hundreds of three-foot-long maggot-like creatures, Strovat larvae, crawled and writhed over each other. From two entrances on the other side, Strovats threw animals, mainly stray dogs and cats, down into the pit. The larvae tore the animals apart, and then fought each other over the scraps.

True to his word, Hans did not beg. He said nothing as the Strovat guard dropped him into the pit. The larvae devoured him like hungry piranhas.

End of book one

D L Bell

APPENDIX A

The Sagobian Revolt

Cousins to the Alamani, the Sagobians have many of the same physical characteristics, except that they are shorter and darker, with bandy legs. Originally from Alaman, the Alamani regard the Sagobians as a lesser race and had subjugated them eons ago. Though the Alamani did not practice slavery, their society did at one time resemble the Human caste system, with the Sagobians being on the bottom of the totem pole.

In old Alamani society, the Sagobians were the lowest of the low. They enjoyed few rights, limited opportunities, only a basic promise of education, and no expectation of advancing beyond the jobs which no one else wanted to do. Even in ancient Rome, the peasant could gain citizen status through service in the army, but for the Sagobians it was not so. They were considered too inferior to be accepted into the Alamani armed services.

Just as the peasants in 14th century England, led by Wat Tyler, had risen up against Richard II's taxation, the Sagobians led a similar revolt on Alaman circa 23,000 BC. The Sagobians rose up, or rather they sat down. Under the leadership of one Marcian, the Sagobians went on an empire-wide strike.

Marcian, realizing that armed revolt would be suicide against the Alamani military machine, had organized a series of strikes and boycotts in an attempt to gain better wages and education for his people. By refusing to perform the undesirable, but necessary jobs in Alamani society, Marcian believed that his people could gain concessions. After all, no respectable Alamani would debase himself by disposing of his own garbage, or his own sewage. Nor was he likely to clean such disposal areas. Nor was he going to dispose of the dead, as well as animal carcasses, all of which were considered unclean.

The idea was sound, and at first successful. The emperor granted wage concessions, but not more education, and the Sagobians would not be afforded any advancement opportunities outside of their unclean, but necessary professions. The idea of advancing Sagobians in their society was more repugnant to the Alamani than having to handle their own sewage. When Marcian attempted to push for more concessions, he and the other instigators were arrested. Marcian and over two thousand of the other Sagobian leaders were publicly executed in a most painful manner. The strikes collapsed, and for the most part the Sagobians went back to work. A few ringleaders managed to escape capture and went into hiding. The king of the Alamani thought that was the end of it.

A new Sagobian leader by the name of Decius rose from the ashes. He was more devious and pragmatic than the honest and non-violent Marcian. Decius promised obedience to the Alamani king and put his people back to work. However, he also secretly helped many Sagobians defect to the Amali, and then used these defectors as both spies and secret negotiators. Through them, Decius cut a deal with the mortal enemies of Alaman, the Burbesenys.

The Burbesenys geared up for another war. The Alamani picked up on their preparations and they made ready as well, but somehow their intelligence completely missed what was brewing right under their noses. On the eve of a massive Burbeseny offensive, Decius ordered an empire-wide sit-down strike. The Sagobians showed up for work and then did nothing, tying up docks, vehicles, ships, communications, and travel routes. The Alamani logistical system ground to a halt, and its military bogged down. When the Burbesenys struck their blow, the Sagobians rioted, destroying much of the equipment which they had tied up. The king of Alaman was forced to pull troops from the front lines to put down the Sagobian revolt, a move which decisively altered the war effort.

In the end, both the Alamani and the Sagobians lost. During the war, the Sagobians who had not been executed were all interred on gulag worlds. The Alamani government destabilized, and the military removed the ruling dynasty. The strongest of the noble families, the Golars, assumed control and negotiated an armistice. Both Alaman and Nephil lost systems to the Burbesenys. The Golars restructured the economy and exiled the Sagobians forever. Hundreds of millions of Sagobians found themselves as refugees in Amali and Burbeseny territory.

The Amali and Burbesenys turned this catastrophe around in their favor. They recognized the Sagobians as a potential ally, and terraformed a new home world for them in the Epsilon Perseus system, which had previously belonged to the Nephilim. The Sagobians became a buffer zone between Burbeseny and Nephil. They had become the mortal enemies of the Alamani, and their occupation of former Nephilim territory caused enmity with that kingdom as well. Over the next twenty-five thousand years, many wars would be fought in this sector.

D L Bell

APPENDIX B

Other alien races

Nephilim
System: Zeta Taurus
Home world: Nephil
Affiliation: Alamani

The Nephilim are an independent kingdom allied to the Alamani, and they have been historically on the front lines of the wars between Alaman and Burbeseny. They also have had many of their own border wars with the Sagobians. The Nephilim average five feet tall, but with long, horse-like bodies over six feet in length, with four powerful legs, large feet, and two powerful arms with three-fingered hands. They have blue or green skin, long necks, high foreheads, and large, toothy mouths. Carnivorous and rather aggressive by nature, the Nephilim do not participate in diplomacy or trade outside of the Alamani or the Heruli. Thus, they have had very little contact with most of the members of the Tellopian League, except through piracy. In fact, recent Tellopian investigations have discovered a money trail linking much of the piracy and organized crime in the quadrant to Nephil.

Amali
System: Delta Lyra I
Home world: Amal
Affiliation: Tellopian League

This is an ancient feudal society dominated by marcher lords who elect a ruling grand duke. They are reptilian, amphibious methane-breathers from a swampy world. Amali possess blue or green scaly skin, large bulbous eyes, long spindly arms, and flattened heads with large mouths. They stand a mere five and a half feet tall, but this is deceiving because they are bow-legged and they walk hunched over. They are allies with the Burbesenys, and are therefore longtime enemies to the Alamani and their allies. The Amali Empire was overrun by the Strovats in 2134, and they became refugees. They joined the Tellopian League and moved to a terraformed world in the Vega system.

Antearian
System: Graffias
Home world: Anteari
Affiliation: Tellopian League
The Antearians are small humanoids, averaging under five feet tall, with fair skin, yellow hair, and either pink or yellow eyes. Theirs was originally an independent kingdom with close ties to the Burbesenys, but they were overrun by the Strovats in the year 2114. However, they were well organized and managed to keep themselves and much of their space fleet intact. They joined the Tellopian League as refugees, and relocated to a terraformed world in the Pollux system.

Gutayids
System: Unukalhai
Home world: Gutay
Affiliation: Tellopian League
This is an old representative democracy and one of the original members of the Tellopian League. However, the Gutayids are a non-aggressive vegetarian species, and joined more for the trade benefits; although they did eventually build a significant fleet to help protect the trade routes. Gutayids are gray-skinned, scaly, tall and lanky aliens which average slightly more than six feet in height. They each possess a lizard-like head, two short arms with four-fingered hands, and three legs in tripod fashion.

Kirharans
System: Alpha Lacertae
Home world: Kirhar
Affiliation: Tellopian League
The Kirharans are a tall, ancient race very closely related to Humans. Their home world is very cold, having a mean temperature of about eleven degrees Celsius. They average six and a half feet in height, and are very much like Humans in appearance, with fair skin, gray or pink eyes, and white hair which covers most of their bodies. They have a reputation as hardy warriors, and circa the year 1200 AD they were one of the charter members of the

Tellopian League. Anciently their planet was balkanized. However, roughly ten thousand years ago, Ivarr the Conqueror consolidated all of the separate kingdoms into one. This single kingdom remained intact until long after joining the Tellopians. Eventually the people of the planet desired to have their world ruled in the same democratic way in which the League operated, and a parliament was granted. By 2000, the Kirharan government had become a constitutional monarchy similar to 19th century Britain.

Zuzims
System: Vega
Home world: Zuz
Affiliation: Tellopian League
The Zuzims are an ancient kingdom of Amphibious humanoids. They are methane-breathers from a swampy world, and distantly related to the Amali. They average between five and six feet tall with smooth, blue skin and webbed hands and feet. They possess small mouths, beady eyes, and crested heads. Their society is very refined, and their leaders have a tendency to be condescending toward other races, with the exception of the Alamani, whom they consider to be their cultural equals. The Zuzims, while always friendly towards the Amali, had remained aloof from any alliances with them before 2134, so that they could trade independently with Alaman. They were among the original five members of the Tellopian League.

ABOUT THE AUTHOR

An author, father of four, and part-time cartoonist, D L Bell (David Lee Bell) is a native of Ludlow, Kentucky, and currently resides in Cincinnati, Ohio. The most important aspects in his life are family, religion, dogs, cats, and writing. An avid historian, he has spent twenty years studying the history of Great Britain, the late Roman Empire, and the Dark Ages.

D L Bell published his first novel, *The Unexpected Witness* (romance/suspense), in 2013. You can view more information on this book at theunexpectedwitness.com. His cartoon can be seen at Facebook.com/ByrdAndElsa.

See more information on *The Outer Rim* and its sequel, *The Return of the Leviathan,* at outrim.com.